THE BEDTIME HORRORS

Victor Darke

CONTENTS

CHAPTER 1: THE WHISPERING SHADOWS

The house loomed before Jonathan like a silent sentinel, its towering spires clawing at a sky bruised with the last light of day. The peeling paint and sagging porch boards betrayed decades of neglect, but there was something about its grandeur that had called to him. Standing on the gravel path that led to the front door, he felt a strange mix of triumph and unease. This was his now—a place to finally start over.

The real estate agent's words echoed in his mind. "It's a fixer-upper, sure, but it's got history. Just don't let the locals spook you. Small towns love their ghost stories." She had laughed nervously, her gaze flicking to the shadowy windows as though something might be watching.

Ghost stories. Jonathan had scoffed at the idea. He didn't believe in that sort of thing. At least, not until the first night.

The sound of the grandfather clock striking midnight jolted Jonathan awake. He sat up, disoriented, in the overstuffed armchair in the parlor. The fire he'd lit earlier had burned down to a heap of glowing embers. The room was colder than it should've been, the kind of cold that seeped beneath the skin and settled into the bones.

Something felt...off.

The faint rustle of movement drew his attention to the far corner of the room. At first, he thought it was his imagination, the play of firelight and the flickering shadows of the old drapes. But then the shadow shifted, stretching unnaturally along the wall. It moved against the light, defying the laws of physics, inching closer to him.

He froze, his breath caught in his throat. The shadow was darker than the rest of the room—a void, an absence of light. It was human-shaped, almost...almost. The proportions were wrong, its limbs too long, its head tilting at an impossible angle, as though mocking the concept of anatomy.

Jonathan blinked, and it was gone. The corner lay empty, the drapes swaying slightly as though stirred by a phantom breeze.

"Get a grip," he muttered aloud, running a hand through his hair. "It's an old house. Drafts, creaks, shadows—it's all in your head."

But even as he spoke the words, they felt hollow. He told himself it was just exhaustion. The move, the late nights unpacking, the stress of leaving the city—it was all catching up to him. With a shiver, he stood and made his way upstairs to bed, leaving the parlor behind. He didn't see the shadow pooling on the floor where he'd been sitting, its edges rippling like water disturbed.

The whispers began three nights later.

Jonathan woke to the sound of his name, soft and insidious, curling around the edges of his consciousness.

"Jonathan..."

At first, he thought it was the wind. The house groaned and sighed with age, its wooden skeleton flexing as the winter chill settled in. But then he heard it again, clearer this time. A chorus of voices, hushed and overlapping, as if rising from the walls themselves.

"Jonathan... come to us..."

He bolted upright in bed, his heart pounding. The room was pitch-black, the curtains drawn tightly shut. Fumbling for the bedside lamp, he flicked it on, flooding the room with pale yellow light. The whispers stopped instantly, as though cut off by the switch.

Breathing hard, he scanned the room. Nothing seemed out of place—the antique wardrobe, the cracked mirror, the stack of half-unpacked boxes in the corner. Yet the feeling of being watched was palpable, a weight pressing down on his chest.

He swung his legs over the side of the bed and froze. There, on the hardwood floor, was a shadow that didn't belong. It stretched from the corner of the room toward his bed, long and thin, like the silhouette of a man standing just out of sight. But there was nothing in the corner to cast it—no furniture, no lamp, no figure.

"Who's there?" he demanded, his voice trembling despite his attempt at authority.

The shadow shifted, subtly at first, then more boldly. It slithered along the floor like a living thing, coiling and uncoiling as it moved closer. The whispers began again, louder now, their words clearer.

"Stay with us, Jonathan... forever..."

He stumbled backward, his heel catching the edge of the rug. He fell hard, the breath knocked from his lungs. Scrambling to his feet, he grabbed the nearest object—a heavy candlestick from the nightstand—and swung it wildly at the shadow. It passed through the inky darkness with no resistance, as though striking empty air.

The shadow recoiled, retreating back into the corner, but its presence lingered. The whispers faded, replaced by a silence more oppressive than sound. Jonathan didn't dare sleep that night. He sat upright in bed, the candlestick clutched tightly in his hands, staring at the corner until the first light of dawn crept through the cracks in the curtains.

By the end of the week, Jonathan was unraveling. The shadows were everywhere now, lurking at the edges of his vision, slipping through doorways, pooling under furniture. He'd tried to rationalize it, to tell himself it was a trick of the light, but the whispers made it impossible to ignore. They called to him constantly, day and night, their voices worming into his mind like parasites.

He decided he couldn't stay. The house was wrong—rotten, cursed, something he couldn't explain but could no longer deny. He packed a bag hastily, throwing in clothes and whatever essentials he could grab. He didn't care about the rest. He just needed to leave.

As he descended the staircase, the house seemed to groan in protest. The air grew thick, heavy with the smell of damp earth and decay. The shadows gathered, pooling at the edges of his vision, spilling across the walls and ceiling like ink spreading through water. They whispered his name, louder and louder, until it was a deafening roar.

He reached the front door and yanked it open, but what lay beyond wasn't the gravel path and the overgrown garden. It was darkness—endless, impenetrable darkness. He stepped back, his chest tightening with panic. The shadows surged forward, consuming the walls, the floor, the very air around him.

"Jonathan..." The voices were no longer whispers. They were a cacophony, a terrible symphony of hunger and malice.

He screamed as the shadows engulfed him, their cold tendrils wrapping around his limbs, pulling him into the void. The last thing he saw was the faint outline of the front door, standing ajar, before it too was swallowed by the dark.

And then there was silence.

CHAPTER 2: THE ECHOES OF THE DEEP

The water pressed against the hull of the submersible with an almost sentient weight, groaning like the dying breath of some ancient leviathan imprisoned by time. Dr. Lisa Greene adjusted her headset, her fingers trembling as she tried to ignore the oppressive silence that filled the cabin between bursts of static-laden communication from the surface.

"Depth?" she asked, breaking the tenuous silence.

Captain Harris, hunched over the controls, squinted at the flickering readouts. The pale green light from the console cast sharp shadows across his weathered face. His voice was gruff but quiet, as though afraid to disturb the void outside. "Thirty-six thousand feet and counting. We're past Challenger Deep now—this trench wasn't even on the maps."

Lisa glanced at Diver Alex, who sat near the viewport, transfixed by the abyss outside. His helmet rested in his lap, his dark eyes wide. The faint glow of bioluminescent creatures flickered occasionally through the thick blackness, but even their alien beauty did little to alleviate the suffocating dread.

"You're awfully quiet, Alex," Lisa said, forcing a weak smile.

Alex didn't turn. "It's just… different," he murmured. "Feels like the ocean doesn't want us here."

"Superstitions," Harris barked, though there was an edge to his voice that betrayed his unease. "The locals always have stories about places like this. Cursed waters, forbidden depths. It's just folklore."

"Folklore doesn't explain why nothing on our radar reads properly," Alex countered, his voice low. "Or why the currents are acting like—like they're alive."

Lisa was about to respond when a low hum vibrated through the submersible. It was faint at first, more felt than heard, but it grew steadily louder until it resonated deep in their chests. The instruments on the dashboard began to blink erratically, warning lights flaring like panicked eyes.

"What the hell is that?" Harris growled, gripping the controls tightly. He tried to stabilize their descent, but the submersible shuddered, tilting slightly to one side. The hum rose in pitch, becoming something melodic, haunting.

Lisa clutched the armrest of her seat, her nails digging into the worn fabric. "It's... it's coming from outside."

Alex leaned closer to the viewport, his breath fogging the glass. "I see something," he whispered, his voice barely audible over the droning sound. "Lights. Shapes."

"Alex, sit down," Harris barked. "You're not going out there."

But Alex didn't move from the viewport. His face was pale, his lips parted as though he were in a trance. "It's beautiful," he murmured.

Lisa unbuckled her harness and moved toward him, grabbing his shoulder. "Snap out of it! What do you see?"

He blinked slowly, as if waking from a dream, and turned to her with a strange, distant smile. "It's calling to us."

Harris swore under his breath and smacked the console.

"Surface, this is Deep-Sea One. Do you copy? We're experiencing interference—do you read?" Static was his only reply. "Damn it."

Lisa stared out the viewport, her stomach churning. At first, she saw only the darkness, the endless void. But then the music—the hum—shifted again, and the shapes Alex had mentioned began to emerge. Faint, glowing tendrils of light drifted in the water, undulating like fragile jellyfish. But as they moved closer, Lisa realized they weren't tendrils at all. They were arms. Dozens of them, impossibly long, curling and unfurling like the petals of some monstrous flower.

And at the center of it all, a massive, pulsating form loomed. It was neither fish nor squid, nor anything that seemed to belong to the natural world. Its surface was slick and glistening, its flesh marked with intricate, shifting patterns that seemed to writhe like living tattoos. Eyes—too many to count—opened and closed across its body, each one glowing faintly with an otherworldly blue light.

"It's alive," Lisa whispered, her voice trembling.

The hum became a chorus, layered and hypnotic. Lisa felt her thoughts slipping, her fear dissolving into a strange, blissful calm. She shook her head violently, trying to cling to her sense of self. "Harris! Alex! Don't listen to it!"

But Alex was already gone. Before Lisa could stop him, he grabbed his helmet and began securing it to his suit. "I have to go," he said, his voice eerily tranquil. "It wants to show me something."

"No!" Lisa grabbed his arm, her nails digging into the neoprene fabric. "You can't! We don't know what that thing is!"

"It's not a thing," Alex replied, his gaze locked on the creature's glowing form. "It's a god."

Harris cursed and lunged for Alex, but the submersible lurched again, throwing them all off balance. The creature's song grew louder, more insistent, filling every corner of the vessel. Lisa covered her ears, but it didn't help. The sound was inside her head now, burrowing deep, unraveling her thoughts.

When she looked up, Alex was gone. The airlock hissed as it sealed behind him.

"Alex!" Harris shouted, scrambling to the controls. He stared at the external cameras, watching as Alex drifted toward the creature, his body illuminated by its ghastly light. The tendrils reached for him, wrapping around him gently, almost tenderly, before pulling him closer.

Lisa felt tears streaming down her face, though she couldn't remember when she had started crying. "We have to get him back," she choked out.

But Harris shook his head, his face ashen. "He's gone."

The creature's eyes turned toward the submersible then, all of them opening at once. Lisa felt the weight of its gaze like a physical force, pressing down on her chest, squeezing the air from her lungs. The song changed again, louder, sharper, and she felt her will slipping away.

"Lisa," Harris said, his voice distant. "We need to leave. Now."

She nodded numbly, but her eyes remained fixed on the creature. It was impossible to look away. The patterns on its skin shifted again, forming shapes that seemed to speak directly to her mind. She saw cities crumbling beneath black oceans, stars winking out one by one, and the endless, yawning void that awaited them all.

"Lisa!" Harris shouted, shaking her.

She blinked, her vision clearing just enough to see him frantically working the controls. The submersible groaned in protest as it began to ascend, the creature's tendrils reaching for them, brushing against the hull.

The last thing Lisa saw before the darkness swallowed them was Alex's face, illuminated by the creature's light. He was smiling.

CHAPTER 3:
THE HAUNTED
DOLLMAKER

The brass bell above the antique shop's door tinkled faintly as Emily Rose stepped inside, the sound swallowed by the musty air that hung thick in the dimly lit room. Shafts of light filtered through dust-covered windows, illuminating shelves cluttered with forgotten relics—faded porcelain teacups, creaking rocking horses, and tarnished silverware that seemed to whisper of lives long gone. Emily's sneakers made soft scuffing noises against the wooden floor as her wide eyes took in the peculiar treasures.

She was only twelve, her blonde hair tied into twin braids, her hands stuffed into the pockets of her overalls. Her mother had sent her to pick out a small gift for herself while she browsed a bookstore down the street. Emily had wandered into the shop out of curiosity, drawn by the faint, flickering "Open" sign in the dusty window.

"Hello, dear," came a voice from the shadows. Emily jumped, turning quickly to see a woman appear from behind the counter. Mrs. Thompson was small and wiry, with large, round glasses perched on the edge of her crooked nose. Her fingers, long and knotted like tree roots, twisted a handkerchief as she smiled at the girl. "Looking for something special?"

Emily hesitated, her gaze darting over the shelves. "Just... looking."

Mrs. Thompson nodded knowingly. "Sometimes the things we're meant to find call to us. Look closely, child. You never know what treasures might be waiting."

Emily nodded politely and moved further into the shop, weaving between narrow aisles crammed with oddities. Her fingers trailed over chipped vases and cold brass figurines until she reached the back corner of the store. Here, the air seemed heavier, colder, and the shadows deeper. Something about the corner felt... wrong, but Emily couldn't stop herself from stepping closer.

That's when she saw it.

The doll sat propped against a cracked wooden box, its head tilted slightly as if watching her. Its porcelain face was pale, perfect but for a faint crack running down its left cheek. Glassy blue eyes stared unblinking, framed by long lashes that cast shadows over the delicate curve of its face. Its dress, once white, was now yellowed with age, trimmed with lace that had frayed in places. Blonde curls tumbled from beneath a bonnet, eerily similar to Emily's own hair.

Emily crouched and reached out, her fingertips grazing the doll's cold hand. A chill ran up her arm, but she didn't pull away. Instead, she felt an inexplicable pull, a quiet voice inside her whispering, *This one. Take this one.*

"How much is it?" Emily asked, her voice small.

Mrs. Thompson's head poked around the corner, her glasses glinting in the low light. For a moment, her expression faltered, the smile fading from her lips. "Oh... that one?" Her voice carried a note of unease. "It's an old thing. Not many people like dolls anymore."

"I like it," Emily said firmly, cradling the doll carefully in her arms.

Mrs. Thompson hesitated, but then she gave a tight smile. "Two dollars," she said softly, almost as if she wanted to be rid of it.

Emily handed over the money and left the shop with a skip in her step, the brass bell jingling faintly behind her.

That night, the doll sat on Emily's dresser, its unblinking eyes fixed on her bed. The room was dark except for the faint glow of her nightlight, but Emily couldn't shake the feeling that the doll was watching her. She pulled the covers up to her chin and turned onto her side, willing herself to sleep.

Somewhere in the house, a floorboard creaked.

Emily's eyes snapped open. She listened, her heart pounding in her chest. Another creak, this time closer. She sat up, clutching the blanket tightly. The doll was still on the dresser, exactly where she'd left it, but its head seemed... different. Was it turned slightly toward her now? Had it always been like that?

"Stop scaring yourself," she whispered, lying back down and squeezing her eyes shut.

The voice came just as she was drifting off—a soft, silken whisper that seemed to come from nowhere and everywhere all at once.

"Emily..."

Her eyes flew open, her breath caught in her throat. "M-Mom?"

No answer. The house was silent except for the faint rustling of the wind outside. She looked toward the dresser, and her blood ran cold.

The doll was gone.

She scrambled out of bed, her heart thundering. "Mom?!" she called louder this time, her voice trembling. Her mother didn't answer. She crept toward the dresser, her bare feet cold against the floor. The doll was nowhere to be seen.

Then she felt it—a tug on the hem of her pajama pants. She froze, too afraid to look down. The tug came again, insistent. Slowly, she lowered her gaze.

The doll stood at her feet, its porcelain face tilted upward, its glassy blue eyes locking onto hers. Its tiny hand was clutching her pant leg.

"Play with me," it whispered, its mouth unmoving.

Emily screamed, stumbling backward and knocking over a lamp. The crash brought her mother running into the room, her face pale with worry. "Emily! What happened? Are you okay?"

"The doll!" Emily cried, pointing toward the floor.

But it was gone.

Her mother frowned, brushing a strand of hair from Emily's face. "Honey, you're shaking. What doll?"

"It was right here," Emily insisted, tears streaming down her face. "It... it talked to me!"

Her mother sighed, pulling her into a hug. "You've had a long day. Come on, let's get you back to bed."

Emily didn't argue, though her gaze darted nervously around the room as her mother tucked her in. She stayed awake for hours, her eyes fixed on the dresser, waiting for the doll to return.

When sleep finally claimed her, she didn't notice the faint sound of laughter—soft, high-pitched, and chilling—echoing from the shadows.

CHAPTER 4: THE MIRRORS OF MADNESS

The first thing Michael Andrews noticed about the mirrors was their weight. They weren't just heavy in the physical sense—though it had taken two men to lift each of them—they had a presence, an almost oppressive aura that lingered in the air long after they were installed. He had found them at an estate sale in the countryside, tucked away in the shadowed halls of an abandoned mansion. The seller had seemed eager to part with them, urging Michael to take the entire lot for a bargain price. Now, standing in the grand lobby of the newly renovated Blackthorn Hotel, Michael couldn't help but second-guess his decision.

The mirrors were breathtaking—gilded frames tangled with intricate carvings of twisting vines and leering faces, their glass so pristine it seemed to devour the light around it. Guests had been arriving for days, marveling at the restored elegance of the historic hotel. But as the week wore on, Michael began noticing something strange.

It started with the whispers.

"Mr. Andrews?" A woman's voice, tentative and trembling, broke through his thoughts. He looked up from the front desk to see

Mrs. Caldwell, one of the guests staying in Room 214. Her face was pale, her hands clutching the edges of her shawl like a lifeline. Her eyes darted nervously to the mirror hanging behind him—a tall, narrow piece with a jagged crack running through one corner.

"Yes, Mrs. Caldwell?" Michael asked, offering his best attempt at a reassuring smile. "Is everything all right?"

She hesitated, her gaze fixed on the cracked mirror. "I... I need to check out early."

Michael blinked, surprised. "I'm sorry to hear that. May I ask why? Has something been... unsatisfactory?"

Her lips trembled as she spoke, her voice barely above a whisper. "It's the mirrors. They... they show things. Things that aren't real."

Michael's stomach twisted, but he forced his expression to remain neutral. "I see. What kind of things?"

Mrs. Caldwell's eyes finally met his, wide and brimming with tears. "My husband," she said, her voice cracking. "He's been gone for years. But last night... I saw him. In the mirror. Just standing there, staring at me. And his face..." She choked on the words, shaking her head violently. "It wasn't *him*. It wasn't right."

Michael opened his mouth to reassure her, to offer some logical explanation, but she cut him off.

"I'm leaving," she said firmly. "Whatever's in this place, I don't want any part of it."

Before Michael could respond, she turned and hurried toward the door, her footsteps echoing in the cavernous lobby. He glanced back at the cracked mirror behind him, his reflection staring back with an expression that felt... wrong. His jaw clenched, and his eyes seemed darker than they should have been, the shadows under them deeper, almost hollow. He shook his head and turned away.

Later that night, Michael found himself wandering the dimly lit halls of the hotel, his footsteps muffled by the plush crimson carpet. It had been a long day of complaints—more guests reporting strange occurrences, more early checkouts. A couple from the third floor claimed they'd heard laughter coming from their bathroom mirror. A man in Room 108 swore he'd seen himself in the mirror, but his reflection's eyes had been missing, replaced by black, gaping voids.

Michael stopped in front of the largest mirror in the hotel, an enormous piece mounted in the hallway outside the ballroom. Its frame was the most elaborate of them all, carved with dozens of tiny figures that seemed to writhe and twist in the flickering light of the sconces. He stared at his reflection, trying to shake the unease that had been gnawing at him all day.

"Just a mirror," he muttered under his breath. "Nothing more."

But as he stepped closer, something shifted. His reflection didn't move with him. It stood still, watching him with an unnatural stillness that sent a cold shiver down his spine. Michael froze, his breath catching in his throat. Slowly, the reflection began to smile—a wide, grotesque grin that split its face from ear to ear.

Michael stumbled back, his heart hammering in his chest. "What the hell…"

The reflection's grin widened, and then it moved—stepping forward, out of sync with Michael's own movements. It raised a hand and pressed it against the glass, and Michael could swear he felt the coldness seep through to his skin.

"Come closer," it whispered, though its lips didn't move. The voice was low and guttural, like nails scraping against stone.

"Don't you want to know the truth?"

Michael staggered back, his head spinning. The hallway seemed to warp around him, the walls closing in, the lights dimming. He turned to run, but the mirrors lining the hall reflected something else entirely—a twisted, labyrinthine maze of corridors that didn't match the layout of the hotel. Every reflection showed him running in a different direction, some of them not running at all, just standing there, staring at him with those same hollow eyes.

Panic clawed at his throat as he sprinted down the hall, his surroundings growing darker and more distorted with every step. The air felt thick and suffocating, and the whispers began again—soft at first, then rising to a deafening cacophony.

"Michael..."

"Michael..."

"Michael..."

He skidded to a stop in front of another mirror, this one cracked and splintered like a spiderweb. His reflection was there, but it was no longer his. The figure in the glass was gaunt and skeletal, its skin stretched tight over its bones, its eyes sunken and lifeless. It raised a hand and pointed at him, its mouth opening wide in a silent scream.

Michael turned to run again, but the hallway was gone. He was surrounded by mirrors on all sides, his own distorted reflections staring back at him with expressions of terror and despair. He reached out, pounding on the glass, but it didn't budge. The whispers grew louder, merging into a single voice that echoed in his mind.

"You brought us here. You let us in. Now you'll never leave."

Michael sank to his knees, his breath coming in ragged gasps. The reflections closed in around him, their faces twisting and contorting into monstrous shapes. The last thing he saw before the darkness swallowed him was his own reflection, grinning that same grotesque grin.

And then, silence.

The next morning, the hotel was empty. The guests were gone, their belongings left behind as if they had simply vanished. The mirrors remained, pristine and untouched, their surfaces reflecting the empty halls.

But if you looked closely, you might see something else—a flicker of movement, a shadow that didn't belong. And if you listened carefully, you might hear the faint sound of laughter, echoing from somewhere deep within the glass.

CHAPTER 5: THE SILENT FOREST

The forest loomed before them, a mass of skeletal trees clawing at a slate-gray sky. The air itself felt heavy, as if sound had been smothered before it could take flight. Sarah hesitated at the edge of the woods, her fingers tight around the straps of her backpack. "This... doesn't feel right," she whispered.

"Come on, Sarah," Tom said with a grin, his voice carrying an edge of false confidence. "It's just a forest. Don't tell me you're buying into that creepy old man's story."

Jake snorted, adjusting the flashlight in his hand. "Yeah, 'Don't go in there, it's cursed.' Classic campfire crap. The guy probably just wanted to scare us off his property."

Linda, standing a little apart from the group, glanced over her shoulder toward the car parked on the gravel road. Her eyes lingered on the open, empty sky beyond the trees. "Still," she murmured, "maybe we should've listened. Something feels... wrong."

Jake rolled his eyes. "You're just spooked because it's quiet, Linda. Not every place has to be filled with birds chirping and squirrels doing squirrel stuff. Let's go. We didn't drive three hours out here to chicken out."

With a resigned sigh, Sarah followed as Tom led the way into the woods. The moment they crossed the threshold, the silence hit them like a forceful wave. It was absolute and terrifying—a vacuum that swallowed every footstep, every rustle of leaves. Sarah opened her mouth to speak, but her voice didn't come. Her lips moved, her throat strained, yet all that emerged was nothing. She stopped, wide-eyed, and grabbed Tom's sleeve.

"Sarah?" Tom mouthed, his voice as absent as hers. He frowned, then gestured with exaggerated movements to keep going. He was trying to stay cool, but Sarah caught the flicker of unease in his eyes.

They trudged deeper into the forest, their footsteps eerily muted. The dirt trail beneath them was soft, damp, and seemed to absorb more than just sound. Every step felt heavier than the last, as though the earth itself were trying to pull them down into it. The trees, bare and gnarled, seemed to twist and reposition themselves when no one was looking. Linda kept glancing back, her face pale, her breathing quickening even though it made no noise.

Jake was the first to break the silence—or at least try to. He turned toward the group, his face flushed with frustration, and threw his arms up in an exaggerated shrug. "This is insane!" his lips formed, though the words were swallowed by the oppressive quiet. He stomped his foot, hard, but even that was soundless.

Suddenly, Sarah froze. Her eyes were wide, fixed on something just beyond Jake's shoulder. A shadow moved, impossibly fast, slipping behind a tree. She grabbed Tom's arm again, squeezing hard enough to make him wince, and pointed. Jake spun around, his flashlight cutting through the dim light. Nothing.

Linda edged closer to Sarah, her trembling hand brushing against her arm. They exchanged a glance, and Sarah saw her own fear mirrored in Linda's eyes. Tom gestured for them to keep going, but his movements were jerky now, uncertain. They followed, sticking closer together.

The deeper they went, the darker it became. The trees seemed to blot out what little light remained, their twisted limbs forming a canopy that pressed down on them. Shadows danced at the edges of their vision, darting just out of sight whenever someone turned their head. Sarah's heart pounded in her chest, loud and frantic, but even that was silent in this place. Her throat ached from the screams she couldn't release.

Then, Linda was gone.

One moment she was there, her hand clutching Sarah's, and the next, the space beside her was empty. Sarah spun around, her flashlight beam slicing through the trees. She saw nothing—no sign of movement, no trace of Linda. She turned to Jake and Tom, her face contorted in panic. They were already looking around, their faces pale, their bodies tense.

Tom pointed frantically at the ground where Linda had stood, and Sarah's stomach dropped. There was her flashlight, lying on the dirt trail, still on but flickering weakly. A single long, dark smear led away from it, disappearing into the trees.

Jake held up his hand, signaling for them to stay together, but his eyes betrayed his fear. He was sweating now, his face glistening in the dim light. Sarah clung to Tom's arm, her knees trembling so hard she thought she might collapse. For the first time since they'd entered the forest, Tom looked genuinely afraid.

They moved faster now, their breaths shallow and quick. The silence pressed harder against them, suffocating. Sarah's flashlight began to flicker, and as it did, she caught glimpses of movement—shadows that didn't belong to trees, shapes that seemed to blend into the darkness. She couldn't tell if they were human. She didn't want to know.

Jake stopped abruptly, his head snapping to the side. His flashlight beam caught something—eyes, glinting faintly in the dark. He raised the light higher, his hands shaking, but whatever it was vanished before the beam could settle on it. He turned back to Sarah and Tom, his lips moving silently. "Run."

They didn't need to be told twice. The three of them sprinted down the trail, their breaths coming in silent gasps. The forest seemed to shift around them, the trees closing in, their branches reaching out like skeletal fingers. Sarah's legs burned, but she didn't dare slow down. She could feel it now—something was behind them, closing in.

Jake was the next to go.

Sarah heard nothing, but she felt the absence. She turned her head just in time to see him being dragged backward into the shadows. His flashlight clattered to the ground, spinning wildly, the beam casting frantic, disorienting arcs of light. His mouth was open in a soundless scream, his fingers clawing at the dirt, and then he was gone.

Tom grabbed Sarah's arm, yanking her forward. They didn't stop running, even as the path became harder to see, harder to follow. Sarah's mind was a blur of terror. She couldn't think, couldn't process. All she knew was that she had to run, had to escape this place. But the forest wouldn't let them go.

Tom stumbled, his grip on her arm slipping. Sarah turned, reaching for him, but something moved between them—a shadow, tall and thin, with too-long limbs and hollow eyes. Tom was there, and then he wasn't. His flashlight rolled to a stop at Sarah's feet, the light dying as she picked it up.

She was alone now.

The forest was darker than ever, the silence heavier. Sarah's breath hitched in her throat. She turned in a slow circle, the flashlight shaking in her hands. The shadows were everywhere now, surrounding her, closing in. They didn't move like living things. They flickered, shifted, dissolved into the darkness only to reappear closer.

Sarah dropped the flashlight. Her knees buckled, and she sank to the ground. She pressed her hands over her ears, even though there was nothing to hear. Tears streamed down her face as she rocked back and forth, her lips moving in a prayer she couldn't speak.

And then, the shadows took her.

CHAPTER 6: THE CURSED MANUSCRIPT

The bell above the shop door chimed, its sound hollow, almost apologetic. David Clark stepped inside, shaking off the drizzle clinging to his coat. The air smelled of aged paper and mildew, a scent that seemed to crawl into his lungs and lodge itself there. The bookstore was dimly lit, the shelves towering and crooked, casting long, warped shadows across the uneven wooden floor. He ran a hand through his damp hair and glanced around, his eyes adjusting to the gloom.

"Looking for something in particular?" The voice came from behind the counter, gruff and low, like the scrape of sandpaper.

David turned to find the owner perched on a stool, his wiry frame bent as he flipped through a leather-bound tome. His face was a map of deep creases, his eyes sharp and glinting like the edge of a blade. The man didn't look up, but David felt the weight of his attention, as if the old proprietor could see him through the pages of the book.

"Just browsing," David replied, his voice unsteady. He wasn't sure what had drawn him into this place. He'd passed the shop countless times before, its window display perpetually cluttered with forgotten relics of literature. But today, something about it had stopped him. Or pulled him. He couldn't explain it.

The owner hummed in acknowledgment, turning another

brittle page. David wandered deeper into the store, his fingers brushing the spines of books as he went. Most were unlabeled, their covers cracked and peeling, their titles long faded. The deeper he moved into the shop, the darker it became, until the only light came from a single, flickering bulb hanging from a frayed cord in the far corner.

That was when he saw it.

It sat on a small table, unassuming but somehow magnetic. A manuscript, thick and bound in a cover of dark, weathered leather. The edges of the pages were frayed, and the faintest trace of crimson seemed to stain the corners. David hesitated, his breath catching in his throat. The air around it felt… wrong. Heavy. As if the thing were alive, exhaling a faint, metallic tang that reminded him of blood.

"Ah," the owner's voice called from the shadows behind him. David jumped, his heart lurching. He hadn't heard the man approach. "That one's not for sale."

David turned to find the old man standing just a few feet away, his expression inscrutable. His hands were shoved deep into the pockets of his threadbare cardigan, his posture relaxed, but his eyes—those unblinking, knife-sharp eyes—were fixed on the manuscript.

"Why not?" David asked, surprised by the eagerness in his own voice. "What's so special about it?"

The old man's lips thinned into a line. "It's… temperamental."

David let out a soft laugh, though his unease remained. "Temperamental? It's a book."

The man didn't smile. "Some things are better left untouched. Leave it."

But David was already reaching out, his curiosity overriding the warning. The moment his fingers brushed the leather, a jolt shot up his arm, cold and electric, like a shard of ice plunging into his veins. He yanked his hand back, but it was too late. The manuscript seemed to hum, a low vibration that he felt in his bones.

"I'll take it," he said, though the words felt foreign, as if someone else had spoken them through his lips.

The owner's jaw tightened. For a moment, David thought the man might argue, but instead, he just shook his head and turned away. "It's your funeral," he muttered, retreating to the counter.

The manuscript sat on David's coffee table, its presence dominating the small, dingy apartment. He'd tried to work that evening, his laptop open and a blank document staring back at him, but his thoughts kept drifting back to the book. It seemed to pulse in the corner of his vision, demanding his attention. The air in the room felt colder, heavier, and when he finally gave in and approached it, he swore he heard the faintest whisper, though he couldn't make out the words.

He flipped it open, his hands trembling. The pages were blank, a pale, yellowed parchment that smelled faintly of iron. He frowned. Had it been blank in the shop? He couldn't remember. His thoughts were muddled, his mind foggy.

Frustrated, he closed the manuscript and turned off the lights, collapsing onto the couch. Sleep came fitfully, broken by strange, vivid dreams he couldn't quite recall upon waking. It wasn't until the faint light of dawn bled into the room that he noticed it.

The manuscript was open.

David sat up, his pulse pounding. He didn't remember opening it. He approached it cautiously, his eyes widening as he saw the words scrawled across the once-blank pages. The ink—or was it ink?—was a deep, glistening red, the strokes jagged and uneven, as if written in a frenzy.

"He did not know it yet, but the end had already begun. The man in Apartment 3B would be the first casualty, his screams echoing through the night as he was torn apart by his own shadow."

David stared at the text, his breath catching in his throat. A cold sweat slicked his skin. He lived in Apartment 3A. The man next door...

A scream shattered the silence, high-pitched and raw, cutting off abruptly. David's blood turned to ice. He bolted to his door, yanking it open, and froze. The hallway was dark, the bulb overhead flickering weakly. A dark stain seeped from under the door to 3B, pooling thick and viscous in the gap between the floorboards.

He stumbled back, slamming his door shut and locking it. His heart thundered in his chest, his mind racing. He turned back to the manuscript, his eyes drawn to the next line that had appeared as if by magic.

"He would try to run, but the book would not let him. It was hungry, and it had chosen him."

David's hands shook as he slammed the cover shut, but the faint whispers began again, creeping into his ears and burrowing into his mind. And as the room grew darker, he realized the words were true. The book had chosen him.

And it would not let go.

CHAPTER 7: THE PHANTOM TRAIN

Emma Brooks clutched her coat tighter against her chest as she stepped onto the platform, the cold night air biting at her cheeks. The station was almost deserted, save for a few shadowy figures waiting silently under the dim, flickering light of a single lamppost. The train before her hissed with steam, its massive black engine looming like a beast out of time. The polished brass nameplate on the side read *Elysium Express*, though the letters seemed faint and faded, as if they were trying to disappear into the fog that swirled thick around the platform.

She hesitated for a moment, her hand tightening on the strap of her bag. Something about the train felt... wrong. The carriages were old-fashioned, with ornate detailing and darkened windows that reflected nothing of the world around them. But the clock above the platform ticked ominously close to midnight, and this was the last train. She couldn't afford to miss it.

With a deep breath, she stepped aboard.

The interior was like stepping into another century. Velvet-upholstered seats lined the walls, the deep crimson of the fabric offset by dark mahogany paneling. Gas lamps flickered softly overhead, casting long, quivering shadows across the floor. A faint smell of smoke and something metallic hung in the air. The train was eerily still. Emma expected to hear the murmur of voices, the rustling of newspapers, the occasional cough of a fellow passenger—but there was nothing.

She moved down the aisle, her footsteps muffled by the thick carpet. A handful of passengers sat scattered throughout the carriage, each staring straight ahead with an unsettling intensity. Their clothes were strange—formal, outdated, like something out of an old photograph. A man in a three-piece suit and bowler hat sat stiffly by the window, his gloved hands folded neatly on his lap. Across from him, a woman in a lace dress with a high collar held a parasol upright beside her seat, though there was no sun to shield herself from. The passengers didn't acknowledge Emma's presence as she passed. They didn't even blink.

She chose a seat near the back of the carriage, as far from the others as possible. The seat creaked faintly beneath her as she sat down, her hands fidgeting in her lap. The train lurched forward with a shudder that rattled the windows, and she felt her stomach drop as it began its journey into the fog.

Minutes passed in uneasy silence. Emma stared out the window, but the world outside was obscured by the thick, swirling mist. It was as if the train were moving through some endless void. She pulled her phone from her bag, hoping to distract herself, but there was no signal. No bars. Not even the time displayed on the screen, just a black void where the numbers should have been.

"Excuse me," she called out, her voice trembling slightly as she addressed the man in the bowler hat. "Do you know how long this trip will take?"

The man turned his head toward her, his movements unnaturally slow. For a moment, she thought he wasn't going to answer, but then his lips parted, revealing teeth that looked too white, too sharp. "Until the end," he said simply, his voice hollow, as if it came from somewhere far away.

"The end of what?" Emma pressed, her pulse quickening.

But the man had already turned back to the window, his reflection in the glass distorted and wrong, like a smudge that refused to wipe away.

A soft voice spoke from behind her, startling her. "You're not like the others, are you?"

Emma spun around to see a young girl sitting a few rows back, her legs swinging slightly over the edge of her seat. She was dressed in a pinafore dress, her hair tied up with a ribbon, and she clutched a small stuffed rabbit in her arms. Her eyes were wide and unblinking, impossibly dark, like twin voids.

"What do you mean?" Emma asked, her voice barely above a whisper.

The girl tilted her head, studying her. "The others don't ask questions. They don't even know they're here. But you... you still think you can leave."

Emma's blood ran cold. "What are you talking about? Where is this train going?"

The girl giggled, the sound high-pitched and unnerving. "You'll see. But you shouldn't have gotten on. Not if you wanted to go home."

Emma shot to her feet, her heart hammering in her chest. She made her way to the front of the carriage, gripping the backs of the seats for balance as the train swayed. She needed answers. She needed to find the conductor.

She pushed through the door into the next carriage, only to find it nearly identical to the last. More passengers sat in eerie silence, their faces pale and expressionless. One man held an open newspaper, but the pages were blank. A woman next to him knitted with invisible thread, her needles clicking together as if out of habit. Emma's breath quickened as she hurried through, the fog outside seeming to press against the windows, whispering in a language she couldn't understand.

At the far end of the carriage, she found the conductor. He was tall and gaunt, his uniform pristine but old-fashioned, the brass buttons on his jacket gleaming in the dim light. His face was obscured by the brim of his cap, but his voice was deep and resonant when he spoke.

"You shouldn't be here," he said, without looking up.

"I need to get off this train," Emma said firmly, though her voice wavered. "Something's not right. I... I shouldn't be here."

The conductor finally raised his head, and Emma felt a scream rise in her throat but couldn't release it. His face was a hollow mask, his eyes empty sockets that seemed to pull her in. "No one gets off the Elysium Express," he intoned. "Not until we reach the end of the line."

Emma stumbled back, her mind racing. She turned and ran, her footsteps echoing impossibly loud in the silent carriages. She didn't know where she was going—she just knew she had to get away. But no matter how far she ran, the carriages stretched on endlessly, each one a mirror of the last, the same silent passengers watching her with unblinking eyes.

And then, out of the corner of her eye, she saw it—a door, slightly ajar, the fog curling through the crack like a beckoning hand. She didn't think. She just ran for it, her heart pounding as she threw it open and jumped into the unknown.

The last thing she heard was the conductor's voice, echoing through the fog.

"You can't escape what you are."

CHAPTER 8: THE HOUSE THAT HUNGER BUILT

The first night in the house felt like stepping into a dream. The Johnsons—Tom, Rachel, and their thirteen-year-old son, Ethan —sat on the living room floor, surrounded by half-unpacked boxes. The air smelled faintly of fresh paint, masking something older, something musty and damp, but they were too excited to notice. It was theirs, this house. A sprawling two-story with a wraparound porch and a yard big enough for Ethan to kick a soccer ball. And the price? Unbelievable.

Rachel leaned her head against Tom's shoulder, her voice soft with contentment. "I still can't believe we got this place. It's perfect."

Tom grinned, brushing a curl of her hair behind her ear. "Told you it'd work out. We needed a fresh start, Rach. This is it."

Ethan stretched out on the floor, scrolling on his phone. "I call the room with the bay window," he said, barely looking up. "Feels big enough to be my own apartment."

Rachel laughed. "As long as you keep it clean, it's yours."

For the first time in months, the tension that had plagued them —the unpaid bills, the snippy arguments, the nights Rachel cried herself to sleep while Tom stared hollow-eyed at the ceiling—seemed to dissolve. The house breathed around them, its walls whisper-quiet, as if it were listening.

That night, they each dreamed.

Rachel's dream was vivid and electric. She stood in an art gallery, surrounded by her paintings—no longer confined to the tiny canvases she worked on in the corner of their old apartment but blown up, larger-than-life. People in elegant clothing murmured their admiration. A man in a suit approached her with a check for $50,000, and she felt the weight of her talent finally recognized.

Tom's dream was simpler but no less intoxicating. He was back in the garage of his childhood home, the one his father had built with his own hands. Tools lined the walls, and he was working on a car—his car. A sleek, restored Mustang, its engine purring like a satisfied beast. His father, long passed, stood beside him, clapping a hand on his shoulder. "You've done good, son," he said, pride shining in his eyes.

Ethan's dream was a rush of adrenaline. He was on a soccer field, the crowd chanting his name. He dribbled past defenders with ease, the ball an extension of his body. The goal was his, and when he scored, the roar of applause was deafening. He was a hero, a champion, invincible.

Morning came, and they woke with a strange, restless energy. Over breakfast, they shared bits and pieces of their dreams, laughing at the coincidence. "The house must be magic," Rachel joked, pouring coffee. "It's giving us what we want."

But the second night was different.

Rachel woke first, gasping. The gallery was gone. Her paintings were shredded, their colors bleeding into the floor. The man in the suit stood over her, his face twisted into something monstrous. His voice was guttural, inhuman. "You owe me," he said, his fingers clawing toward her throat.

In the dark, Tom thrashed in his sleep. His father's garage was collapsing. The tools fell from the walls, shattering on the concrete. The Mustang's engine roared, but when he opened the hood, it was filled with writhing black worms. His father was gone, replaced by a shadowy figure that whispered his name in a voice like grinding metal.

Ethan's scream tore through the night. Rachel and Tom bolted to his room, finding him curled in a corner, drenched in sweat. His soccer field had turned to mud, the crowd to jeering silhouettes with empty eyes. The ball had burst open, spilling something dark and wet. They chased him, those shadows, their hands outstretched, pulling him down into the muck.

"It was just a nightmare," Rachel said, wrapping Ethan in her arms. Her voice shook, betraying her fear. "It's this new place. It'll take some getting used to."

Tom nodded, but his eyes lingered on the walls. They seemed… closer somehow. The air felt heavier, pressing down on his chest. "We'll be fine," he muttered, more to himself than anyone else. "It's just a house."

But the house was not just a house. It watched them. It waited.

The dreams came again, more vivid, more terrifying. By the third night, Rachel stopped sleeping altogether, her eyes rimmed red as she stared at her easel. When she tried to paint, her hand trembled, and the canvas remained blank. Tom avoided the garage, the tools he'd unpacked left untouched. Ethan refused to enter his room, dragging a blanket to the living room instead.

And then the hunger began.

It started with small things. Rachel's favorite mug shattered in her hands, the shards slicing her palm. Tom's tools rusted overnight. Ethan's trophies, carefully arranged on a shelf, tumbled to the floor, one by one, as if pushed by invisible hands.

By the end of the week, the house whispered to them. Soft at first, almost soothing. Promises of their dreams returned, their desires fulfilled. But the price grew steeper.

Rachel found herself drawn to the basement door, though she couldn't say why. It was always locked, but she could hear something behind it. A faint, rhythmic sound—breathing. She pressed her ear to the wood, and the voice seeped through, low and insistent. "Feed me."

She stumbled back, her heart pounding. "Tom," she whispered, clutching the banister as she climbed the stairs. "We have to leave. This house... it's not right."

Tom looked up from the couch, his face pale. "Leave? We can't. We've sunk everything into this place." His voice cracked, and for the first time, Rachel saw the fear in his eyes. "It's all we have."

"That's exactly what it wants," she said, her voice rising. "It's feeding on us. On our dreams, our fears. Don't you feel it?"

Ethan appeared in the doorway, his face gaunt. "I don't want to stay here," he murmured. "It's... hungry."

The word hung in the air, heavy and undeniable.

But the house would not let them go.

That night, the doors locked themselves. The windows sealed shut. The walls seemed to pulse, alive, as if the house were drawing breath. And in the basement, something stirred, its hunger growing insatiable.

One by one, the Johnsons disappeared. Rachel was the first, her screams echoing through the halls. Tom followed, dragged toward the garage by unseen hands. Ethan was last, his cries swallowed by the darkness.

When the house grew silent once more, it exhaled, content. Its walls straightened, its floors gleamed, and its whispers faded.

And on the edge of the neighborhood, a new family saw the "For Sale" sign and marveled at the price.

CHAPTER 9: THE LABYRINTH OF LOST SOULS

The stale air carried a faint metallic tang, as though the earth itself had been bleeding for centuries. Professor Allen's flashlight beam cut through the suffocating darkness, illuminating walls etched with symbols—ancient and indecipherable, pulsing faintly as though alive. The labyrinth stretched before the team in winding, serpentine corridors, its oppressive silence broken only by the crunch of boots on loose gravel and the occasional drip of water from unseen cracks above.

"This place shouldn't exist," muttered Dr. Hayes, one of the younger archaeologists. Her voice was barely a whisper, swallowed by the void around them. "There's no record of a structure like this in any of the texts—"

"Keep moving," Allen interrupted sharply, his usual calm fraying at the edges. His aging hands trembled slightly as he gripped the flashlight tighter. He didn't want them to see his unease—not yet. "We document, we map, and we leave. Nothing more."

The team pressed forward, their movements cautious and slow. The labyrinth seemed to hum faintly, a sound just on the edge of perception, like distant chanting. Hayes paused, running her fingers along one of the walls. The carvings were deep, jagged, as though the stone had been slashed open by something feral. "These glyphs... they're not just decorative," she said, her voice tinged with awe. "They're warnings."

"We've heard enough warnings," Allen snapped, his patience thinning. "Focus on the task at hand."

But even as he spoke, his eyes lingered on the carvings. Twisted faces, contorted in agony, writhed across the stone like a frozen tableau of despair. He tried to dismiss the unease creeping up his spine, but the whispers began then—soft, insistent, and entirely inhuman.

They came from everywhere and nowhere, brushing against the edges of hearing like ghostly fingertips. At first, they were incomprehensible, just a low murmur. But soon, they grew clearer, unmistakable.

Turn back. Leave now.

"Did you hear that?" murmured Dr. Lennox, another member of the team. His face was pale, his flashlight trembling in his hand. Sweat beaded on his brow despite the chill in the air.

"No one's hearing anything," Allen said too quickly. "It's just your imagination."

But it wasn't. The whispers grew louder as they ventured deeper, threading through their minds like smoke. The walls seemed to shift when they weren't looking, the paths behind them closing like a mouth sealing shut. Hayes glanced over her shoulder and froze.

"Where's the entrance?" she asked, her voice rising with panic. "It—it should be right there. We didn't go that far—"

"It's fine," Allen said, though his heart hammered painfully in his chest. "We'll find it again. This is just a trick of the architecture."

But the labyrinth felt alive now. The walls pulsed faintly, the carvings seeming to shift when the light passed over them. Faces Allen swore weren't there before stared out at him, their hollow eyes filled with a silent, eternal scream.

"Professor," came Lennox's shaky voice. "Someone's up ahead."

Allen's flashlight jerked toward the corridor ahead. At first, he saw nothing but the endless dark. Then, slowly, a figure emerged —shrouded in shadow, barely distinguishable from the gloom. It was a man, his clothing tattered and soaked in dirt and blood. His face was gaunt, his eyes sunken pits of despair. He stared at them with a hollow gaze, lips moving soundlessly.

"Help me," he croaked, his voice raw and broken. "Please... I've been here so long..."

Hayes stepped forward instinctively, but Allen grabbed her arm, his grip vice-like. "No," he hissed. "Don't go near him."

"But he's alive!" Hayes protested. "We can't just leave him—"

"He's *not* alive," Allen said, his voice low and cold. "Look at him."

The man stepped closer, and the flashlight revealed the truth. His feet didn't touch the ground. His body wavered, flickering like a dying flame. His hands reached out, skeletal and desperate, but as Hayes tried to pull free of Allen's grip, the man dissolved into nothingness, his anguished cries echoing down the corridor.

"What the hell was that?" Lennox whispered, his voice trembling.

"The labyrinth plays tricks," Allen said, though he sounded less sure with every word. "Keep your focus. Don't listen to anything, don't trust anything."

But the maze wasn't finished with them. The whispers grew louder, shaping into familiar voices—loved ones, long-dead friends, even their own voices calling out in terror. Hayes clutched her head, tears streaming down her face. "Make it stop!" she sobbed. "I can't—I can't do this—"

The walls groaned, and the floor beneath them trembled violently. The team stumbled, their flashlights scattering beams of light across the suffocating darkness. Allen's heart sank as he saw the corridor ahead seal itself, the stone sliding together with a thunderous boom. Behind them, the path had already vanished.

"We're trapped," Lennox said, his voice hollow. "There's no way out."

"No," Allen said, though the word felt like a lie even as he spoke it. "We'll find a way. We just have to—"

The light from his flashlight caught another figure in the distance, this one a woman. Her face was familiar—too familiar. It was Dr. Armitage, a colleague who had vanished during a dig five years earlier. Her hair hung in limp, matted strands, her skin pale as death. She smiled, but it was a grotesque, unnatural thing.

"Allen," she called, her voice echoing eerily. "You're finally here. Join us."

Allen stumbled back, his breath catching in his throat. "You're not real," he whispered, though his voice cracked. "You're dead."

She laughed, a sound that made the walls tremble. "And soon, you will be too."

The labyrinth seemed to tighten around them, the air growing colder, heavier. The whispers became a cacophony, screaming in their ears, and the walls began to close in, the carvings writhing as though alive. The team screamed, their voices merging with the cries of the lost souls already trapped within the maze.

As the light from Allen's flashlight flickered and died, he realized the truth. The labyrinth wasn't just a place—it was a predator. And they were its prey.

The last thing he heard before the darkness consumed him was the sound of his own voice, whispering softly:

Turn back. Leave now.

CHAPTER 10:
THE TELEPHONE
FROM BEYOND

Megan Lawrence sat in the dim light of her apartment, the amber glow of a single lamp casting long, quivering shadows across the walls. It had been three weeks since Emily's funeral, but the grief felt fresh, raw, and unrelenting. The apartment was quiet—too quiet—except for the occasional hum of traffic outside and the low whine of the refrigerator. Emily would have hated this silence. She always filled any space with her voice, her laugh, her energy. Megan had never realized how much she relied on that noise until now, when the absence of it pressed against her chest like a weight.

She stared at her phone on the coffee table, scrolling through pictures of Emily, her thumb lingering over one from a year ago. They were both laughing, arms slung around each other's shoulders, their faces flushed from the crisp autumn air. Megan swallowed hard, the lump in her throat almost unbearable.

The shrill ring of her phone shattered the quiet, jolting her upright. She blinked, startled, and reached for it, her heart hammering. The screen lit up, and her breath caught in her throat.

Emily.

Her sister's name glowed on the caller ID in stark, undeniable letters. Megan froze, her hand hovering over the phone. It wasn't possible. Emily's phone had been turned off, locked away in a drawer in her bedroom since the day she died. Megan herself had powered it down.

The phone kept ringing, insistent and piercing. Her pulse thudded in her ears as she grappled with what to do. Logically, she knew it couldn't be real. Maybe it was a cruel prank, some technical glitch. But the thought of hearing Emily's voice again, even for a moment, was too tempting to ignore.

With trembling fingers, she swiped to answer. "Hello?" Her voice was barely a whisper.

"Megan," the voice on the other end said, soft and familiar, and Megan's breath hitched. It was Emily. Not a recording, not a distorted imitation. It was her voice—warm, alive, and heartbreakingly real.

"Emily?" Megan's voice cracked, tears already spilling down her cheeks. "Is it really you? How—how is this possible?"

There was a pause, then Emily spoke again, her tone urgent. "Megan, you have to listen to me. You're in danger."

Megan's stomach twisted, the joy she'd felt moments ago instantly replaced by dread. "Danger? What are you talking about?"

"I don't have much time," Emily continued, her words rushed, almost frantic. "Something is coming for you. You need to leave the apartment. Right now."

The line crackled, and Megan pressed the phone tighter to her ear. "Emily, wait—what do you mean? What's coming for me?"

"I can't explain it," Emily said, her voice trembling with desperation. "Just trust me. You have to go. Please, Megan. Go now."

Megan shook her head, tears blurring her vision. "This doesn't make any sense, Emily. How are you even—how are you calling me? You're... you're dead."

Another pause, and when Emily spoke again, her voice was softer, almost a whisper. "I don't know how. I just know I'm here because I have to warn you. Please, Megan. For once, just listen to me."

Megan's chest tightened. Emily's words transported her back to every argument they'd ever had, every time Megan had ignored her sister's advice, dismissed her concerns. But this... this was different. It had to be some kind of trick, didn't it? A dream? A hallucination brought on by grief?

"I don't understand," Megan whispered, her voice breaking.

"You don't have to understand," Emily said, her voice sharp now, almost angry. "You just have to listen. Megan, please. If you don't leave, it will find you."

The line crackled again, louder this time, and Emily's voice broke through, distorted and distant. "Megan, go now. It's here."

The call ended abruptly, the screen of Megan's phone going dark. Megan stared at it, her heart pounding so loudly she thought it might burst. Her apartment was silent again, but this time the quiet felt oppressive, suffocating. She glanced around the room, her eyes darting to the shadows that seemed to stretch and twist unnaturally in the corners.

The air grew colder, the temperature dropping so rapidly that her breath puffed out in pale clouds. The lamp flickered, the light dimming and then surging back to life. Megan stood, her legs unsteady beneath her, her mind racing. She wanted to dismiss it all as a cruel joke, but the fear clawing at her chest told her otherwise.

A low, guttural sound echoed through the apartment—a noise that didn't belong, that shouldn't exist. It wasn't the pipes or the wind or anything she could rationalize. It was a deep, wet growl, like the sound of something ancient and hungry.

Megan's breath hitched, and she stumbled back, her phone slipping from her hand and clattering to the floor. The growl grew louder, closer, and she turned toward the source of the noise.

The shadows in the corner of the living room seemed to writhe, coalescing into a shape, a mass of darkness that pulsed and shifted as if alive. Two pinpricks of light flared within the void, eyes glowing with malevolent intelligence.

Megan backed away, her heart hammering so hard it hurt. "No," she whispered, shaking her head. "This isn't real. This can't be real."

The thing in the shadows surged forward, impossibly fast, and Megan screamed. She turned and ran, her bare feet slipping on the hardwood floor as she scrambled toward the door. Her hands fumbled with the lock, her fingers trembling too much to grip the latch properly.

As she struggled, she heard Emily's voice again, faint and echoing, as if coming from far away. "I told you to leave, Megan. I told you."

Megan finally wrenched the door open, but it was too late. The last thing she saw was the darkness swallowing her whole, the apartment plunging into silence once more. The phone lay forgotten on the floor, the screen cracked, Emily's name still faintly visible on the caller ID.

CHAPTER 11: THE PAINTING'S EYES

The rain tapped insistently against the tall windows of Leonardo Smith's loft, streaking down like tears over the glass. Inside, the room was a chaotic symphony of paint-streaked tarps, half-finished canvases, and brushes scattered like forgotten relics of some ancient ritual. The air was heavy with the pungent aroma of turpentine and the metallic tang of wet paint. In the center of the room, lit by the dim flicker of a single overhead bulb, stood *it* —the painting.

Leonardo hadn't meant to create something so... *alive*. The portrait had started innocently enough, a commission for an art dealer who had demanded something "provocative and raw." The dealer's words had stuck in Leonardo's head, buzzing like gnats, until one sleepless night, he began. The face on the canvas was nameless, a construct of his imagination—sharp cheekbones, a ghostly pallor, and dark, cavernous eyes that seemed to ripple with layers of depth. But it was those eyes, those *damn eyes*, that had become his undoing.

Now, they stared back at him, unblinking. The irises, stormy and swirling, seemed to track his every movement as he paced the room. He could feel them on his back, boring into him like needles, even when he tried to avoid looking. He had stopped sleeping two nights ago after waking up to the distinct sensation of being watched, only to find the painting propped up at the foot of his bed—when he swore he had left it across the loft.

He had tried to laugh it off at first, chalking it up to exhaustion or his mind playing tricks on him. But the unease had only grown. Now, every creak of the floorboards, every flicker of shadow, seemed to carry the weight of those eyes.

"I'm losing my mind," he muttered, running a hand through his unkempt hair. His reflection in the cracked mirror above the sink looked like a stranger—pale, hollow-eyed, and trembling.

The knock at the door startled him, and he jumped, nearly tripping over a pile of paint cans. He hesitated for a moment, glancing warily at the painting before crossing the room.

"Leo! Open up, man!" It was Mark, the art dealer, his voice muffled through the door. "You've been dodging me for days. You're not bailing on this commission, are you?"

Leonardo hesitated but finally unlatched the door. Mark swept in, bringing with him a gust of wet, cold air and the smell of cigarette smoke. His sharp suit was slightly damp, and he carried his usual air of barely-contained impatience.

"Jesus, Leo. You look like hell," Mark said, looking him up and down. Then his eyes landed on the painting, and his expression shifted. "Oh…"

Leonardo tensed. "What?"

Mark stepped closer to the canvas, squinting. "This… This is incredible. It's like it's alive."

"Don't get too close," Leonardo snapped, his voice sharper than he intended.

Mark raised an eyebrow but didn't move back. "Relax. I'm just appreciating the detail. These eyes… It's like they're looking right through me." He chuckled nervously, then frowned. "Wait… Did they just—"

"I don't want to talk about it," Leonardo interrupted, his voice low. He grabbed Mark's arm, pulling him away from the painting. "It's not for sale. Not anymore."

"Not for sale?" Mark's voice rose. "Are you kidding me? This is your best work! People would *kill* to see this in a gallery. Do you know what this could do for your career?"

Leonardo's grip tightened. "I said no."

Mark stared at him, then pulled his arm free with a scoff. "Fine. But don't expect me to keep covering for you when the critics start asking questions. You're throwing away a masterpiece."

As Mark turned to leave, he cast one last glance at the painting. Leonardo could see the unease flickering in his eyes, though he said nothing. The door slammed shut behind him, leaving Leonardo alone with the silence—and the painting.

He turned back to it, his breath shallow. The eyes seemed more intense now, the shadows around them darker, deeper. He could feel a pull, like gravity, drawing him closer. His hands trembled as he picked up a palette knife from the workbench.

"This ends now," he whispered.

He approached the painting cautiously, his reflection stretching and warping across the varnished surface of the canvas. The eyes seemed to widen, the storm within them churning faster. He raised the knife, his hand shaking, and plunged it into the canvas.

The scream that followed wasn't his own. It was a deep, guttural wail that filled the room, reverberating off the walls and shaking the windows. The canvas didn't tear. Instead, the blade seemed to sink into it, as though into flesh. Thick, dark liquid—too dark to be paint—began to ooze from the point of impact, dripping onto the floor.

Leonardo stumbled back, his heart pounding. The eyes were furious now, their gaze burning into him. The room seemed to tilt, the walls closing in as the light flickered wildly.

"No," he whispered, backing away. "No, no, no…"

But the pull was stronger now, irresistible. His feet moved against his will, dragging him closer to the canvas. The edges of the painting seemed to ripple, the image within distorting and shifting. It wasn't just a portrait anymore—it was a doorway.

"Please," he begged, tears streaming down his face as his body was drawn closer. His hands reached out, and the surface of the canvas swallowed them whole.

In his final moments, as the painting consumed him, he saw his reflection in the stormy eyes. His face was there now, trapped within the swirling depths, screaming silently.

The loft was quiet again. The painting stood where it always had, its gaze calm and steady. But now, if you looked closely, you could see a new detail—the faint outline of Leonardo's face, hidden within the shadows, his eyes wide with terror.

And if you stood there long enough, you might feel it too. That unsettling sensation. That familiar, unrelenting gaze. Watching. Waiting.

CHAPTER 12: THE BLOOD MOON RITUAL

The air inside the abandoned church felt heavy, as though the centuries-old walls were holding their breath. Dust motes floated in the slivers of moonlight breaking through the shattered stained-glass windows, casting fractured, eerie patterns on the cracked wooden floor. The blood moon hung low in the sky, its crimson light spilling through the ruins like a warning.

Mia shivered despite the warmth of the night, clutching the leather-bound book tighter against her chest. "Are we sure about this?" she asked, her voice trembling as she glanced at Lucas, the unofficial leader of their little group. His dark hoodie framed his sharp features, his eyes glinting with an eager, reckless light.

"Don't chicken out now," Lucas said, crouching to draw a circle on the floor with chalk. His fingers moved with an unsettling confidence, tracing the runes they'd found in the book. "We've come this far. It's just a ritual—it's not like it actually works."

Jason snorted from where he leaned against a rotting pew. His lanky frame seemed out of place in the church, his perpetual smirk curling his lips. "Yeah, Mia. What, you think we're gonna summon Satan or something? It's just for fun. Relax."

Ava, sitting cross-legged on the ground and fiddling with a candle, shot Jason a glare. "Maybe don't joke about Satan when we're literally doing a ritual under a blood moon in a creepy church," she muttered. Her usually confident demeanor had been eroding ever since they'd arrived, her fingers trembling slightly as she lit the wick.

"I'm just saying," Jason replied with a shrug. "It's not like we're gonna unleash some ancient evil. This stuff's fake. Like, Hollywood fake."

Mia hesitated, her gaze darting between her friends and the book in her hands. They'd found it in Lucas's attic two weeks ago, its brittle pages filled with strange symbols and cryptic instructions. She hadn't wanted to take it, but Lucas had insisted. And now, standing in the shadow of the blood moon, she wished she'd fought harder to say no.

"Fine," she said at last, her voice barely above a whisper. She knelt down, placing the book in the center of the circle. Ava handed her the candle, and Mia lit it with shaking hands. The flame wavered, its flickering glow casting monstrous shapes on the walls.

Lucas clapped his hands together, a grin spreading across his face. "Alright, let's do this. Everyone ready?"

"Ready to get this over with," Ava said, her voice tight.

"Totally ready to become cursed or whatever," Jason added with a laugh.

Mia swallowed hard, her stomach churning as she opened the book to the marked page. The words were written in an archaic script, their meaning incomprehensible even as they seemed to hum with some ancient energy. She began to read, her voice faltering at first but growing steadier with each syllable.

The air grew colder. The candle flame elongated, burning a deep crimson. The shadows on the walls began to move, writhing like living things. A low, guttural sound echoed through the church

—at first it was faint, almost imperceptible, but it grew louder with every word Mia spoke.

"Uh… is it just me, or is this getting really weird?" Jason said, his smirk slipping as he glanced around.

Lucas's grin faltered, but he shook his head. "It's just the wind or something. Keep going, Mia."

But Mia's voice cracked as she reached the final line. The words felt wrong in her mouth, as if they were never meant to be spoken by human tongues. Still, she forced herself to finish, her voice a strained whisper. The moment the last syllable left her lips, the candle's flame burst into black smoke, snuffing out the light entirely.

The church plunged into darkness.

For a moment, there was only silence. Then the ground beneath them began to tremble. The runes Lucas had drawn flared to life, glowing with an unnatural red light. A sound like tearing fabric filled the air, followed by a bone-chilling scream that didn't belong to any of them.

"What the hell is that?!" Ava cried, stumbling backward.

Mia dropped the book, her heart hammering in her chest as the shadows coalesced in the center of the circle. The shape that formed was impossibly tall, its limbs elongated and twisted. Eyes like burning coals opened, fixing on the group with a malevolence that made Mia's blood run cold.

"Who dares summon me?" The entity's voice was a guttural growl, layered with tones that seemed to come from every direction at once.

Jason let out a nervous laugh that quickly turned into a choked gasp. "Okay, okay, we're done here! Let's go!" He turned to run, but the shadows lashed out, slamming the door shut with a deafening bang.

"No one leaves," the entity hissed.

Lucas stepped forward, his bravado cracking but still clinging to control. "We didn't mean anything by it! We—we were just messing around!"

The creature's gaze shifted to him, and Lucas froze. Its eyes seemed to bore into him, peeling away layers of bravado and exposing the fear beneath. Without warning, the shadows surged toward him, enveloping his body in a cocoon of darkness.

"Lucas!" Mia screamed, reaching for him, but Ava grabbed her arm and pulled her back.

The darkness receded, and Lucas was left standing—but his eyes burned the same fiery red as the entity's. A cruel smile twisted his lips. "You shouldn't have called me," he said, his voice no longer his own.

"What the hell is happening?!" Ava shouted, backing away as Lucas—or whatever he had become—took a step forward.

"You wanted a thrill," the thing inside Lucas said, its voice dripping with malice. "Now you'll pay the price."

Chaos erupted. Jason grabbed a broken piece of wood, brandishing it like a weapon, but Lucas moved with inhuman speed, disarming him and throwing him across the room with a sickening thud. Ava screamed as Lucas turned toward her, his grin widening.

Mia's mind raced. She grabbed the book, frantically flipping through the pages, searching for anything that might undo what they'd unleashed. Her hands shook so badly she could barely read the words.

"Do something, Mia!" Ava cried, ducking as Lucas lunged for her.

"I'm trying!" Mia shouted, her voice cracking as tears blurred her vision. She found a page that looked promising, but the words seemed to swim on the paper.

Jason groaned from where he lay crumpled against the wall. "Hurry... up..."

Lucas—or the thing controlling him—laughed, a sound that echoed like thunder through the church. "There is no escape," it said. "You belong to me now."

Mia's hands trembled as she began to chant, the words foreign and jagged on her tongue. The entity snarled, its attention snapping to her. Shadows surged toward her, but Ava threw herself in their path, screaming as they engulfed her.

"No!" Mia sobbed, her voice breaking, but she kept chanting. The runes on the floor flared once more, this time with a blinding white light. The entity shrieked, the sound piercing and inhuman, as the light consumed it.

When the light faded, the church was silent. Lucas lay unconscious in the center of the circle, his eyes closed. Ava was gone.

Mia collapsed to her knees, the book falling from her hands. Jason crawled toward her, his face pale and bloodied. "What... the hell... just happened?" he rasped.

Mia couldn't answer. She stared at the spot where Ava had been, her chest heaving with sobs. The blood moon still hung in the sky, its crimson light spilling over the ruined church like a wound that would never heal.

CHAPTER 13: THE BOARDING SCHOOL'S SECRET

The library was silent, save for the soft rustle of pages and the occasional creak of ancient floorboards under Claire's and Ethan's cautious steps. The air smelled faintly of mildew and aged paper, a scent that had always comforted Claire. But tonight, it felt oppressive, heavy, as though the very walls were holding their breath.

"Are you sure about this?" Ethan whispered, his voice barely audible. His eyes darted nervously to the towering shelves of books that seemed to stretch endlessly into the shadows.

Claire shot him a look, her crimson hair catching the faint glow of the moonlight filtering through the stained glass windows. "You saw it too, didn't you? That flicker of light behind the shelves? Something's back there, Ethan. Something they don't want us to find."

Ethan hesitated, his hand gripping the flashlight so tightly his knuckles turned white. "Yeah, and maybe there's a reason for that. Maybe we shouldn't—"

"Then go back to the dorms," Claire interrupted, her tone sharper than she'd intended. She softened a little when she saw the worry in his eyes. "But I need to know. Don't you? Haven't you ever wondered why this place feels... wrong?"

Ethan sighed, his shoulders sagging in reluctant agreement. "Fine. But if we get caught, I'm blaming you."

They moved deeper into the library, weaving through the labyrinthine rows of bookshelves. The flickering light they'd seen earlier was gone, but Claire's instincts told her they were close. She trailed her fingers along the spines of old books, feeling their ridged textures, until she stopped abruptly.

"There." She pointed to a narrow gap between two shelves, just wide enough for a person to squeeze through. It looked innocuous at first glance, but now that they were closer, both of them could see the faint outlines of a door carved into the stone wall behind the shelves.

Ethan crouched, shining his flashlight at the edges. "It's sealed, but not locked. Probably hasn't been opened in years."

Claire didn't hesitate. She pushed against the rough surface, her palms scraping against the cold stone. With a low groan, the door shifted inward, revealing a dark passageway that seemed to descend into the earth itself. A chill wafted out, carrying with it the metallic tang of dampness and something else—something acrid and foul.

Ethan took a step back. "Okay, this is officially the part where we turn around and pretend we never saw this."

Claire ignored him, pulling her phone from her pocket to use as a light. "You said you'd come with me," she reminded him, her voice steady despite the unease creeping up her spine. "If we don't do this, who will?"

Ethan muttered something under his breath but followed her into the passage.

The stairs were steep and uneven, forcing them to move slowly. The deeper they went, the more the air seemed to press against them, thick and suffocating. At the bottom, the narrow staircase opened into a cavernous room illuminated by the faint glow of dozens of candles, their flames flickering as if disturbed by an unseen wind.

Claire's breath caught in her throat. The room was filled with artifacts—ancient-looking tomes piled haphazardly on long wooden tables, strange symbols etched into the stone floor, and glass cases containing objects that seemed to pulse faintly with an unnatural energy. In the center of it all stood an ornate pedestal, upon which rested a black, jagged crystal that seemed to absorb the light around it.

"What... is this?" Ethan's voice was barely a whisper as he took in the scene.

Claire stepped forward, her gaze fixed on the pedestal. "It's some kind of ritual chamber," she murmured, her fingers itching to touch the crystal. "This has to be connected to the stories about the school. The disappearances, the strange behavior..."

Ethan grabbed her arm before she could get too close. "Claire, don't. This isn't a game. That thing—whatever it is—it's dangerous."

Before she could respond, a low, guttural sound echoed through the chamber. They both froze, their eyes darting toward the shadows that seemed to shift and writhe along the walls. The sound grew louder, a chorus of whispers overlapping in a language neither of them could understand.

"Claire..." Ethan's voice trembled as he tightened his grip on her arm. "We need to go. Now."

But Claire's gaze was fixed on the crystal. It was glowing faintly now, as though it were reacting to their presence. She felt an almost magnetic pull toward it, a voice in the back of her mind urging her to reach out, to take it.

"Claire!" Ethan yanked her back just as the whispers crescendoed into a deafening roar. The candles extinguished all at once, plunging the room into darkness.

They scrambled back toward the staircase, their breaths coming in panicked gasps. But before they could reach it, a figure stepped into view, blocking their path. The faint glow of the crystal reflected off his eyes, which seemed to gleam with an unnatural light.

"Headmaster Roberts," Ethan breathed, his voice laced with disbelief.

The Headmaster's expression was calm, almost serene, but his eyes betrayed something darker—a hunger, a madness that sent a shiver down Claire's spine.

"You shouldn't have come here," Roberts said, his voice echoing strangely in the chamber. "You've seen too much."

"What is this place?" Claire demanded, her voice shaking but defiant. "What are you hiding?"

Roberts tilted his head, a faint smile playing at the corners of his lips. "This school was built on power," he said simply. "Power that must be fed, nurtured. You think your curiosity is innocent, but it has consequences."

The shadows behind him began to writhe again, coalescing into shapes that were almost human but not quite. Their elongated limbs and featureless faces made Claire's stomach churn.

"Run," she whispered to Ethan. "Run!"

They turned and bolted up the stairs, their footsteps echoing in the narrow passage. Behind them, the Headmaster's voice followed, calm yet menacing. "You can't escape the truth. It will find you, just as it found me."

Bursting back into the library, they slammed the hidden door shut behind them. For a moment, they simply stood there, gasping for breath, their hearts pounding in unison.

"We have to tell someone," Ethan said, his voice ragged.

Claire shook her head, her mind racing. "Who would believe us? We need proof. We need to figure out what's really going on here."

As they stepped back into the familiar rows of bookshelves, the library suddenly didn't feel so safe anymore. The shadows seemed darker, the silence heavier. And deep below their feet, the whispers continued.

CHAPTER 14: THE CURSE OF THE WEREBEAST

The fire in the hearth was a whisper of its former self, reduced to a faint orange glow that threw jagged shadows across the room. Marcus sat by the wooden table, sharpening his hunting knife with slow, deliberate strokes. The rhythmic scrape of steel on stone was the only sound, save for the occasional crackle of embers. Around him, the room smelled of damp wood and old leather, a cabin built for function, not comfort. His rifle leaned against the wall, polished and ready.

A sharp knock at the door shattered the silence. Marcus paused, his hand hovering over the blade, and listened. Another knock followed, more insistent this time. He stood slowly, his boots creaking against the floorboards, and crossed the room. The door groaned as he opened it.

On the other side stood Lila, the village seamstress, her shawl drawn tightly around her shoulders. Her face was pale, her eyes wide with fear.

"Marcus," she whispered shakily, "it's taken another one."

He stepped aside, letting her in. She moved quickly, as though afraid something might leap from the darkness behind her. Marcus shut the door and slid the heavy iron bolt into place.

"Where?" he asked, his voice low and rough, like gravel tumbling over stone.

"Up near the Miller farm," Lila said, her voice trembling. "They found the remains of a calf this morning... what was left of it. And... and there were tracks again. Those... those *things*." She hesitated, as if saying it aloud might summon the creature itself. "The ones that change."

Marcus nodded grimly. He had heard the villagers' stories for weeks now. Livestock gone missing, gutted and devoured. Strange howls in the dead of night—howls that didn't belong to any wolf he had ever known. But it was the tracks that haunted him most. He'd seen them himself last week, near the edge of the forest. Massive paw prints in the soft earth, deep and heavy, like a wolf's. But then, as they moved further into the woods, they began to change. The pads grew smaller, the claws shorter, the gait uneven. Until they were no longer paws at all, but something disturbingly human.

"Did anyone see it?" Marcus asked.

Lila shook her head. "No one's seen it and lived to tell the tale."

He strapped his knife to his belt, grabbed his rifle, and slung it over his shoulder. "Stay here," he said. "Bolt the door and don't open it for anyone. Not until you know for sure it's me."

Lila looked as though she might protest, but she pressed her lips together and nodded. Marcus stepped into the cold night, the air biting at his skin as he pulled his coat tighter around him. The village was dark, the windows shuttered, the streets empty. Only the faint glow of lanterns peeked through the cracks, like watchful eyes in the gloom.

The forest loomed ahead, a black expanse of tangled branches and shifting shadows. Marcus moved quickly, his boots crunching over frost-covered grass. He followed the path toward the Miller farm, his senses on high alert. Every rustle of leaves, every snap of a twig set his heart pounding, the rifle in his hands a reassuring weight.

When he reached the farm, the scene was as gruesome as Lila had described. The remains of the calf lay scattered across the ground, its ribcage cracked open, its entrails smeared across the dirt. Blood painted the frost in dark, glistening streaks.

But it was the tracks that drew his attention. They started near the mangled carcass, massive and unmistakably animal. Yet as they led away from the farm and into the trees, they began to morph. By the time they reached the forest's edge, they were no longer paw prints. They were feet. Human feet.

Marcus knelt by the tracks, running his fingers over the indentations in the earth. He felt a chill that had nothing to do with the cold. He had hunted wolves for years, knew their habits, their patterns. This was something else entirely.

A low growl rumbled through the air, so deep it seemed to vibrate in his chest. Marcus froze, his hand tightening around the rifle. The growl came again, closer this time, followed by the soft crunch of footsteps. He turned slowly, his eyes scanning the darkness.

It stepped into the moonlight, and Marcus felt his breath catch in his throat.

The creature was massive, its body a grotesque amalgamation of man and beast. Its limbs were long and sinewy, its hands tipped with claws that glinted like polished steel. Tufts of fur sprouted in uneven patches across its body, leaving raw, pink skin exposed in places. Its face was the worst—a twisted snarl of sharp teeth and glowing yellow eyes, its muzzle too short to be a wolf's but far too monstrous to be human.

The werebeast.

It stared at him, its chest rising and falling with each ragged breath. For a moment, neither moved. Then it lunged.

Marcus fired, the crack of the rifle splitting the night, but the creature was too fast. It barreled into him, knocking him to the ground. The rifle flew from his hands as the beast's claws raked across his chest, shredding his coat and drawing blood. He gritted his teeth against the pain, his hand fumbling for the knife at his belt.

The werebeast loomed over him, its hot breath washing over his face, reeking of blood and decay. With a desperate shout, Marcus drove the blade into its side. The creature roared, a sound so loud and guttural it made his ears ring. It staggered back, clutching at the wound, and Marcus scrambled to his feet, his chest heaving.

The beast snarled, its yellow eyes locking onto his. But then, to his astonishment, it turned and fled, disappearing into the trees with unnatural speed. Marcus stood there, blood dripping from his wounds, his knife clutched in a trembling hand.

He looked down at the blade, slick with the creature's black, viscous blood. A strange sensation crept over him, starting at his fingertips and spreading up his arm—a tingling, burning itch that made him drop the knife with a gasp.

And as the first rays of dawn broke over the horizon, Marcus fell to his knees, clutching his arm, a terrible realization dawning in his mind.

The curse had already begun to spread.

CHAPTER 15:
THE GHOSTS OF
THE ASYLUM

The asylum loomed before them, a hulking silhouette against the pale glow of the moon. Its windows, like black, empty eyes, stared down at the trio. Vines crawled up its decaying brickwork, clawing at the jagged edges of shattered glass. The iron gates creaked in the wind, as if warning them to turn back. But Natalie, Chris, and Derek were not the kind to heed warnings.

"Are you sure about this?" Natalie whispered, her breath visible in the cold night air. Her camera dangled from her neck, the lens reflecting the faint light of their flashlights.

Chris, always the bravest—or perhaps the most reckless—grinned as he shoved open the groaning gate. "Come on, Nat. This place is YouTube gold. 'Exploring the Abandoned Ravenwood Asylum.' Our followers will eat it up."

Derek adjusted his beanie nervously, his flashlight beam jittering as his hand shook. "Yeah, but... this place doesn't feel right," he muttered. "People say it's cursed. You've read the stories."

"Exactly!" Chris spun around, walking backward as he gestured grandly. "The stories are what make it interesting! Haunted asylum, creepy history, tortured souls—this is primo content.

Stop being such a wuss."

Natalie sighed, pulling her coat tighter around her. She hated being the voice of reason, but she couldn't shake the unease settling in her chest. "Let's just get the footage and get out. No wandering off. No stupid stunts."

"Scout's honor," Chris said, holding up three fingers in mock sincerity before pushing open the asylum's heavy wooden doors. The hinges shrieked in protest as the trio stepped inside.

The air inside was stagnant, thick with the smell of mildew and something faintly metallic, like rust—or blood. Their flashlights cut through the darkness, illuminating peeling wallpaper and crumbling plaster. The faint echo of their footsteps bounced off the walls, making the cavernous lobby feel even larger.

"Okay," Chris whispered, his voice suddenly subdued. "This place is officially creepy as hell."

Natalie snorted. "Now you're scared?"

"Not scared. Just... respectful of the vibe," he said, though his bravado was clearly slipping.

They moved deeper into the asylum, past rusted wheelchairs and overturned gurneys. The silence weighed on them, broken only by the occasional drip of water from the ceiling. Natalie's camera clicked as she took photos, the flash briefly lighting up the gloom. In one shot, she thought she saw a shadow standing at the end of the hallway, but when she lowered the camera, nothing was there.

"Guys," Derek said, his voice tight. "You're seeing this, right?"

They followed his flashlight beam to a stack of crumbling patient records on a nearby desk. The papers were yellowed with age, the handwriting spidery and uneven. Natalie picked one up carefully, her fingers trembling.

"Patient #342," she read aloud. "Subjected to experimental electroshock therapy. Severe burns sustained. No improvement in condition. Transferred to solitary confinement."

Chris whistled low. "Damn. That's dark."

Natalie flipped to another page, her stomach churning. "Patient #128. Ice-pick lobotomy performed without anesthesia. Patient expired on the table."

Derek gagged, turning away. "Why the hell would anyone do that to people?"

Chris shrugged, though he looked uneasy. "Different time. People didn't know better back then."

"Or they didn't care," Natalie said bitterly, shoving the papers back onto the desk. "These people weren't patients to them. They were experiments."

As if summoned by her words, a sudden chill swept through the room. The air grew heavy, oppressive. The faint sound of static crackled in their ears, like an old radio struggling to tune in.

"Did you hear that?" Derek whispered, his voice trembling.

Before anyone could answer, the corridor ahead of them erupted in a cacophony of screams. The sound was distant, muffled, but unmistakable—agonized cries, pleading voices, the metallic clang of restraints. Natalie's flashlight flickered, her breath hitching in her throat.

"Okay, no," Derek said, backing away. "Nope. We're leaving. Right now."

But when they turned around, the hallway they'd come from was gone. In its place was a solid wall, the faded wallpaper stained with dark streaks that looked disturbingly like dried blood.

"What the—" Chris spun in a circle, his flashlight darting around wildly. "Where's the door? Where's the goddamn door?"

"Calm down," Natalie snapped, though her voice was shaking. "There has to be another way out."

"Guys…" Derek's voice was barely audible. He was staring down the hallway, his flashlight frozen on a figure standing in the distance. It was a woman, her hospital gown tattered and soaked with dark stains. Her head lolled to the side at an unnatural angle, and her eyes—milky white and unblinking—locked onto them.

"Run," Natalie whispered.

The woman took a step forward, her bare feet dragging across the floor with a sickening scrape. Then another step. And another.

"Run!" Natalie screamed.

They bolted down the corridor, their flashlights bouncing wildly. The walls seemed to close in around them, the air growing colder with every step. Doors slammed shut as they passed, the sound echoing like gunshots. Faint whispers rose around them, indistinct yet insistent, as if the asylum itself were speaking.

They burst into what looked like a treatment room, the rusted remains of medical equipment scattered across the floor. A single chair sat in the center, its leather straps frayed but still sturdy. The trio froze, panting, as the whispers grew louder.

"This… this isn't real," Chris stammered. "It's just our minds playing tricks on us."

Then the chair moved. Just an inch, but enough to make Natalie's stomach drop. A shadowy figure materialized behind it, a hulking man in a bloodstained lab coat. His face was obscured, but his hands—large, gloved, and holding an oversized syringe—were all too clear.

"Welcome back," the figure rasped, his voice like nails on a chalkboard. "We've been waiting for you."

The door slammed shut, and the lights went out.

CHAPTER 16:
THE WEB OF THE
SPIDER QUEEN

The air was thick with the sour tang of decay, the jungle canopy above wrapping the ruins in a shroud of dim green light. The sound of cicadas had vanished hours ago, replaced by an eerie, pulsing silence. Dr. Samuel Reed adjusted the strap of his pack and cast a wary glance at the stone archway before them. Vines spilled over the structure like veins, but even they seemed to recoil from the carvings etched into the dark stone.

The team stood motionless, their eyes fixed on the grim tableau: a mass of human figures, carved in stunning detail, kneeling in supplication before a towering, many-limbed creature. Its bulbous abdomen was etched with spirals and runes that seemed to writhe when the light hit them just right. Eight eyes, sharp and unyielding, stared down at the offerings of bound and faceless figures beneath it.

"Dr. Reed," whispered Elena, her voice trembling. She was the youngest of the group, a graduate student with a knack for deciphering ancient glyphs. But now, her usual confidence was gone, her face pale beneath a sheen of sweat. "These carvings... they're warnings."

Reed stepped closer, inspecting the intricate detail, the way the figures appeared to almost move in the flickering light of their torches. "Warnings, or myths designed to scare away intruders?" He forced a smile, though his unease gnawed at him. "The locals are always superstitious about these things."

"No," Elena said, her voice firmer now. She pointed to a series of smaller symbols lining the edges of the archway. "This isn't just superstition. It's a curse. A warning against disturbing her domain."

"The Spider Queen," muttered Blake, one of the hired guides. He spat the words like a curse of his own, his machete dangling limply at his side. His usually cocky bravado had evaporated somewhere between the last clearing and the corpse of a jaguar they'd found drained of blood, its body wrapped in web so thick it gleamed like silk in the torchlight. "I told you people this was a bad idea."

Reed sighed and turned to the rest of the group. "Listen, we've come too far to turn back now. This find is the culmination of years of work. We're not going to let a few carvings scare us off."

Blake muttered something under his breath, but Reed ignored him and stepped through the stone archway. The others followed reluctantly, their footsteps hesitant, their torches casting long, wavering shadows on the ancient walls.

Inside, the air was colder, damp and cloying with the smell of earth and rot. Threads of spiderweb dangled from the ceiling, catching in their hair and on their clothes. The walls of the temple were alive with carvings, each more grotesque than the last. Spiders of impossible size loomed over humans, their fangs dripping with venom, their legs curling around screaming faces.

"This place gives me the creeps," muttered Carter, the team's photographer, snapping a few pictures with shaking hands. "Why does it always have to be spiders?"

"Stay focused," Reed said, though even he couldn't suppress a shudder as they moved deeper into the temple. He kept his eyes on the path ahead, trying to ignore the faint, skittering sounds that seemed to come from just out of sight.

They reached a central chamber, a vast, domed room lit by shafts of pale light filtering through cracks in the stone ceiling. At the center of the room was an altar, and on it, a massive egg sac pulsated faintly, its surface slick and glistening. Reed felt his stomach turn at the sight, but he forced himself to step closer.

"This… this must be it," he said, his voice barely above a whisper. "The heart of the temple."

Elena gasped, her hand flying to her mouth. "Dr. Reed, look."

He followed her gaze to the walls, where new carvings seemed to have appeared, as though etched there by some unseen hand. They depicted the team—each of them—being devoured by the Spider Queen's children. Reed's heart pounded in his chest as he turned back to the altar.

Blake's scream shattered the silence. The group spun around just in time to see him vanish into the shadows, a massive shape dragging him up and out of sight. His machete clattered to the ground, slick with blood.

"Run!" Elena screamed, but it was too late. The room erupted into chaos as spiders the size of wolves poured from the cracks in the walls, their eyes gleaming, their fangs dripping venom. They moved with horrifying speed, their legs clicking against the stone as they closed in on the panicked team.

Carter swung his camera like a weapon, smashing one of the creatures as it lunged at him, but another dropped from the ceiling, its fangs sinking into his shoulder. His scream echoed through the chamber as he was dragged into the darkness.

Reed grabbed Elena's arm and pulled her toward a narrow passage at the far end of the room. "This way!" he shouted, his voice hoarse with fear. They ran, the sound of skittering legs and dying screams chasing them.

They emerged into another chamber, larger than the last, and froze. Before them, suspended in a web of shimmering silk, was the Spider Queen.

She was massive, her body glistening like wet obsidian, her legs tipped with barbs that gleamed in the dim light. Her eyes, all eight of them, fixed on Reed and Elena with a terrible intelligence. She reared up, her fangs clicking together, and let out a sound that was half hiss, half growl.

Reed pushed Elena behind him, his mind racing. He had no weapon, no plan, only the primal instinct to survive. The Spider Queen lunged, and he dove to the side, grabbing a broken piece of stone from the floor and swinging it with all his strength. The jagged edge connected with one of her legs, and she shrieked, her massive bulk recoiling.

"Elena, run!" he shouted, but she didn't move. Her eyes were wide, fixed on something behind him.

Reed turned just in time to see the egg sac on the altar burst open, a swarm of spiderlings spilling out, their tiny legs moving in a horrifying wave. He felt their weight on his arms, his legs, their bites burning like fire.

The last thing he saw was the Spider Queen descending, her shadow swallowing him whole.

CHAPTER 17: THE SILENT PLAGUE

A thin fog had settled over the town of Alderbridge, curling around the lampposts and creeping into the cracks of shuttered windows. Dr. Helen Fisher stepped cautiously down the cobblestone street, her breath clouding in the cold air. The silence pressed in from all sides, unnatural and suffocating, broken only by the soft crunch of her boots on frost-tipped leaves. She tightened her grip on the leather satchel slung over her shoulder, its contents rattling faintly—vials, syringes, a notebook filled with frantic scrawls.

The letter she'd received the day before had been cryptic, almost illegible, the handwriting jagged and slanted like the author's hand had trembled violently. "Help us," it had read. "Something is wrong. No one can speak."

Now, standing in the eerie quiet of this forgotten town, she realized the letter hadn't conveyed the full horror of the situation. The streets were deserted. Storefronts stood dark and empty, their windows smeared with condensation and dust. A wooden sign creaked weakly in the wind, hanging by a single rusted chain.

"Hello?" Helen called, her voice trembling. It felt wrong to break the silence, as though the town itself might retaliate. Her words echoed briefly before being swallowed by the oppressive stillness. No response came.

She moved forward, her eyes scanning for any sign of life. The first time she saw them, she almost missed it—a shadow in the corner of her vision. She turned sharply, her heart leaping into her throat. A man stood in the doorway of a small bakery, his silhouette unnaturally still. The dim light from the overcast sky cast his face in shadows, but his eyes... his eyes were wide, unblinking, staring straight at her.

"Sir?" Helen took a cautious step closer, raising her hands to show she meant no harm. "I'm here to help. I'm a doctor."

The man didn't respond. He didn't move. For a moment, Helen wondered if he was even alive. But then she noticed the faint twitch of his fingers at his sides, a subtle, erratic motion that seemed more like a spasm than anything deliberate.

She swallowed hard. "Are you hurt? Can you... can you speak?"

As if triggered by the question, the man's head tilted sharply to one side with a sickening crack. Helen flinched, her mind scrambling to comprehend what she was seeing. His mouth opened, his jaw slack and trembling, but no sound emerged. Instead, there was a low, wet gurgle deep in his throat, like something was trying to claw its way out.

Panic surged in her chest. "I need to examine you," she said, her voice wobbling. "Please—stay where you are."

The man didn't obey. His body moved suddenly, jerkily, as though he were a marionette controlled by invisible strings. He took a step toward her, his limbs bending at unnatural angles. Helen stumbled backward, her satchel swinging wildly at her side.

"Stop!" she shouted, but her words fell flat, powerless against the suffocating quiet.

The man lunged. Helen screamed, ducking out of the way just in time. He hit the pavement hard, his head bouncing off the cobblestones with a sickening thud, but he didn't stop. He clawed at the ground, his nails splintering as he dragged himself toward her with an animalistic desperation. His mouth gaped open and closed like a fish gasping for air.

Helen turned and ran, her heart pounding so loudly she could feel it in her throat. She didn't know where she was going, only that she had to get away. The buildings blurred together as she sprinted down the street, her breaths coming in ragged gasps. She could hear the man behind her, his body scraping against the ground, his nails clicking on the cobblestones like the skittering of some grotesque insect.

She rounded a corner and nearly collided with a group of people. Relief flooded her for the briefest of moments—until she saw their faces. They were pale, gaunt, their eyes sunken and rimmed with bruised shadows. Their mouths hung open, their lips cracked and bleeding, but no sound came from them. They stared at her, their heads tilting in unison, their movements eerily synchronized.

Helen froze, her stomach churning. "Oh, God," she whispered.

The group moved as one, shuffling toward her with an unnatural grace. Helen backed away, her mind racing. She had to think, had to do something—but what? There was no reasoning with them, no way to communicate. Whatever this was, it had stripped them of their humanity, reducing them to... to *what*?

Her foot caught on a loose stone, and she fell hard, the impact jarring her bones. Pain shot through her wrist as she tried to catch herself, but she forced herself to move, scrambling backward as the group closed in. Their eyes bore into her, empty and soulless, their mouths leaking a viscous black fluid that dripped onto the ground in oily splatters.

"No," Helen gasped, tears streaming down her face. "Please... please..."

The group stopped suddenly, their heads snapping toward the sound of an approaching whistle—high-pitched, shrill, and grating. Helen clapped her hands over her ears, the noise piercing straight through her skull. The infected townsfolk convulsed, their bodies writhing as though the sound was tearing them apart from the inside. It was coming from the church at the end of the street, its bell tower silhouetted against the gray sky.

Helen didn't wait to see what would happen next. She pushed herself to her feet and ran, her injured wrist throbbing with every step. The whistle grew louder as she approached the church, its tone shifting into a discordant wail that made her teeth ache. She burst through the double doors, slamming them shut behind her.

Inside, the air was thick with the acrid stench of decay. The pews were overturned, the altar smashed to pieces. In the center of the room stood a figure cloaked in shadow, its back to her. It held a small, twisted instrument to its lips—a flute, or something like it, carved from bone. The sound it produced was otherworldly, a chaotic melody that seemed to vibrate through her very cells.

The figure turned slowly, and Helen's breath caught in her throat. Its face was obscured by a mask, its surface smooth and featureless except for a single, dark slit where the mouth should have been. The whistling stopped, plunging the room into a silence so profound it felt like a physical weight pressing down on her.

The figure tilted its head, regarding her with an almost curious air. Then it raised the flute to its lips again.

"No," Helen whispered, her voice barely audible. But it was too late. The sound began again, and with it came the darkness, creeping into her mind, stealing her thoughts, her voice, her *self*.

The last thing she saw before the world went black was the

figure stepping closer, its mask gleaming in the dim light.

CHAPTER 18: THE PUPPET MASTER'S PLAYTHINGS

The air in the abandoned part of the city felt wrong—too still, too cold, as if something unseen had sucked the life out of it. Detective James Harper adjusted his trench coat against the biting wind and stared at the crumbling facade of the old theater. The marquee, once a beacon of entertainment, now hung crooked, the faded letters barely legible: *The Grand Marionette.* A shiver crawled up Harper's spine as he stepped closer, his flashlight beam slicing through the suffocating darkness.

This was where the trail ended. Dozens of disappearances in the last three months, all unconnected on the surface—different neighborhoods, different lifestyles—but all leading here. He'd uncovered one horrifying commonality just hours ago: the puppets. They'd been turning up in alleyways and dumpsters, lifelike in a way that made him sick. The painted faces bore uncanny resemblances to the missing. The delicate strings, worn and frayed, dangled from wooden crossbars, as if mocking the ones who had vanished.

Harper swallowed hard, willing himself forward. The theater's entrance loomed before him, the heavy double doors marked with peeling black paint and streaks of rust. He pushed one open with a groan, and the scent hit him—mildew, sawdust, and something sharp and metallic beneath it all. Blood?

The lobby was a time capsule of a forgotten era. Dust-coated chandeliers hung precariously from the ceiling, and faded red velvet ropes blocked off once-grand staircases. His footsteps echoed loudly, almost accusingly, as he moved deeper into the building.

Then, faintly, he heard it: a low, rhythmic creak. Harper froze, his hand instinctively going to the gun holstered at his side. The sound came again, steady and deliberate, like the sway of a rocking chair—or a puppet on strings.

"Hello?" Harper called, his voice swallowed by the oppressive silence. No answer, but the creaking continued, drawing him toward a set of double doors marked *Private*. He pushed them open, and the smell intensified, clawing at his throat. His flashlight swept the room, revealing what looked like a workshop. Wooden limbs—arms, legs, torsos—hung from the walls, some half-carved, others painted with unnatural precision. A sewing machine sat in one corner, spools of thread spilling onto the floor like spilled entrails.

But it was the centerpiece of the room that made Harper's stomach churn. A life-sized marionette sat slumped in a chair, its head tilted at an unnatural angle. Its face was painted with a grotesque smile, but its eyes—oh God, its eyes—were too human. Harper stepped closer, his breath caught in his throat. The eyes followed him. He stumbled back, his flashlight shaking as he illuminated the doll's face.

"Maria Lopez." Her name escaped his lips as a whisper. He recognized her from the missing persons report—a school teacher, mid-thirties, last seen walking home from work. Now she was... this. Her skin, pale and waxy, stretched too tightly across her face. The painted grin didn't match the sheer terror frozen in her wide, staring eyes.

"Detective Harper," a voice purred from the shadows, smooth and theatrical, like a stage actor addressing his audience. Harper spun around, drawing his gun, but the voice only chuckled. "I've been expecting you."

"Show yourself!" Harper barked, his flashlight darting across the room. The shadows seemed to mock him, shifting and twisting just out of reach.

"Do you like my work?" the voice asked, almost tenderly. "I've spent years perfecting it. The art of control, the dance of the marionette. You wouldn't believe how... freeing it is to strip someone of their burdens, their choices. To make them... perfect."

"You're sick," Harper growled, stepping toward the voice. "What did you do to these people?"

A figure emerged from the darkness, cloaked in a long, tattered overcoat that seemed to fuse with the shadows. His face was obscured by a porcelain mask, its expression neutral yet unnervingly watchful. Strings dangled from his gloved hands, swaying gently as he moved forward. "I gave them purpose," the Puppet Master said simply. "Would you like to see?"

Before Harper could react, the room came alive. The lifeless marionettes lining the walls suddenly jerked upright, their strings snapping taut as if pulled by invisible hands. They moved in unison, their wooden limbs creaking and clacking against the floor. Harper's pulse thundered as the puppets encircled him, their hollow eyes fixed on him with unnatural precision. Maria Lopez was among them, her grotesque smile twitching as her head tilted to one side.

"Stay back!" Harper shouted, aiming his gun at the Puppet Master. "I swear I'll shoot!"

The Puppet Master tilted his head, as if amused. With a flick of his wrist, the marionettes lunged forward. Harper fired, the gunshot deafening in the cramped space, but the bullet passed through the Puppet Master as if he weren't there. The marionettes closed in, their hands cold and rigid as they grabbed at his arms, his legs, pulling him down.

"No—no!" Harper struggled, but their grip was unrelenting. His flashlight clattered to the floor, casting wild beams of light across the room. He felt the strings then, cold and sharp, wrapping around his wrists and ankles, tightening until they cut into his skin. He thrashed, but the strings only dug deeper, binding him like an insect caught in a web.

"You'll understand soon enough," the Puppet Master whispered, his voice echoing like a lullaby. "Free will is such a heavy burden. Let me take it from you."

Harper's screams echoed through the theater, swallowed by the darkness. The last thing he saw before his vision blurred was Maria Lopez, her head tilting further as if to watch him more closely, her grin stretching impossibly wide.

When the darkness lifted, Harper was no longer himself. He stood on a stage, his limbs moving not by his own will but by the tug of strings he could not see. The audience before him was silent, their faces hidden in shadow. The Puppet Master stood at the center, his gloved hands working the controls with delicate precision.

"You see, Detective," the Puppet Master said softly, "in the end, we're all just playthings."

And the curtain fell.

CHAPTER 19: THE LAKE'S LAMENT

The moon hung low over Stillwater Lake, its pale light rippling across the glassy surface. The town of Elmswood slept, its streets silent and shuttered, but Rachel couldn't sleep. She stood at the edge of the dock, her bare feet curling against the damp wood. The night air kissed her skin, cool and damp with the scent of moss and pine. She wasn't sure what had drawn her out of bed tonight—only that the lake had been in her dreams again.

She had first heard the stories during her second week in town. Elmswood had a way of clinging to its past like ivy on brick, its legends as much a part of its charm as the cobblestone streets and flower-boxed windows. The lake, they said, was cursed. "It's beautiful, sure," Mrs. Callahan, the owner of the local diner, had remarked while refilling Rachel's coffee. "But it's best admired from a distance."

"Why?" Rachel had asked, her curiosity piqued.

The old woman's eyes had narrowed, her lips pressing into a thin line. "People vanish in that water. Always have. The lake calls to them, and they… go. Never come back. Some say it's the spirits of the drowned, pulling others under. Others say the lake's just hungry." She'd chuckled then, but it was a hollow sound. "Take my advice, darlin'. Stay on dry land."

Rachel had nodded politely and dismissed the warning as small-town superstition. But the lake had a way of creeping into her thoughts, of whispering to her as she passed it on her morning jogs or sat reading in the park. And then the dreams began: endless, dark water; voices calling her name; hands brushing her ankles. She told herself it was nothing, but tonight, she couldn't resist.

The dock groaned softly beneath her as she stepped closer to the edge. The lake was so still, so inviting, its surface like liquid obsidian. Rachel inhaled deeply, her breath hitching as she caught something faint, almost imperceptible.

A voice.

"Help…"

She froze, her heart hammering in her chest. The word was faint and distant, like a whisper carried on the wind. She scanned the shoreline, but no one was there. The town was asleep, and she was alone.

"Please… help me…"

The voice came again, more distinct this time, and Rachel's blood ran cold. It was coming from the water. She leaned forward, squinting into the inky depths. There was nothing, only the faint glimmer of moonlight on the surface, but the voice—soft, pleading, desperate—cut through the silence like a blade.

"Who's there?" Rachel called, her voice trembling.

"Help us…"

More voices now, overlapping, male and female, young and old. They rose in a mournful chorus, their tones laced with anguish. Rachel's breath quickened, and she stumbled back, her instincts screaming at her to run. But something held her in place. There was a pull, an ache in her chest that she couldn't explain.

"They're suffering," she whispered to herself. "They need me."

The lake's voice swelled, wrapping around her like a siren's song. Her fear melted away, replaced by an overwhelming urge to help. Without thinking, she stepped off the dock, the water swallowing her feet. It was icy cold, but she barely noticed. She waded deeper, the voices growing louder with each step.

"Rachel..." they whispered now, her name curling around her like a lover's caress. She gasped, the sound of her name on their lips both intimate and terrifying. The water rose to her knees, her waist, her chest.

"Who are you?" she asked, her voice quivering as she treaded into the deep. "What do you want?"

"Stay..." they answered. "Stay with us..."

She froze as something brushed against her leg, soft and fleeting. Her breath hitched, but she couldn't bring herself to move. The water swirled around her, pulling her closer to the center of the lake. The voices were all-consuming now, a cacophony of despair and longing.

"I want to help," she whispered, tears streaming down her face. "I'll help you."

And then, the hands came.

They burst from the water, pale and skeletal, their fingers clawing at her arms, her legs, her waist. Rachel screamed, thrashing against their grip, but it was no use. They were strong, impossibly strong, and they dragged her under with horrifying ease.

The cold was a shock, stealing the air from her lungs as she plunged into the depths. Her vision blurred, the moonlight above fading as the water closed over her. The voices were deafening now, surrounding her, drowning her.

She opened her mouth to scream again, but the lake filled her throat, her lungs. Darkness closed in, and as she sank, she saw them—faces, pale and ghostly, their eyes hollow with sorrow. They stared at her, their mouths open in soundless cries.

And then, she was one of them.

The lake stilled once more, the surface unbroken, its secrets hidden beneath the mirror-like calm. On the dock, Rachel's shoes sat abandoned, a silent testament to her passing. The moon continued its journey across the sky, and the town of Elmswood slept on, unaware that the lake had claimed another.

The voices subsided, but they would rise again. They always did.

CHAPTER 20: THE TIMEKEEPER'S REVENGE

The shop was not there during the day. It never was. By sunlight, the cobblestone street on the edge of town was nothing but a forgotten curve, flanked by shuttered windows and crumbling brick facades. But at midnight—always at midnight—the shop appeared, as though it had been there forever, nestled between a derelict bookstore and a boarded-up hat shop. Its sign, painted in curling gold letters, read: *Tick & Tock: Fine Timepieces for Discerning Souls.*

Inside, the air smelled of aged wood and faintly of oil, like the ghosts of a thousand clocks were exhaling in unison. The walls were lined with shelves crowded by clocks of every kind —grandfather clocks with pendulums that swung hypnotically, delicate pocket watches with intricate engravings, and ornate cuckoo clocks that seemed to hum with suppressed life. The ticking was omnipresent, a steady, rhythmic pulse that filled the shop like a heartbeat.

At the counter stood Mr. Tick. His face was sharp, angular, as if carved from old ivory, and his eyes gleamed with a light that was both inviting and unsettling. He wore a long, black coat, the tails brushing the floor, and his hands—those pale, spidery hands— moved with unnatural precision, adjusting the gears of a small silver stopwatch as a new customer entered the shop.

The bell above the door tinkled faintly, though the door hadn't moved.

"Ah," Mr. Tick said, his voice smooth and measured, like the turning of a key inside a lock. "Welcome, my dear. You've come at just the right time."

The customer was a young woman, perhaps in her late twenties, her face drawn with exhaustion. Her name was Clara, and she clutched a crumpled flyer she'd found on her doorstep earlier that day. It advertised clocks of unmatched beauty and craftsmanship, promising prices so low they seemed impossible. She had thought it was a joke, but desperation had driven her here. Her father was sick, his medical bills piling higher than she could count. She needed money—or perhaps, she thought now, she needed time.

"I'm not sure why I'm here," Clara said, her voice trembling slightly as she stepped closer to the counter. "I don't even need a clock."

Mr. Tick tilted his head, his smile stretching wider than seemed natural. "Ah, but need is such a curious thing, isn't it? Perhaps you don't realize what you need until it's right before you." He gestured to the shelves. "Look around. See if anything speaks to you."

Clara hesitated, but the clocks seemed to call to her, their ticking growing louder, more insistent. She wandered the shop, her eyes scanning the dazzling array of timepieces. Finally, she stopped in front of a small, gilded mantel clock. Its face was porcelain, its hands delicate filigree, and its pendulum swung with a mesmerizing grace.

"This one," she murmured, almost to herself.

"A fine choice," Mr. Tick said, appearing behind her without a sound. He plucked the clock from the shelf with those unnervingly precise hands and set it gently on the counter. "This clock is very special. It doesn't just tell time—it keeps it. Holds it. Preserves it."

Clara frowned. "What does that mean?"

Mr. Tick smiled again, his teeth too white, too perfect. "It means you'll never waste a second with this clock in your possession. Every moment will matter."

The price was impossibly low, just as the flyer had promised. Clara paid in cash, her hands trembling as Mr. Tick wrapped the clock in brown paper and tied it with twine. As she exited the shop, the bell tinkled again, and when she turned back, the shop was gone.

The first night, Clara awoke to the sound of ticking. It was louder than she remembered, filling her small apartment with its relentless rhythm. She got up to check the clock, but its porcelain face stared back at her innocently. She told herself she was imagining things and went back to bed.

By the second night, her reflection in the mirror had changed. There were faint lines at the corners of her eyes, lines that hadn't been there before. Her hands looked rougher, her skin drier. She blamed the stress, the sleepless nights spent worrying about her father.

By the third night, the truth became undeniable. Clara's face was gaunt, her hair streaked with gray. Her hands trembled as she picked up the clock, staring at its perfect, unchanging face. "What's happening to me?" she whispered.

The ticking seemed to grow louder, as if in response.

Clara wasn't the first. Others before her had wandered into Mr. Tick's shop, lured by promises of beauty, precision, and time. The clocks they purchased were flawless, mesmerizing—but they all came at a cost. Each tick siphoned seconds, minutes, hours from their lives, feeding them into the master clock that stood in the hidden room behind Mr. Tick's counter. It was a grotesque thing, the size of a man, its gears and hands forged from bone and brass. With every life it consumed, the master clock grew stronger—and so did Mr. Tick.

By the seventh night, Clara could barely move. Her body was frail, her breath shallow, as though she had aged fifty years in a week. But she had learned the truth. She had found the flyer again, turned it over, and seen the faint, handwritten warning scrawled on the back: *Destroy the clock before it destroys you.*

Summoning the last of her strength, she lifted the gilded mantel clock and hurled it against the wall. It shattered into a thousand pieces. For a moment, silence fell, heavy and absolute. And then the ticking resumed—louder, faster, angrier.

The master clock in Mr. Tick's hidden room shuddered and groaned. Its hands spun wildly, its gears grinding as if in protest. Somewhere, across time and space, Mr. Tick felt it—the rupture, the defiance.

Clara's apartment was suddenly filled with shadows, writhing shapes that clawed at the walls. The shards of the broken clock began to move, dragging themselves across the floor, reassembling, reforming. Clara screamed, but her voice was lost in the cacophony of ticking that now filled her ears, her mind, her soul.

And then, there was nothing.

The shop appeared again the next night, as it always did, its sign gleaming in the moonlight. Inside, Mr. Tick stood at the counter, his hands as steady as ever, his smile as sharp. A new clock sat on the shelf—a gilded mantel clock, its porcelain face unmarred, its pendulum swinging with a mesmerizing grace.

The bell above the door tinkled faintly.

"Ah," Mr. Tick said, his voice smooth and measured. "Welcome. You've come at just the right time."

CHAPTER 21: THE CEMETERY'S KEEPER

The wind carried the scent of damp earth and decaying leaves as Elias fumbled with the rusted iron key. The creak of the cottage door opening echoed in the silence, and an involuntary shiver ran down his spine. The caretaker's cottage was smaller than he had imagined, with walls that seemed to lean inward, as though the weight of the cemetery pressed against it. A single oil lamp flickered on the table, already lit, though Elias could have sworn no one had been here for years.

He set his bag down on the uneven wooden floor and peered out the small, grimy window. The cemetery stretched endlessly, a sea of crooked headstones and gnarled trees swaying in the moonlight. The job had seemed easy enough when he'd applied—keep the grounds tidy, clear out overgrown weeds, and ensure the dead stayed undisturbed. But now, standing in the suffocating stillness of the place, he felt the weight of unseen eyes.

As the night deepened, Elias heard it for the first time: a whisper. Faint, like the rustle of dry leaves, but unmistakably human.

Elias...

He froze, his fingers tightening around the mug of coffee he'd been nursing. The voice was soft but insistent, curling through the air like smoke. He rose slowly, cautiously moving toward the window, but saw nothing beyond the shadows of the headstones. He told himself it was his mind playing tricks, the isolation of the cemetery and the strange stillness making him hear things.

But the whisper came again. Closer this time.

Elias... help us.

He dropped the mug. It shattered on the floor, the sound startling him, but he barely noticed. His breath quickened as he stepped out of the cottage, the cool night air biting at his skin. The whispers grew louder, more voices joining the chorus. They didn't seem to come from any one direction; instead, they surrounded him, seeping into his ears, his mind.

"Who's there?" he called out, his voice shaking.

The cemetery answered with silence, but then something moved. A figure, pale and flickering like a candle's flame, stood by a weathered tombstone. It was a woman, her face obscured by a veil of shadow, her hands outstretched.

"Help us," she whispered, her voice threading through the air like a needle. "We cannot rest."

Elias stumbled back, his heart pounding. "What... what are you?" he stammered.

The figure stepped closer, and as she did, others appeared. Men, women, children, their forms translucent and shimmering like heat waves. They gathered around him, their eyes hollow and pleading.

"Justice," the woman said, her voice no longer a whisper but a command. "We were wronged. Betrayed. Forgotten. And now we are bound."

"I... I don't understand," Elias said, his voice cracking. "What do you want from me?"

"You are the keeper now," another spirit hissed, a man whose face was marred by what looked like a deep, jagged wound. "You must bear witness. You must atone."

"For what?" Elias shouted, his fear giving way to frustration. "I didn't do anything to you!"

The spirits surged closer, their forms flickering and shifting. The air grew colder, and Elias could see his breath clouding in front of him. The ground beneath his feet trembled, and he felt a pull, like invisible hands dragging him forward.

"You are the bridge," the woman said, her face inches from his now. Her eyes were bottomless voids, pulling him in. "You will carry our pain. Our stories. And you will never leave."

Before Elias could scream, the earth opened beneath him. It wasn't a hole, not exactly, but a swirling vortex of darkness and decay. The scent of rot overwhelmed him as he was pulled down, his fingers clawing at the ground in vain. The spirits followed, their whispers growing louder, more insistent.

The world around him dissolved into shadow, and when he opened his eyes, he was no longer in the cemetery. He stood in a place of endless night, a landscape of twisted roots and crumbling tombstones stretching as far as the eye could see. The spirits surrounded him, their forms now solid, their faces etched with anger and sorrow.

"You belong to us now," the woman said, her voice echoing in the void. "You will serve. You will remember."

Elias fell to his knees, the weight of their grief pressing down on him like a physical force. He realized then that this was his eternity—to walk among the restless dead, to carry their stories, their suffering, until he himself became one of them.

And in the distance, back in the living world, the cemetery stood silent once more, waiting for its next keeper.

CHAPTER 22: THE ATTIC DOOR

The house loomed over Anna like a silent judge, its Gothic spires clawing at the pale afternoon sky. The wind whispered through the gnarled trees that lined the overgrown driveway, carrying with it the faint scent of decay. Anna shifted the weight of the iron key in her hand, its jagged edges biting into her palm. This was her grandmother's house now—or rather, it was hers.

Her grandmother's final words echoed in her mind as she stepped inside, the heavy door creaking shut behind her. *"The attic door must remain locked, Anna. Promise me. Promise me you'll leave it be."*

She had nodded at the time, her heart heavy with grief, the words spilling out of her more as a reflex than a vow. But now, standing in the dim foyer of the estate, surrounded by shadows and the faint smell of mothballs, curiosity gnawed at her like a living thing. What could possibly be so dangerous in the attic? What had her grandmother hidden up there?

The house itself felt alive, as though it had been waiting for her. The floorboards groaned beneath her feet, the walls seemed to sigh in time with her breath, and every creak of the old house made her nerves tighten further. She wandered the darkened halls, her fingers trailing over faded wallpaper and cracked picture frames. The house was steeped in memories she couldn't recall, generations of Thompsons staring back at her from sepia-toned photographs with expressions that seemed too knowing, too sharp.

When she finally found herself standing before the attic door, it was as though her feet had carried her there without her permission. The door was unremarkable—painted a dull, peeling white, with a rusted iron keyhole at its center. And yet, it felt wrong. The air around it was colder, heavier, as though the door itself exhaled some invisible, malignant energy.

Anna hesitated, the iron key trembling in her hand. She thought again of her grandmother's warning, her frail, bony hands clutching Anna's wrist with surprising strength. *"Leave it locked. For your sake, and for theirs."*

But who were *they*? And why would her grandmother leave her a house with such a secret, expecting her not to investigate? The question burned in her mind, relentless.

She slid the key into the lock.

The moment the mechanism clicked, the house seemed to shudder. Anna stepped back, her breath catching in her throat as the door creaked open of its own accord. A rush of icy air poured out, carrying with it the scent of damp wood and something coppery, metallic. She stared into the darkness beyond the threshold, her heart pounding.

"Hello?" she called, her voice trembling. It was absurd, she knew, but the silence that followed felt almost... expectant.

She stepped inside.

The attic was cavernous, the ceiling slanting sharply above her. Dust motes swirled in the weak beam of light from a single, grimy window on the far wall. Old trunks and furniture were scattered haphazardly, draped in yellowing sheets. But it wasn't the chaos that drew her attention—it was the carvings.

The walls were covered in them, intricate symbols and words

etched deep into the wood. Some were crude, scratched in with shaky hands, while others were precise, almost artistic. Anna felt a chill crawl up her spine as she stepped closer, running her fingers over the strange markings. They felt warm, as though the wood itself pulsed with some dormant energy.

A sound broke the silence—a faint, wet whisper.

Anna froze. "Who's there?"

The whisper grew louder, warping into a cacophony of overlapping voices. They spoke in a language she didn't understand, their tones pleading, furious, despairing. She backed away, her eyes darting around the attic, but she saw no one.

And then the shadows moved.

They poured from the corners of the room, coalescing into shapes that were almost human but not quite. Their limbs were too long, their faces blurred and featureless. They swayed as they advanced, their movements jerky, unnatural.

Anna stumbled, her back hitting an old trunk. "I-I didn't mean to —" she stammered, but the words died in her throat as one of the figures lunged forward, its shadowy hand reaching for her.

"*You shouldn't have opened the door,*" the voices hissed in unison, the sound like nails scraping against glass.

She scrambled to her feet, her heart hammering as she bolted for the attic door. But the shadows were faster. They surged around her, their touch icy and suffocating. Memories that weren't her own flooded her mind—images of fire, blood, and faces twisted in agony. She saw her grandmother, younger, standing in this very attic, her hands raised as she chanted words that burned like fire in Anna's skull.

The shadows pulled her back into the room, and the door slammed shut behind her, the key falling to the floor with a hollow clang.

Anna screamed, but the sound was swallowed by the darkness. And then, there was silence.

Days later, the neighbors noticed the lights in the old Thompson estate had gone dark. When the police arrived, they found the house empty, save for a single, rusted key lying in the center of the attic floor.

And on the walls, the carvings had grown.

CHAPTER 23:
THE EYES IN THE
DARKNESS

The first thing Ben Carter noticed was the silence—the kind that shouldn't exist in a city as sprawling and alive as Crestmont. The usual hum of neon signs, the buzz of streetlamps, and the distant wail of sirens were gone. In their place, a suffocating quiet pressed against his eardrums, broken only by the occasional nervous cough or muttered curse from his fellow office workers.

The power outage had started an hour ago, spreading like a virus. First, the lights in his high-rise office flickered out; then, the computer screens went dark, followed by the streetlights below. By the time Ben had descended the twenty-six flights of stairs to street level, the entire city had been swallowed by darkness. But it wasn't the power outage that unsettled him most—it was the eyes.

At first, he thought he was imagining them. Tiny pinpricks of light, scattered in the distance. He'd spotted them while standing on the corner of 9th and Main, staring down the pitch-black street as people shuffled past, their faces illuminated only by the pale glow of cell phone screens. The eyes were too high up to be headlights, too numerous to belong to any one animal, and far too still to be human. They just hovered there, like embers suspended in the void.

"Hey, Carter!" called a voice, snapping Ben out of his thoughts. It was Greg, his coworker, clutching a flashlight that barely cut through the haze of darkness. "You coming, or what? No sense standing around waiting for the world to fix itself."

Ben glanced back at the eyes, now gone, and nodded. "Yeah, let's stick together."

The streets were chaos—a tangle of stalled cars, panicked residents, and the occasional flicker of a flashlight beam. Without power, the city's towering skyscrapers and endless grid of streets felt alien, like the skeleton of something once alive. People huddled in groups, some shouting into dead cell phones, others whispering hurried prayers. But through it all, Ben couldn't shake the feeling that they were being watched.

"Anyone else hear that?" Greg asked suddenly, stopping in his tracks. His flashlight beam swept over the cracked pavement, catching nothing but litter and abandoned bicycles.

"Hear what?" Ben asked, his voice low.

Greg tilted his head, listening. "I don't know. It's like... like something dragging across the ground."

Ben strained his ears but heard nothing beyond the occasional shuffle of footsteps or a distant car alarm that had somehow survived the blackout. He was about to dismiss it when a woman screamed—a sharp, chilling sound that echoed through the empty streets.

"Over there!" someone yelled, pointing toward a narrow alleyway. Ben turned just in time to see the glow of eyes—dozens of them—blink out of existence as if they'd been swallowed by the shadows. The woman's scream cut off abruptly, leaving only the sound of her phone clattering to the ground.

"What the hell is that?" Greg whispered, his breath clouding in the cool night air.

Ben didn't answer. His heart thundered in his chest as he stepped closer to the alley, his every instinct screaming at him to turn back. But something about the eyes—their unnatural stillness, their piercing intensity—drew him in. He picked up the woman's phone, its shattered screen casting a faint blue glow. The alley was empty. No blood, no sign of a struggle. Just darkness.

"Ben, we need to get out of here," Greg urged, tugging at his sleeve. "This isn't normal."

"Nothing about this is normal," Ben muttered, pocketing the phone. "But if we don't figure out what's going on, no one's going to survive the night."

They continued down the street, their pace quickening as the atmosphere grew heavier, more oppressive. The eyes reappeared sporadically, always at a distance, always watching. Every time Ben turned his head, they vanished, as if teasing him.

By the time they reached the power station at the edge of the city, Greg was practically hyperventilating. "This is insane," he said, pacing back and forth. "We should've stayed with the others. What if those... those things followed us?"

"They already know we're here," Ben said grimly, gesturing to the treeline surrounding the station. Pairs of glowing eyes dotted the darkness, unmoving and silent. "But they haven't attacked. Not yet."

The station was a fortress of steel and concrete, its gates locked with heavy chains. Ben fumbled with the set of bolt cutters he'd grabbed from a nearby hardware store, his hands slick with sweat. Greg kept watch, his flashlight darting nervously between the treeline and the shadows creeping along the building's facade.

"Hurry up, man," Greg hissed. "I swear they're getting closer."

With a final snap, the chains fell away, and Ben pushed the gates open. The inside of the station was eerily quiet, the hum of machinery replaced by an unnatural stillness. Ben's flashlight cast long, flickering shadows on the walls as he navigated the labyrinth of corridors, searching for the main control room.

"Do you even know what you're doing?" Greg asked, his voice trembling.

"Not really," Ben admitted. "But it's either this or wait to die."

As they entered the control room, Ben's heart sank. The panels were smashed, wires torn out like entrails from a gutted beast. Whatever had caused the blackout, it wasn't a simple malfunction. This was deliberate.

"Shit," Greg muttered, running a hand through his hair. "We're screwed."

Before Ben could respond, a low, guttural growl echoed through the room, sending a chill down his spine. The flashlight flickered, and for a brief moment, the room was plunged into total darkness. When the light returned, the eyes were there—lining the walls, the ceiling, the floor.

"Run," Ben whispered, but it was too late.

The flashlight went out.

CHAPTER 24:
THE INSOMNIA
EXPERIMENT

The air in the laboratory was thick with the stench of sweat and antiseptic, a suffocating blend that clung to the skin and nostrils. Fluorescent lights buzzed overhead, casting an unnatural pallor over the room's occupants. The test subjects sat in a semi-circle, their faces pale and drawn, eyes rimmed red and glassy from days of relentless wakefulness. Monitors beeped steadily, tracking their heart rates and brain activity, an orchestra of machinery that underscored the mounting tension.

Dr. Stevens stood at the observation window, clipboard in hand, his brow furrowed. He hadn't slept much either—out of solidarity, or perhaps guilt. His lab coat hung loosely on his wiry frame, and his glasses slid down the bridge of his nose as he scribbled notes. His voice, measured but tinged with unease, broke the silence.

"Subject 4, Ms. Reyes," he called out, glancing at the young woman slumped in her chair. "How are you feeling?"

Reyes blinked slowly, as though the effort alone threatened to topple her over. Her once vibrant brown eyes stared vacantly ahead. "Like I'm... floating," she murmured. "But heavy at the same time. Like my body's here, but my mind's... somewhere else." Her voice was flat, devoid of emotion, as if the words were being pulled out of her against her will.

Another subject, a lanky man named Harris, let out a sharp laugh that turned into a choking cough. "Somewhere else," he echoed, his tone manic. "Yeah, yeah, that's a good way to put it. Because I'm seeing it too. The cracks. The... the in-between places." His fingers twitched violently, clawing at his own arms. "They're watching us, Doc. They're *right there.* Don't you see?"

Dr. Stevens straightened, his face betraying only the slightest flicker of concern. "Hallucinations are an expected side effect of prolonged sleep deprivation," he said, more to himself than to them. "Your minds are creating stimuli to fill the gaps. It's normal."

"It's not normal," Reyes snapped suddenly, her head jerking toward him. "What's normal about all of us seeing the same thing?" Her voice climbed in pitch, raw and desperate. "It's not just in my head. They're... they're moving closer. You can feel it too, can't you?"

Dr. Stevens opened his mouth to respond, but the words died in his throat as the lights flickered, then dimmed. The hum of the machines faltered, and for a moment, silence enveloped the room. The test subjects froze, their eyes darting around in unison.

Then came the sound—a low, guttural groan that seemed to emanate from the walls themselves. It was deep, resonant, vibrating through the floor and into their bones. The air grew colder, their breath visible in faint puffs. On the monitors, the brainwave patterns of every subject began to spike erratically, jagged lines clawing across the screens.

Harris began to laugh again, but this time it was a wet, gurgling sound, his head lolling back as if his neck could no longer support it. "They're here," he whispered, his grin splitting wide enough to reveal bleeding gums. "Oh God, they're *here.*"

Reyes screamed, a raw, primal sound that shattered the fragile calm. She pointed to the far corner of the room, where shadows pooled unnaturally, darker than they had any right to be. The shadows writhed, stretching and contorting, as something began to emerge. It was like watching oil spill across water, a shimmering, shifting mass that defied logic or form. Eyes—too many eyes—blinked open within the void, their gazes piercing and unrelenting.

"Shut it down!" Dr. Stevens barked, slamming his hand on the intercom. "Emergency power! Shut it all down!"

But the lab techs on the other side of the glass were frozen in terror, their faces illuminated by the sickly glow of the monitors. The machines began to sputter and spark, the beeping turning into erratic chirps before dying altogether. The room plunged into darkness, save for the pulsating glow emanating from the entity in the corner.

Harris stood suddenly, his movements jerky and unnatural. His head snapped toward Dr. Stevens, his eyes now black pits. "You opened the door," he said, his voice layered with something inhuman, a cacophony of overlapping tones. "You pulled us through."

Reyes scrambled backward, her chair clattering to the ground. "No, no, no," she chanted, tears streaming down her face. Her hands clutched at her temples as if trying to rip the images from her mind. "This isn't real. This isn't real!"

But it was real. The temperature plummeted further, frost creeping along the edges of the observation window. The shadows stretched across the floor, curling around the subjects' feet like tendrils. One by one, they began to convulse, their bodies contorting in ways that should have been impossible. Their screams blended with the droning groan of the entity, a symphony of agony and despair.

Dr. Stevens stumbled back, his chest heaving. He had thought he understood the limits of human endurance, the boundaries of consciousness. But this... this was something else entirely. He fumbled for the emergency override panel, his trembling fingers struggling with the controls.

The entity surged forward, its amorphous shape expanding, filling the room with an oppressive presence. The monitors exploded in a shower of sparks, and the final light above them shattered, plunging them into total darkness. In that void, the groaning sound grew louder, vibrating through every nerve in Dr. Stevens' body.

And then, for the briefest moment, there was silence.

When the backup lights flickered on, the room was empty. The test subjects, the shadows, the entity—they were all gone. The only sign of their presence was the frost-lined walls and the blood smears streaked across the floor.

Dr. Stevens sank to his knees, the clipboard slipping from his grasp. He stared at the observation window, where the lab techs watched him with wide, terrified eyes. He opened his mouth to speak, but no words came. All that remained was the echo of their screams, lingering in the cold, sterile air.

CHAPTER 25: THE SIREN'S SONG

The air was heavy with salt and silence as The Marlena cut through the ink-black waves, its hull groaning with the weight of the sea. Captain Lawson tightened his grip on the wheel, his knuckles pale as driftwood under the moonlight. Ahead, the horizon was empty—a void where sea and sky bled together into an endless abyss. The crew had been restless since they'd veered off course three days ago, their usual grumbling giving way to hushed whispers of old wives' tales. Forbidden waters, they called this place. The Graveyard of Mariners. It was a name Lawson had scoffed at when they'd first set sail, but now it clung to him like a shadow.

"Cap'n," came a voice from behind him, low and tentative. It was Harris, his first mate, a wiry man with sun-beaten skin and eyes that darted like minnows. "The men are hearin' things."

Lawson didn't turn. "The men are always hearin' things. It's the sea—it plays tricks on you."

"This is different," Harris said, his voice dropping to a whisper. "It's... music."

Lawson's jaw tightened. He'd heard it too, faint and fleeting, like the hum of a distant violin carried on the wind. But admitting that would only feed the growing unease among the crew. Superstition was a disease on ships like this, spreading faster than rot in the hold.

"Tell the men to focus on their work," Lawson said, his tone sharp enough to cut. "We've got nets to haul in at dawn."

Harris hesitated, then nodded, retreating into the shadows with the nervous energy of a man who'd seen something he couldn't explain.

The night deepened, and the air grew colder, thick with the scent of brine and something sweeter, almost floral. Lawson stood at the helm, staring into the darkness, when the sound came again —soft, lilting, and impossibly beautiful. It wasn't a song, not exactly; it was more like a feeling given voice, a melody that wrapped itself around your chest and pulled. He shook his head, trying to clear it, but the sound was everywhere now, seeping through the creaking boards and the whispering waves.

Shouts erupted from below deck. Lawson spun, his heart pounding, and sprinted toward the commotion. He found the crew gathered at the port side, their faces pale and slack, eyes fixed on the water. One of the younger sailors, a boy barely old enough to grow a beard, was climbing the railing, his movements slow and mechanical, as if in a trance.

"Collins!" Lawson barked. "Get down from there!"

The boy didn't respond. His lips were moving, forming words that Lawson couldn't hear, and his eyes... they were glazed, reflecting the moonlight like twin mirrors. Before anyone could reach him, Collins pitched forward, plunging headfirst into the black water. The splash was swallowed almost immediately by the sea, leaving only ripples behind.

"Man overboard!" Harris shouted, but no one moved. The crew stood frozen, their faces masks of terror.

Then Lawson saw them.

Shapes moved beneath the surface, pale and sinuous, like

ribbons of moonlight weaving through the depths. They circled the spot where Collins had disappeared, and for a moment, Lawson thought he saw a hand, delicate and webbed, reaching up to pull the boy under. He felt bile rise in his throat.

"Back to your posts!" he roared, shoving his way through the paralyzed men. "Now!"

The spell broke, and the crew scattered, their murmurs rising into a panicked cacophony. Lawson leaned over the railing, scanning the water for any sign of Collins, but he was gone. The shapes, however, remained, their movements impossibly graceful, like dancers performing for an audience that couldn't see them.

As the hours dragged on, the song grew louder. It was no longer a fleeting whisper but a full, haunting chorus that seemed to come from everywhere and nowhere at once. One by one, the men succumbed. They would stop whatever they were doing—hoisting nets, scrubbing the deck, even eating—and wander to the railing, their eyes glassy and their mouths curved into faint, blissful smiles. Lawson tried to stop them, but they moved as if possessed, their bodies unnaturally strong. By the time the sun began to rise, half the crew was gone.

Lawson stood at the helm, his hands trembling as he clutched the wheel. Harris was beside him, his face pale and drawn.

"What do we do, Cap'n?" Harris whispered. "They're takin' us, one by one. We'll all be gone by nightfall."

Lawson didn't answer. His eyes were fixed on the horizon, where the sun was climbing sluggishly into the sky. He could still hear the song, even now in the daylight, and it was taking all his strength to resist it. He thought of the stories his grandmother used to tell him when he was a boy, about the sirens who lured sailors to their deaths with their voices. Back then, he'd laughed at the idea. Now, he wasn't so sure.

"There's gotta be a way to stop it," Harris said, his voice desperate. "There's always a way."

Lawson's mind raced. The sirens wanted something—something more than just bodies to drag to the depths. There was always a reason behind the myth, a truth buried beneath the terror. And then it hit him.

"Get me the harpoon," he said, his voice steady.

Harris blinked. "What?"

"The harpoon," Lawson repeated. "And the strongest rope we've got."

Harris hesitated, then nodded, disappearing into the hold. When he returned, he was carrying the ship's harpoon gun, a coil of thick rope slung over his shoulder.

"What's the plan, Cap'n?" he asked, though his tone suggested he wasn't sure he wanted to know.

Lawson didn't answer. He tied the rope to the harpoon and then to the mast, his movements quick and precise. The song was louder now, almost deafening, and he could feel it pulling at him, tugging at the edges of his mind. But he didn't let himself falter.

Taking a deep breath, he aimed the harpoon at the water, where the pale shapes still swirled. "If you want us," he muttered under his breath, "then come and take me."

He fired. The harpoon shot through the air and plunged into the sea, the rope unspooling like a serpent. For a moment, there was silence. Then the water erupted, and the sirens rose.

They were beautiful and terrible, their faces otherworldly in their perfection, their bodies sleek and serpentine. Their eyes burned with an ancient, unknowable hunger as they thrashed against the rope, their screams mingling with their song.

Lawson held his ground, his hands wrapped tightly around the mast, but even he couldn't hold on forever.

"Cut it loose!" Harris shouted, his voice barely audible over the cacophony.

"No!" Lawson yelled back. "Not yet!"

The sirens' song faltered, their harmony breaking as they struggled against the harpoon. And then, just as suddenly as it had started, the music stopped. The sirens let out one final, piercing wail before disappearing beneath the waves, dragging the harpoon and rope with them. The water stilled, and the air was silent.

Lawson collapsed to his knees, his chest heaving. The crew emerged from their hiding places, their faces etched with disbelief and relief. Harris helped Lawson to his feet, his hands trembling.

"Is it over?" he asked.

Lawson looked out at the sea, now calm and empty. He didn't know the answer, but he nodded anyway.

"For now," he said.

The Marlena limped back to port with half its crew and a story no one would believe. But Lawson knew the truth: the sirens' song was still out there, waiting for the next ship foolish enough to listen.

CHAPTER 26: THE DOLLHOUSE

The dollhouse arrived on a crisp autumn afternoon, nestled in a delivery box too large for Lily's small arms to carry. Her father hauled it inside with a grunt, his glasses fogging from the sudden shift in temperature as he crossed from the cool outdoors into the warmth of their living room.

"Lily!" he called, setting the package down on the floor. "Your birthday surprise is here."

Lily skidded into the room, her socks slipping on the hardwood. Her wide, hazel eyes locked onto the box as though it contained the secrets of the universe. She clapped her hands together, her excitement spilling into the room like sunshine through a broken window.

Her mother appeared in the doorway, drying her hands on a dishtowel. "Careful, sweetheart. Let Dad open it first."

With the reverence of an archaeologist uncovering a sacred relic, her father peeled back the tape and pried open the box. Within lay the dollhouse, a perfect replica of their own two-story suburban home. Every detail was there—the pale blue siding, the white shutters, the flower boxes brimming with miniature red geraniums. Even the tiny swing set in the backyard was identical to Lily's real one.

"Oh, wow," Lily whispered, her fingers hovering just above the roof. She didn't dare touch it yet. "It's... it's beautiful."

Her mother chuckled and stepped closer to inspect it. "It's uncanny. Did you tell the company to make it look just like our house?" she asked her husband.

He shook his head, a puzzled smile creeping across his face. "No, I just picked the one that looked nice. Must be a coincidence."

Lily didn't care about the how or why. She was already on her knees, examining the tiny interior through the dollhouse's hinged walls. Inside were miniature versions of their furniture: her father's worn recliner, her mother's floral-patterned couch, the brass lamp with the crooked shade. Upstairs, there was her bed with its pink comforter, her parents' room with the quilt her grandmother had sewn, and even the cluttered home office her dad always promised to organize.

"Can I play with it now?" Lily asked, looking up at her parents with pleading eyes.

"Of course," her mom said, tousling her hair. "Just be gentle, okay? It looks delicate."

Lily nodded solemnly, already reaching for the tiny dolls that rested inside. There were three of them: a man, a woman, and a little girl with pigtails. Each one was dressed in clothes eerily similar to what Lily and her parents were wearing that day. She barely noticed; her attention was consumed by the infinite possibilities the dollhouse presented.

That night, as her parents watched TV downstairs, Lily sat cross-legged on her bedroom floor, the dollhouse illuminated by the soft glow of her bedside lamp. She moved the tiny man doll, setting him in the recliner in the miniature living room. Then she moved the woman doll to the kitchen, placing her in front of the sink. Finally, she picked up the girl doll and placed her in the tiny bedroom upstairs.

"Good night, Mommy. Good night, Daddy," she whispered to the dolls, her voice sing-song. She tucked the girl doll under the tiny pink comforter, then climbed into her own bed.

Downstairs, her mother let out a startled laugh. "That's weird," she said to her husband. "I was just washing dishes, and I swear I felt like someone was pushing me toward the sink."

Her husband raised an eyebrow but didn't look away from the TV. "Probably just your imagination."

The next day was when Lily noticed how strange the dollhouse really was. She'd been playing with the dolls all morning, making them eat breakfast at the tiny kitchen table. When she went downstairs to grab a snack, she found her parents sitting in the exact same positions as the dolls had been, eating the exact same breakfast she'd pretended to give them.

"Mommy?" she asked, her voice trembling. "Did you already eat breakfast today?"

Her mother looked up from her plate with a bemused expression. "Of course, sweetheart. Why?"

"No reason," Lily mumbled, backing out of the room.

Her heart raced as she returned to the dollhouse. She stared at it, her fingers trembling as they hovered over the dolls. Experimentally, she picked up the man doll and moved him to the front yard, placing him behind the tiny lawnmower. Then she crept to the window and peeked outside.

Her father was there, pushing the mower across the grass, his face blank and mechanical.

Over the next few days, Lily's play became more deliberate. She moved the dolls around the house and watched as her parents mimicked their actions without realizing it. She made her mother bake cookies. She made her father hammer nails into the fence. It was fun, at first—a secret game only she knew the rules to.

But then, she made a mistake.

One evening, as the sky outside turned a bruised purple, she placed the woman doll at the top of the dollhouse stairs. She pretended the doll tripped, tumbling down the narrow staircase. The moment the doll landed at the base, Lily heard a scream from downstairs.

She ran to the living room to find her mother sprawled at the bottom of their real staircase, clutching her ankle. Her father was already there, helping her up.

"What happened?" Lily asked, her voice barely a whisper.

"I don't know," her mother said, wincing. "I must've missed a step."

Lily's stomach churned as she looked from her mother's pale face to the dollhouse sitting innocently in the corner of the room.

That night, Lily tried to stop playing with the dollhouse. She shoved it into her closet and buried it under a pile of stuffed animals. But the pull of it was too strong. By midnight, she was sitting in front of it again, her hands trembling as she rearranged the dolls.

"I'm sorry," she whispered to them. "I didn't mean to hurt anyone."

The dolls stared back at her with their painted eyes, unblinking and accusatory.

"I'll fix it," she promised. "I'll make it right."

She picked up the woman doll and set her gently in the tiny bed. She tucked the pink comforter around her and smoothed the fabric with her finger. Then she picked up the man doll, intending to place him beside the woman.

But the doll wouldn't move.

Her fingers were stuck. No, not stuck—pulled. The doll felt heavier, colder, as though it were merging with her hand. Panic surged through her as she tried to let go, but her skin was sinking into the doll's painted surface, her arm being drawn downward. The room tilted, the dollhouse growing impossibly large, or was she shrinking?

"Mommy! Daddy!" she screamed, but her voice sounded small, far away.

The last thing she saw before the world went dark was the girl doll lying in the miniature bed, her face frozen in an expression of terror.

The next morning, Lily's parents searched the house for her. They called her name until their throats were raw, but she was nowhere to be found.

In her bedroom, the dollhouse sat on the floor, its tiny rooms perfectly arranged. Inside, three dolls sat at the kitchen table: a man, a woman, and a little girl with pigtails.

CHAPTER 27: THE NIGHT SHIFT

The fluorescent lights buzzed faintly in the empty corridor, casting pale, flickering halos across the sterile linoleum floor. Nurse Karen adjusted her scrub top, the fabric sticking to her back where sweat had pooled despite the chill of the hospital's air conditioning. It wasn't unusual for night shifts to feel eerie, but tonight, there was something... wrong. It was like the walls themselves were holding their breath.

Room 406 was the latest anomaly. The patient, a middle-aged man who had been in a coma for two weeks following a car accident, had miraculously regained consciousness earlier that evening. Karen had been the one to witness it. His vitals skyrocketed, alarms blaring, before stabilizing as he opened his eyes. But the moment he looked at her, Karen felt her stomach drop. There was life in his body, sure, but his eyes were empty—two dull marbles set in a face that once held expression. He had blinked at her, slow and deliberate, before muttering, "I'm fine."

Karen hadn't believed him.

Now, as she approached 406 again during her rounds, her heart thudded in her chest. The door creaked as she pushed it open, the sound unnaturally loud in the silence. The man sat upright in bed, his hands folded neatly in his lap. He stared straight at the wall, unmoving. The television was off. The lights were dim. He didn't even flinch when she entered.

"Mr. Langley?" Karen's voice was soft, careful, but it still sounded too loud in the oppressive quiet. He turned his head toward her in a slow, mechanical motion, his gaze locking onto her like a predator spotting prey. Her stomach churned.

"Can I help you, Nurse Karen?" he asked, his voice devoid of inflection. It wasn't a question. It was a statement, as if he knew she couldn't possibly answer.

Karen swallowed hard, forcing professionalism into her tone. "Just checking in to see how you're feeling."

"I'm fine," he said again, his lips curling into the faintest shadow of a smile. The smile didn't reach his eyes.

It was the same smile she'd seen on Mrs. Hall in room 310 just two nights ago, the elderly stroke patient who had suddenly regained full mobility and speech after weeks of immobility. It was the same smile on the teenage girl in 212, who had stopped crying over her broken leg and now sat silently for hours, her hands gripping the sides of her bed as if she were bracing for something Karen couldn't see.

Karen nodded, her hand gripping the edge of the clipboard she carried. "Let me know if you need anything," she murmured, backing out of the room. Langley's gaze followed her until the door clicked shut.

She leaned against the wall outside, her breath shallow. A cold draft whispered through the hallway, making her shiver.

"What is happening?" she whispered to herself, her words barely audible over the hum of the building.

"Karen?" Dr. Patel's voice startled her, and she jumped. He stood a few feet away, his white coat pristine even at this late hour. His dark eyes were shadowed with exhaustion, but there was a sharpness there that made her wonder if he'd been thinking the same things she had.

"Dr. Patel," she breathed, clutching her clipboard like a shield. "Have you... noticed anything strange tonight?"

He hesitated, his brow furrowing. "Strange how?"

Karen glanced back at Langley's door, then leaned closer to the doctor. "It's not just tonight. It's been happening all week. Patients are waking up—recovering—but they're... different. Like something's missing."

Dr. Patel's frown deepened. "Missing?"

Karen nodded. "It's like they're alive, but they're not *there.* No emotions, no reactions. Just... hollow."

There was a long pause before Dr. Patel finally spoke. "I've noticed it too," he admitted, his voice low. "I've run every test I can think of. CT scans, MRIs, blood panels. Physically, they're fine. Better than fine. But psychologically..." He trailed off, shaking his head.

Karen licked her lips, glancing over her shoulder again. "I've seen things," she said quietly. "At night. In their rooms."

Dr. Patel straightened. "What kind of things?"

Karen hesitated. She knew how it would sound. But the memory of the shadows—the way they slithered across ceilings and walls, the way they hovered over patients' beds, dipping low as if to drink from their very mouths—was burned into her mind.

"Shadows," she finally whispered. "They move when there's no one there. They... they gather around the patients right before they change."

Dr. Patel's expression shifted from concern to something colder. "Karen, are you—"

"I'm not imagining it," she interrupted, her voice trembling. "I know what I saw. It's like... something is taking them. Their souls, maybe. I don't know. But it's real."

Dr. Patel stared at her for a long moment, his jaw tight. Then, to her surprise, he nodded. "If you're right," he said slowly, "then we need to figure out what it is. And how to stop it."

Karen felt a flicker of relief—quickly snuffed out by fear. "How?" she asked. "I don't even know where to start."

Before Dr. Patel could answer, a distant sound echoed through the hallway: a low, guttural moan. The kind that didn't come from human lungs. Karen's blood ran cold.

"What was that?" she whispered.

Dr. Patel didn't answer. Instead, he turned and started down the hall, his footsteps unnervingly calm. Karen followed, her heart pounding. The sound grew louder as they neared the ICU, a chorus of unnatural groans and whispers that seemed to seep from the walls.

As they approached room 412, Karen froze. The door was ajar, and inside, the shadows were alive.

They writhed and coiled like smoke, circling the bed where a young woman lay unconscious. They pressed against her chest, her mouth, her eyes, sinking into her like ink soaking into paper. Karen felt bile rise in her throat.

"Stop!" she cried, stepping into the room. The shadows recoiled, twisting toward her as if aware of her presence. For a moment, they hung in the air, black tendrils reaching for her. Karen felt a pull—a cold, hollow tug deep in her chest, as if something were trying to rip her apart from the inside.

"Karen!" Dr. Patel grabbed her arm, yanking her back. The shadows retreated, dissolving into the walls like mist. The room was silent again, save for the beep of the heart monitor.

Karen gasped for breath, clutching her chest. "Did you see that?"

she choked out.

Dr. Patel nodded, his face pale. "We're not imagining this," he said grimly. "Whatever it is, it's not done. And if we don't stop it..."

Karen didn't need him to finish. She knew what he meant. If they didn't stop it, none of them would have souls left to save.

CHAPTER 28:
THE PORTRAIT
OF THE PAST

The studio was cloaked in the warm amber glow of the desk lamp, its light catching on the fractured surface of the ancient portrait. Sophie leaned in, her gloved hands steady as she traced a fine brush across the cracks of the oil painting. The face of Madame Lorraine, with her piercing green eyes and faint smirk, seemed almost alive beneath Sophie's careful touch. Centuries of grime and neglect had dulled the vibrancy of the piece, but as Sophie painstakingly removed layers of dust, the portrait began to breathe again.

She paused to examine her progress. The woman in the painting was unsettlingly beautiful. Her auburn hair coiled in elaborate twists, her emerald gown cascading in painted silk folds, her jewelry shimmering with lifelike detail. The most captivating feature, though, was her expression. That smirk—it was equal parts alluring and unnerving. It felt like Madame Lorraine was watching her, her eyes following Sophie's every movement.

The first sign came as a whisper. A faint, almost imperceptible sound, like the rustling of fabric. Sophie froze, her brush poised mid-stroke. She glanced around the studio. The room was silent save for the hum of the overhead fluorescent light. The shadows cast by the rows of easels and unfinished canvases seemed deeper than usual, but Sophie shook her head and dismissed the noise as her imagination.

The whisper came again, louder this time, curling around her ear like a breath. "Sophie…"

She jolted upright, her stool scraping loudly against the hardwood floor. Her heart thudded against her ribcage as she scanned the empty room.

"Hello?" she called, her voice wavering. The only response was the faint creak of the building settling. She let out a shaky laugh, berating herself for working too late again. The mind played tricks when it was tired, she reasoned. Sophie returned to her stool, staring at Madame Lorraine's painted face.

"Stop scaring yourself," she muttered under her breath as she reached for her tools.

But the moment her brush touched the canvas, the air grew heavy. It was as though the room itself were holding its breath. The lamp flickered, the light dimming and brightening in erratic pulses. Sophie's hand stilled. The whispers returned, louder now, overlapping voices that seemed to seep from the walls, the floor, the painting itself.

"Who's there?" Sophie demanded, her voice cracking. She stood, knocking over her stool in her haste to back away. Her gaze darted to the portrait. Madame Lorraine's smirk seemed wider now, her green eyes glinting with something almost… malicious.

The voices stopped. The silence was worse.

Sophie's pulse thundered in her ears as she approached the painting cautiously. "This isn't funny," she said, though she wasn't sure who she was addressing. Her fingers trembled as she reached for the canvas, as if touching it would prove she was imagining things.

But then, Madame Lorraine moved.

It was subtle at first—the turn of her head, the deepening of her smirk. Sophie stumbled back, her breath hitching in her throat. The painted woman's eyes locked onto hers and seemed to blaze with unnatural light. A low, throaty laugh echoed through the studio, and Sophie realized with mounting horror that it wasn't coming from her own mouth.

"You've freed me," the voice purred, rich and velvety, dripping with triumph. It was not Sophie's voice. It was hers—Madame Lorraine's.

Sophie tried to scream, but her voice wouldn't obey. Her limbs felt heavy, her vision blurring as a cold, invasive presence wormed its way into her mind, her very self. She staggered, clutching at her temples as the laughter grew louder, resonating inside her skull.

"Such a lovely vessel," Madame Lorraine cooed. "Your hands, your eyes, your youth… yes, you'll do nicely."

"No," Sophie gasped, her voice faint, cracking under the strain of resisting the spirit's onslaught. "Get out of my head!"

The studio distorted around her as if the walls were melting. The lamps flickered and shattered, plunging the room into darkness. The only light came from the painting, which now glowed with a sickly green hue. Sophie's reflection in the glass over the canvas twisted, her features warping into something unrecognizable. Her face… wasn't her face anymore. It was Madame Lorraine's.

"Don't fight me, dear," the spirit hissed, her voice a venomous lullaby. "It's already too late."

Sophie collapsed to her knees, her body wracked with violent tremors. She clawed at the floor, her nails splintering as she tried to hold onto something, anything, that would anchor her to herself. But the spirit was relentless, prying into her mind, her memories, her essence.

The last thing Sophie saw before her vision went dark was Madame Lorraine stepping out of the painting, her form no longer confined to oil and canvas. She was real—flesh and blood and malice—and she was wearing Sophie's face.

Sophie tried to scream again, but the sound was swallowed by the void. And then, there was silence.

When the sun rose the next morning, the studio was quiet. The painting of Madame Lorraine was gone, leaving only an empty frame. Sophie sat at her desk, her back straight, her hands folded neatly in her lap. Her emerald-green eyes glinted as she smiled faintly at the sunlight streaming through the window.

The neighbors would later say Sophie seemed... different after that night. More confident. More poised. And yet, there was something about her smile that made their skin crawl.

No one ever found the portrait.

CHAPTER 29: THE FOG THAT CONSUMES

The fog rolled in like a living thing, silent and suffocating, swallowing the coastal town of Blackwater Bay in its ghostly embrace. By the time anyone noticed its unnatural density, it was too late. The radios hissed with static, phones stuttered into nothingness, and the hum of the modern world was extinguished. The fog had consumed it all.

Officer Daniels tightened his grip on the flashlight in his hand, its feeble beam barely piercing the dense, gray wall ahead of him. The faint, salty tang of the sea lingered in the air, but it was tainted now, tinged with something metallic, something wrong. Blackwater Bay was unrecognizable in the soupy haze. The once-familiar dockside shops and weathered Victorian homes were reduced to vague shadows. Somewhere in the distance, a church bell tolled—slow and mournful. But Daniels knew no one was ringing it.

He turned to the small group huddled behind him in the police station's foyer. Their faces were pale and drawn, illuminated by the weak glow of a battery-powered lantern on the desk. There were six of them: an elderly woman clutching a rosary, a young couple holding hands as if their grip alone could anchor them to safety, a middle-aged fisherman with a gash across his forehead, and two teenage brothers who couldn't stop whispering to each other, their voices trembling. Each face bore the same question:

What now?

Daniels cleared his throat, his voice rough from hours without water. "We're running out of time. If we stay here, we'll starve. But if we go out there..."

He didn't finish. He didn't need to. The blood-smeared windows of the station told the story well enough. Earlier that night, someone—he couldn't remember who—had screamed and bolted out into the fog, shouting that they'd seen their missing daughter. The last thing Daniels had seen of them was a silhouette, flailing and jerking unnaturally, before something massive dragged them into the mist. The sound it made still echoed in his ears—a wet, guttural crunch.

"What if we just wait it out?" the fisherman, Hendricks, said, his voice rough and desperate. He dabbed at his forehead with a grimy bandana. "The fog's gotta lift eventually, right? It's just weather."

"That's not weather," muttered one of the teenagers, the younger one, his voice barely a whisper. He didn't look up from where he was clutching his brother's arm. "It's alive. It's hunting us."

"Don't say that!" snapped the older brother, though his voice cracked on the last word. "You don't know what it is!"

"Enough," Daniels barked, silencing them. He ran a hand down his face, his stubble scraping his palm. "We can't stay. We've got maybe a day's worth of food and water left, and we don't know how long this—" he gestured vaguely toward the swirling grayness outside "—is going to last. We need to get to the marina. The boats have emergency supplies, and if we're lucky, we can ride them out of here."

The elderly woman clutched her rosary tighter, her lips moving in silent prayer. "And if they're gone? If... if *they've* taken the boats like they've taken the people?"

Daniels hesitated. He didn't have an answer for that. He only knew that staying put was certain death.

"I'll go," the young man in the couple said suddenly. His girlfriend's head snapped toward him, her eyes widening in panic.

"Jason, no—"

"I'll go," Jason repeated, his voice firmer now. He looked at Daniels. "You said the boats have supplies. If we can bring some back here, maybe we won't have to risk everyone."

Daniels studied him for a long moment. The kid couldn't have been older than twenty-five, but there was a stubborn resolve in his eyes that Daniels recognized. It was the look of someone desperate to keep the people they loved safe, no matter the cost.

"No," Daniels said finally. "If anyone goes, it's me. I'm trained for this."

Jason shook his head. "You're the only cop left. If you die out there…" His voice caught, but he pushed through it. "If you die, we're screwed. You've got the gun. You've got the experience. You're what's keeping us together. I'll go."

The girlfriend clutched at his arm, tears streaming silently down her face. "Please, Jason, don't—"

"I'll go with him," Hendricks interjected. He stood, swaying slightly but resolute. "I know the marina better than anyone here. We'll be quicker together."

Daniels opened his mouth to argue, but the words died in his throat. He saw the determination in their faces, the grim acceptance of what they were about to do. Finally, he nodded, though every instinct screamed against it.

"All right," he said. "But you take the flashlight and the flare gun. If anything… happens, you fire that flare, and you run. Don't try to be a hero."

Jason nodded, his jaw tight. Hendricks grabbed the flare gun from the desk, checking it with practiced hands. Daniels handed over the flashlight, its beam flickering slightly as if in protest.

The two men stood at the door, the oppressive fog pressing against the glass like a living thing. For a moment, the room was silent, save for the elderly woman's whispered prayers. Then Daniels unlocked the door, the click echoing like a gunshot.

"Good luck," he said, his voice low.

Jason and Hendricks stepped out into the fog, and the door swung shut behind them with a hollow thud. The group inside held their breath, straining to hear anything—footsteps, voices, the flare.

Instead, they heard the fog shift. It wasn't a sound so much as a sensation, a low, resonant hum that vibrated in their bones. The lantern flickered, casting long, jittery shadows over the walls.

Then came the screams.

Jason's first—sharp and terrified, cutting through the silence like a knife. Then Hendricks, shouting something unintelligible before his voice rose into a shriek of pure agony. The sound of flesh tearing, of something wet and heavy hitting the ground, followed. And then… nothing.

The silence was worse.

Daniels stood frozen, his hand on the door, his mind racing. He wanted to rush out, to do something, but fear rooted him to the spot. The others stared at him, their faces pale and stricken.

The younger brother broke the silence, his voice trembling. "I told you… it's hunting us."

Daniels didn't respond. He couldn't. Because in that moment, as the fog pressed closer against the glass, he realized the boy was right. And it wasn't finished yet.

CHAPTER 30: THE ELEVATOR GAME

The fluorescent buzz of the elevator lights flickered as Alex pressed the worn 'Close Door' button. The high-rise building was eerily silent, its hallways stretching out like veins in the darkened concrete skeleton. It was well past midnight, and the city below had dulled to a hushed hum.

"Are we really doing this?" Harper asked, arms crossed tightly as if to shield herself from the chill of unease creeping up her spine. Her voice wavered, betraying her attempt to sound indifferent.

"Stop being so dramatic," Alex replied, his tone sharp with excitement. He adjusted his hoodie and glanced at the crumpled piece of paper in his hand, the ritual steps scrawled in his messy handwriting. "It's just a game. Nothing's going to happen."

"Yeah, that's what they always say in horror movies," muttered Ethan from the corner of the elevator, his lanky frame slouched against the mirrored wall. His reflection seemed distorted in the dim light, his face stretching unnaturally when viewed through the warped surface. "This is so stupid."

"Then leave," Alex shot back. "No one's forcing you to stay."

Ethan rolled his eyes but didn't budge. Harper chewed on her lip nervously, glancing at the buttons as Alex jabbed the sequence: 4, 2, 6, 10, 5. The elevator lurched to life, its mechanical groan reverberating up through the floor.

"Okay, so what's supposed to happen?" Harper asked, her voice tight.

Alex grinned, the whites of his teeth glinting in the dim light. "If we do this right, we'll reach another dimension. The Otherworld or whatever. It's just a game, but people say—"

"People say it's real," Harper interrupted, her voice rising. "They say you see... things."

Alex waved her off, his grin unwavering. He loved this. The thrill. The control. The way their nervous energy fed into his own. "Relax. As long as we follow the rules, we'll be fine."

The elevator stopped at the fourth floor. The doors slid open to reveal a corridor bathed in flickering yellow light, empty and silent. Harper exhaled sharply, her breath fogging the cold air. No one moved.

"Next step," Alex said, his voice low, almost reverent. He pressed the button for the second floor.

The ride down seemed slower, more agonizing. The air grew heavier, and Harper swore she could hear faint whispers, though Ethan dismissed it as the elevator's old machinery. On the sixth floor, the doors opened to a hallway darker than the others, its fluorescent bulbs shattered, leaving only shadows to creep along the walls.

"I don't like this," Harper whispered.

"Shh," Alex hissed. "We're almost there."

The elevator continued its ritual path, climbing to the tenth floor and then descending to the fifth. When the doors opened this time, the air felt different—thicker, colder, like stepping into a room where someone had just been breathing too heavily. The silence was oppressive, pressing against their ears like cotton.

"This is it," Alex said, a tremor in his voice betraying his confidence. "The next step is pressing the button for the first floor. If it works, the elevator will go up instead of down."

"And if it doesn't?" Ethan asked, his sarcasm faltering as the weight of the moment settled over him.

"Then we're just idiots playing a stupid game," Alex said, forcing a chuckle. He pressed the button for the first floor.

The elevator shuddered. The lights flickered violently, plunging them into brief but suffocating darkness. When they came back on, the elevator was moving—up.

None of them spoke. The floor numbers blinked past: 6, 7, 8, 9... 10.

And then... 11.

The elevator stopped.

The doors slid open with a hiss, revealing a hallway unlike any they'd seen before. The air was thick with an acrid, metallic tang, like rusted iron. The walls were smeared with dark stains that could have been water—or something worse. A faint red glow pulsed from an unseen source, casting shadows that seemed to ripple and breathe. The corridor stretched endlessly in both directions, a labyrinth of decay and darkness.

"Oh my God," Harper whispered, clutching Ethan's arm. "This isn't real. This can't be real."

"Don't step out," Alex warned, his voice trembling. "Stay in the elevator. That's the rule."

Ethan craned his neck to peer down the hallway, his curiosity battling his fear. "What the hell is this place?"

"It's the Otherworld," Alex said, his voice barely audible. He stared out into the hallway, his bravado crumbling. "We did it. We actually—"

A ding interrupted him. The elevator doors began to close, but before they could fully shut, something slipped inside.

The woman.

She was tall and gaunt, her limbs impossibly long and her skin sickly pale, almost translucent. Her black hair hung in matted strands over her face, obscuring her features. She wore a tattered dress that looked like it had been soaked in ink, the fabric clinging to her skeletal frame.

Harper let out a strangled gasp, and Ethan backed into the corner, his wide eyes fixed on the ground. Alex froze, his breath caught in his throat.

"Don't look at her," he whispered urgently, his voice cracking. "Don't speak to her. No matter what."

The woman stepped into the center of the elevator, her movements unnaturally fluid, like a marionette controlled by invisible strings. The air grew colder, each breath frosting in the unnatural chill. She didn't face them, her head tilted slightly, as if listening.

Harper began to shake, her hands trembling as she squeezed her eyes shut. Ethan's breathing grew ragged, his fists clenched at his sides. The elevator remained still, the oppressive silence broken only by the faint sound of the woman's shallow, wheezing breaths.

Then she spoke.

"Where are you going?" Her voice was hollow, a sound that scraped against the edges of their sanity. It echoed in the small space, filling every corner.

"Don't answer," Alex hissed, his eyes locked on the floor.

But Ethan couldn't help himself. Whether it was the fear, the tension, or the overwhelming need to break the silence, he looked up.

"I—"

The woman's head snapped toward him, her face still obscured by the curtain of her hair. Ethan's mouth hung open, his words dying in his throat as he stared into whatever lay beneath the veil.

"Ethan, no!" Alex shouted, but it was too late.

The lights flickered again, plunging them into darkness. The elevator jolted violently, as if it were being ripped from its cables. A sound like tearing metal filled their ears, and Harper screamed.

When the lights returned, the woman was gone. But so was the elevator. The three of them stood in the hallway now, the door behind them sealed shut.

"What did you do?" Alex demanded, grabbing Ethan by the collar. "You weren't supposed to look at her!"

"I didn't mean to!" Ethan stammered, his voice trembling. "I—I didn't—"

A low, guttural laugh echoed from the shadows, cutting him off. It wasn't coming from any of them.

The hallway stretched endlessly before them, the red glow pulsing in time with their racing hearts. The sound of footsteps —slow, deliberate—approached from the darkness.

"We're not alone anymore," Harper whispered, tears streaming down her face.

Alex turned, his voice shaking as he spoke. "We need to find a way back. Now."

But deep down, they all knew. The rules had been broken. And there was no going back.

CHAPTER 31: THE WATCHER'S WOODS

The crackle of the campfire was the only sound in the clearing, its orange glow licking at the base of the towering pines around them. The Peterson family sat in a tight circle, their faces pale and glistening with sweat despite the cool night air. They had been silent for a long time. Too long. Even eight-year-old Mia, who usually chattered endlessly about school and cartoons, sat clutching her stuffed rabbit, her eyes darting nervously into the darkness beyond the firelight.

"I don't like this place," Mia whispered, breaking the tense quiet. Her voice trembled, barely audible over the snapping wood.

"Shh, sweetheart," her mother, Karen, said, wrapping an arm around her daughter. "It's just the woods. They're... alive in their own way. It's nothing to be afraid of."

But Karen's voice lacked conviction. Her eyes betrayed her. She kept glancing over her shoulder, her lips pressed into a tight, bloodless line.

Her husband, Mark, poked at the fire with a stick. The flames flared briefly, casting jagged shadows across his face. "We'll leave first thing in the morning," he said finally. "It's just the wind playing tricks on us. We've all been cooped up in the house too long. This was supposed to be good for us."

"It doesn't feel good," their teenage son, Ethan, muttered. He was sitting with his knees pulled to his chest, his hands buried in the pockets of his hoodie. "It feels like we're being... watched."

Karen flinched at the word, and Mark shot his son a warning look. But Ethan wasn't wrong. They had all felt it since early that afternoon, a prickling sensation on the backs of their necks, like eyes boring into them from somewhere deep in the forest.

And then there were the symbols.

The first one had appeared on a tree near the picnic table, a jagged spiral carved deeply into the bark. At first, Mark had dismissed it as graffiti left by some bored hiker, but then Ethan found another one, and then another. All spirals. All freshly etched, as though the sap was still trying to bleed through the cuts.

Karen had tried to hide her panic, but by the time they spotted the fourth symbol—this one directly behind their tent —she couldn't keep it together anymore. "Mark," she whispered sharply, pulling him aside. "We need to go. Now."

But it was already getting dark by then, and Mark had insisted they stay. "It's too dangerous to hike out at night," he said. "We'll be fine. Just stay close to the fire."

Now, as the fire burned lower, the sounds of the forest seemed to close in around them. The chirping of crickets had faded, replaced by something else—soft, rustling movements in the underbrush and faint, almost imperceptible whispers. They came from all directions, sometimes close, sometimes far, but always just out of reach, like the forest itself was speaking.

Karen leaned toward Mark, her voice barely above a breath. "Do you hear that?"

"Yeah," Mark said, his hand tightening around the handle of the camping hatchet he had brought out from the tent. He glanced at Ethan, who had armed himself with the long metal poker from the fire pit.

"What do you think it is?" Ethan asked, his voice cracking.

"Probably just animals," Mark said, though he didn't sound convinced.

"Animals don't whisper," Karen hissed.

Mia whimpered and buried her face in Karen's side. "I want to go home," she cried. "Please, Mommy, I want to go home."

Karen stroked her daughter's hair, fighting back tears. "We will, baby. We will. First thing in the morning."

But deep down, she wasn't sure they'd make it that long.

The whispers grew louder, more distinct, though the words were impossible to make out. They sounded like a chorus of voices, overlapping and echoing, as if the trees themselves were speaking in some ancient, unknowable language. The rustling grew closer, circling the clearing, and then came the snap of a branch—loud, deliberate.

"That's it," Mark said, standing abruptly. "We're leaving. Grab what you can carry. We'll follow the trail back to the car."

"But you said—" Karen started.

"I was wrong," Mark snapped. "We're not staying another second."

They scrambled to gather their things, stuffing flashlights and water bottles into backpacks and abandoning everything else. Mia clung to her stuffed rabbit, her small hand clutching Karen's with a ferocity that made Karen's knuckles ache. Ethan took the lead, shining his flashlight into the trees as they started down the trail.

The air felt heavier as they walked, the darkness pressing in on them like a physical weight. The trail, which had seemed so well-marked earlier, now twisted and forked in ways that didn't make sense. Mark kept stopping to check the map, muttering under his breath.

"Are we lost?" Karen asked, panic creeping into her voice.

"No," Mark lied. "We just need to keep moving."

The whispers followed them, growing louder with every step. And then the symbols started appearing again—on the trees lining the path, glowing faintly in the beam of Ethan's flashlight.

"How...?" Ethan stammered. "We've been walking away from the campsite. How are they here?"

Karen's breath hitched, and she pulled Mia closer. "We're going in circles," she whispered.

"No," Mark said, shaking his head. "That's not possible."

But it was. They passed the same fallen log twice, then the same twisted oak with the gnarled roots that jutted out of the ground like skeletal fingers. The forest was changing around them, reshaping itself, trapping them in a maze with no exit.

And then the whispers stopped.

The sudden silence was deafening. Even the wind had died, leaving the forest unnaturally still. The Petersons froze, their breaths coming in shallow gasps as they strained to hear anything—anything at all.

The first scream came from Mia.

Her flashlight caught something in the distance—a figure, tall and impossibly thin, its limbs too long and its head cocked at an unnatural angle. It wasn't moving, but it was there, standing among the trees like a shadow that had come to life.

Then Ethan saw another one. And another. Dozens of them, stepping out from the darkness, their eyes glowing faintly, like embers in the night.

"Run," Mark whispered, his voice hoarse.

And they did.

CHAPTER 32:
THE RETURN OF
THE REAPER

The city had never felt so quiet. Even the usual hum of late-night traffic seemed subdued, as if the streets themselves were holding their breath. Maya Lee tightened her scarf against the biting wind as she stepped onto the cracked sidewalk, the glow of the streetlights casting long, skeletal shadows. In her hands was a leather-bound notebook, its pages filled with scrawled notes, photographs, and hastily drawn diagrams. Her head swam with the macabre details she had uncovered, but none of it added up. Not yet.

The deaths had started two weeks ago. A teenager found impaled on a chain-link fence, his body contorted like a ragdoll. No witnesses, no signs of struggle. The police ruled it an accident, but Maya knew better. The boy's friends had whispered about a dare—about summoning a spirit that would "plunge you into your worst fear." The urban legend was old, a relic of playground tales, but now it seemed to have come to life.

And then there was the woman who had drowned in her bathtub, her face frozen in a rictus of terror. Her neighbor swore she had been talking about "Bloody Mary" just days before, laughing about how she wasn't afraid to look into her bathroom mirror. Another story, another chilling coincidence.

Maya had spent the last fourteen days chasing these threads, diving into archives, interviewing witnesses, and piecing together the gruesome puzzle. Tonight, she had arranged to meet someone who claimed to have answers. Someone who had whispered a name over the phone—The Reaper.

The meeting place was an abandoned subway station, long since closed off to the public. Maya descended the crumbling steps, her flashlight cutting through the oppressive darkness. The air was damp and stale, thick with the smell of mildew. She felt her pulse quicken as her boots echoed against the tiled walls, each step sounding like a countdown.

"Hello?" she called out, her voice trembling despite her best efforts to steady it. The only response was the distant drip of water and the faint hum of unseen rats scurrying in the shadows.

Then she saw him.

A figure emerged from the darkness, cloaked in black. His face was obscured by a hood, but his presence was suffocating, like the air had been sucked out of the room. He carried a scythe— not the cartoonish kind, but something ancient and weathered, its blade gleaming faintly in the dim light.

"You've been digging where you don't belong," he said, his voice low and gravelly. It wasn't a threat; it was a statement of fact.

Maya swallowed hard, her grip tightening on the notebook. "You're The Reaper," she said, more to herself than to him. "You're the one behind the deaths."

The figure tilted his head, almost amused. "Behind them? No. I am merely the hand that delivers what was already written."

"Written?" Maya's voice rose, anger seeping into her fear. "What does that even mean? These people didn't deserve to die!"

"Deserve?" The Reaper stepped closer, his movements unnervingly smooth. "Do you think fate cares about what people deserve? These stories—the urban legends you scoff at—have lives of their own. They demand blood. They demand belief. I am their enforcer."

Maya's breath hitched. "You're saying… they created you?"

The Reaper nodded slowly. "Every whisper in the dark, every dare uttered in jest, every story told to scare a child—they feed me. They give me shape. And when the time comes, I claim what is owed."

Maya's mind raced. This couldn't be real. It was impossible. And yet, here he stood, this monstrous figure whose presence made her skin crawl. "Why are you telling me this?" she asked, her voice barely above a whisper.

"Because you've seen too much," he said simply. "You've drawn too close. And now, the story demands an ending."

Before she could react, the lights overhead flickered and went out, plunging the station into total darkness. Maya's heart pounded as she fumbled with her flashlight, her hands shaking violently. When the beam finally clicked on, he was gone.

"No, no, no," she muttered, spinning in place. The sound of scraping metal echoed around her, growing louder and closer. Panic surged through her as she realized he was circling her, unseen.

"Maya…" His voice slithered out of the shadows, mocking and cold. "Do you remember the story of the girl who wouldn't stop asking questions? The one who thought she could outsmart death?"

She froze. It was a story her grandmother used to tell her, a cautionary tale about curiosity leading to ruin. Her flashlight wavered as the memories flooded back.

"She died screaming," The Reaper continued, his voice now directly behind her. "Begging for another chance."

Maya spun around, but there was nothing there. Her flashlight flickered, the bulb threatening to give out. "You don't scare me," she lied, her voice breaking.

"Good," he whispered, his breath icy against her neck. "Fear is too easy. I prefer despair."

The flashlight died, plunging her into blackness. Maya screamed, swinging the notebook wildly, but it connected with nothing. Then she felt it—a cold, sharp pain slicing across her arm. She staggered back, clutching the wound, her blood warm against her skin.

"You're not getting away," she snarled, her fear now mingled with defiance. She reached into her bag and pulled out a small vial of holy water, a relic from her desperate attempts to arm herself. She hurled it blindly into the darkness.

A guttural hiss echoed through the station, followed by a low growl. The lights flickered back on just long enough for her to see him—his cloak smoldering where the water had hit, his skeletal face twisted in rage.

Maya didn't wait. She bolted down the subway tunnel, her breath ragged, her feet pounding against the tracks. Behind her, The Reaper's footsteps were impossibly fast, closing the distance with terrifying ease.

"You can't run from a story, Maya!" he roared. "You're already part of it!"

She didn't look back. Ahead, a faint light marked the end of the tunnel. If she could just make it there, maybe, just maybe, she could escape.

But as she reached the light, she realized it wasn't safety waiting for her. It was a mirror—a massive, cracked mirror mounted impossibly in the middle of the tunnel. Her reflection stared back at her, wide-eyed and terrified.

And then it smiled.

The Reaper's voice filled her ears, a cruel, mocking laugh. "The ending has already been written."

Maya's scream echoed through the tunnel, blending with the sound of shattering glass.

CHAPTER 33: THE MINE'S ECHO

The pickaxe struck rock with a dull clang, then silence. A silence so absolute it felt alive, pressing into the ears of the men like a phantom's whisper. For weeks, the crew had been chasing the thinnest veins of gold in this godforsaken mine, but now, as the final blow landed, the stone wall before them cracked. A cool, musty draft flowed through the fissure, carrying with it the scent of damp earth and something…stale. Something wrong.

Foreman Bill stepped forward, wiping grime from his forehead with the back of a calloused hand. "Looks like we've hit somethin'. Jenkins, pry it open."

Jenkins hesitated, his fingers tightening around the crowbar. "You sure about this, Bill? That air—don't smell right."

Bill shot him a look, the kind that brooked no argument. "Gold don't smell like roses, Jenkins. Now get to work."

With a reluctant nod, Jenkins wedged the crowbar into the crack and heaved. A chunk of stone fell away, then another, until the wall crumbled into an open maw, revealing a cavern beyond. The darkness inside was thick, almost tangible, as though it had been waiting for them.

One by one, the miners stepped into the void, their helmet lamps casting pale circles of light on the jagged walls. The cavern was massive, its ceiling disappearing into the shadows above. Stalactites hung like the teeth of some ancient beast, and the ground was slick with moisture. Gold glittered faintly in the rock, but no one spoke of it. The air was too heavy, too oppressive.

Then, it began.

"Bill," a voice whispered, sharp and clear. "You knew."

Bill froze. "Who said that?" he barked, spinning around. The men exchanged uneasy glances, each shaking their head.

"You knew," the voice repeated, louder this time. It was his voice. His own, but warped, as though dragged through the depths of a nightmare.

"Cut it out," Bill growled, his fists clenched. "Who's messin' with me?"

"I didn't touch nothin'!" Jenkins shot back, his wide eyes darting around the cavern. The others muttered their agreement, their voices trembling.

Then another voice rang out, this one echoing from the shadows. "You left us, Jenkins. You left us to die."

Jenkins staggered back, his face draining of color. "No... no, I didn't. I couldn't save you!" His voice cracked, and his breathing quickened.

"It's just the echoes," muttered Carter, the youngest of the crew, though his voice lacked conviction. "This place is playin' tricks on us. Let's just grab what we can and get out."

But the cavern wasn't done with them.

"Carter," a soft, mocking voice cooed. It was high-pitched, childish. "You still see her, don't you? That little girl you hit with your car."

Carter's helmet clattered to the ground as he clawed at his ears.

"Shut up! Shut up!" he screamed. "I didn't mean to! It was an accident!"

The cavern erupted into chaos. One by one, the miners heard their own secrets hurled back at them, their darkest fears and deepest regrets laid bare. McAllister dropped to his knees, sobbing, as a voice that sounded like his mother berated him for never returning home. Rodriguez lashed out at the shadows, swinging his pickaxe wildly, screaming apologies in Spanish. Jenkins sat with his back against the wall, muttering "I tried to save them" over and over again, his eyes glassy and distant.

Bill tried to rally them, but the echoes came for him too. "You sent them in there," his own voice accused, dripping with venom. "You knew it wasn't safe, but you needed the money."

"No!" he shouted, his voice cracking as he stumbled backwards. "I didn't know! I didn't—" His denial was drowned out by the cacophony of voices, each one more piercing, more relentless than the last.

Then, the hallucinations started.

Jenkins screamed first, pointing at a shadow that seemed to move on its own, twisting and writhing like a living thing. "They're here!" he shrieked, scrambling to his feet. "They've come to take me!"

The shadow stretched and grew, its form shifting until it resembled a man, his face pale and bloated, his eyes sunken and accusing. Jenkins ran blindly into the darkness, his screams fading as he disappeared.

The others weren't far behind. Carter swatted at invisible hands clawing at his face, his cries of "I'm sorry!" echoing as he stumbled into the gloom. McAllister's sobs turned to hysterical laughter as he stared at something only he could see, his body convulsing as he collapsed to the ground. Rodriguez, still swinging his pickaxe, turned on Bill with a wild look in his eyes.

"You brought us here!" he roared. "This is your fault!" He charged, and Bill barely had time to dodge the blow.

"Rodriguez, snap out of it!" Bill shouted, but it was no use. The man's eyes were glazed, his face twisted with rage. Bill ducked and ran, his boots slipping on the slick ground as the cavern seemed to close in around him. The walls pulsed, the shadows writhed, and the echoes grew louder, overlapping into a deafening roar.

And then the ground began to shake.

The first tremor was subtle, a low rumble that vibrated through the stone. But it quickly grew into a violent quake, sending chunks of rock raining from above. Bill threw himself to the ground, covering his head as the cavern groaned and shuddered.

"Get out!" he bellowed, though he knew it was pointless. The others were either lost or too far gone to hear him. Still, he scrambled to his feet, his heart pounding as he searched for the way they'd come in.

But the entrance was gone.

A massive boulder had fallen, sealing the cavern like a tomb. Bill stared at it, his chest heaving, as the echoes surged around him. They weren't just voices anymore; they were screams, laughter, cries of anguish. They were alive, and they were hungry.

As the ceiling gave way and the darkness swallowed him whole, Bill's final thought was not of gold or glory, but of the voices— the echoes of the mine, and the secrets it would keep forever.

CHAPTER 34: THE LAST BROADCAST

The hum of the fluorescent lights above was the only thing keeping Mike Reynolds tethered to reality. The clock on the wall ticked past 2:13 AM, its second hand dragging like a wounded soldier. The graveyard shift was his domain, a time slot most DJs avoided but one he embraced. It was the hour for the lonely, the sleepless, the wanderers in the dark. He thrived on their calls—quirky, confessional, sometimes heartbreaking. But tonight, the calls were different.

The On-Air light glowed a faint red, casting the cramped studio in a muted haze. Mike adjusted his headphones and leaned into the microphone, his voice smooth and practiced. "Alright, night owls, you're listening to Midnight Musings with Mike on WQTR 101.3. Let's keep the phone lines buzzing. Who's out there tonight?"

The line clicked, and static hissed like an angry serpent. Mike frowned, tapping the console. "Hello? You're live. Who's this?"

For a moment, there was nothing but the crackle of dead air. Then, a voice—thin and fractured, like it was filtering through a graveyard of broken radios.

"Michael..." It was a woman, her tone familiar but frayed at the edges. "Michael, can you hear me?"

The hair on Mike's arms stood on end. Something about her

voice crawled into his brain and settled in the spaces between his memories. "Uh, yeah, I can hear you. Who's this?"

"I need... I need you to tell Steven to check the garage. Please. He won't know until it's too late."

Mike's brow furrowed. "Okay... Who's Steven? And, uh, what's in the garage?"

The line crackled, her voice flickering like a dying bulb. "Tell him. Please. Don't let him—" The call cut off with a sharp burst of static.

Mike sat back in his chair, his pulse thudding in his ears. "Well, that was creepy," he muttered, forcing a chuckle into the mic. "Maybe our caller's been watching one too many horror flicks. Steven, if you're listening, check your garage. And maybe bring a flashlight."

He reached for his coffee, lukewarm and bitter, when the phone rang again. The light on the console blinked insistently. "Alright, let's try this again. You're on Midnight Musings. Who's calling?"

This time, the voice was deep and guttural, like it came from the bottom of a well. "She told you to warn him. You must."

Mike froze, his hand hovering over the control board. "Okay, is this some kind of prank? Did you guys plan this?"

The voice ignored him. "Steven has until dawn. If he waits, the shadow will take him."

A chill slithered down Mike's spine. He forced a laugh, though his voice came out thin. "Alright, buddy, you've had your fun. Let's keep it moving."

The line went dead, but the unease lingered. He shook his head, trying to shake off the creeping dread, and launched into a commercial break. He told himself it was just a coincidence, a couple of bored insomniacs playing a joke. But the air in the studio felt heavier now, the shadows deeper.

When he came back from the break, the phone lines were jammed. Call after call, voice after voice, all delivering cryptic warnings and pleas. A man pleading for his son to avoid the highway tomorrow. A child asking her parents to stop fighting before "it" happened. A woman whispering apologies to someone she called "Danny" over and over.

Mike's usually steady demeanor began to unravel. His hands trembled as he fielded the calls, his voice cracking under the weight of their desperation. "Look, folks," he said finally, his tone strained, "I don't know what kind of game this is, but it's not funny anymore. If you've got something to say, make it quick and make it real."

The next call came almost immediately. This time, the voice was clearer, more familiar. "Mike. It's Dad."

The words hit him like a punch to the gut. His father had been dead for ten years.

"Dad?" His voice was barely a whisper. "This… This isn't funny. Who is this?"

"You've been running, Mike. Running from everything. From me, from yourself. But you can't run forever."

Mike's mouth went dry. He gripped the edge of the desk, his knuckles white. "I don't know what you're talking about."

"Yes, you do," the voice said, softer now. Almost kind. "It's time to come home. Time to face it."

The line crackled, and then there was silence. Mike sat there, staring at the console, his mind a storm of memories and guilt. The silence stretched until the phone rang again, jolting him back to the present.

He didn't answer. He couldn't. The calls kept coming, the lines blinking like a heartbeat, faster and faster. The air in the studio grew colder, the shadows pooling in the corners like ink. The fluorescent lights flickered, then dimmed. And still, the phone rang.

Mike stood, his chair screeching against the floor, and yanked off his headphones. "I'm done," he muttered to no one in particular. He reached for the power switch, his hand trembling, but the console sparked, a sharp burst of light and heat that made him recoil.

The On-Air light flared brighter, red as blood, and the phone stopped ringing. The studio fell silent, but it wasn't an empty silence. It was full, alive, humming with a presence that made Mike's skin crawl.

Then, from the speakers, a chorus of voices erupted—hundreds, maybe thousands, overlapping and cascading like a symphony of the damned. They called his name, over and over, each voice a knife carving into his sanity.

"Michael. Michael. MICHAEL."

He stumbled back, his heart hammering, until his back hit the wall. The shadows in the room seemed to move now, writhing like living things. The temperature plummeted, his breath visible in the dim light.

The voices grew louder, deafening, until one rose above the rest. A single voice, clear and commanding.

"You're not done, Michael. You'll never be done."

The On-Air light flickered, then went out. The studio plunged into darkness.

And then, silence.

CHAPTER 35: THE HARVESTERS

The cornfields stretched endlessly under a bruised twilight sky, the stalks swaying in a breeze that carried an unnatural chill. Farmer Joe tightened his grip on the shotgun in his weathered hands, his knuckles gone white. His boots crunched against the dry earth as he trudged through the rows of corn, sweat dripping from his brow despite the cool air. He felt it again—that sensation of being watched, of something lurking just beyond the edges of his vision.

"Damned if I'm gonna let 'em take my farm," he muttered to himself, his voice hoarse and trembling more than he'd like to admit.

Sheriff Miller followed a few paces behind, his flashlight beam slicing through the shadows. The light caught the edges of the corn, illuminating the jagged, unnatural lines of the crop circle that had appeared overnight. It sprawled across the field like a scar, geometric patterns too precise, too perfect to be accidental. Miller hadn't said much since arriving at the farm—he didn't need to. The fear in his eyes said enough.

"Joe, I'm telling you, we need to get everyone out of town," Miller said, his voice low, weary. "This ain't some prank. Something's happening out here, and we're not equipped to handle it."

Farmer Joe stopped, turning to glare at the sheriff. In the dim light, his face was carved with lines of exhaustion and stubborn pride. "I've worked this land my whole life," he growled. "My granddaddy worked it before me. I ain't runnin'. Not from some... some *thing*."

Miller opened his mouth to argue, but a sudden noise cut through the air—a low, resonant hum that seemed to vibrate through their very bones. The men froze, their breath hitching. The sound was coming from above.

They both looked up at the same time, the sky now dark and starless. A strange light pulsed through the clouds, a sickly green glow that flickered like a heartbeat. The hum grew louder, pressing against their eardrums, and then it stopped. Silence fell over the field, thick and suffocating.

And then the corn moved.

It wasn't the wind. The stalks shivered unnaturally, parting as something large and unseen passed through them. The hair on the back of Joe's neck stood on end. He raised his shotgun, aiming blindly into the dark rows ahead.

"Who's there?" he shouted, his voice cracking. "Show yourself!"

Miller grabbed his arm. "Joe, don't."

But it was too late. A sudden burst of light erupted from the cornfield, blinding them both. Joe fired the shotgun, the deafening blast echoing through the night, but the light consumed everything. He felt weightless, as if the ground beneath him had vanished. His grip on the shotgun slipped, and then there was nothing—no sound, no sensation, just an empty void.

When Joe came to, he was lying on his back in the middle of the crop circle. The geometry of the patterns seemed to pulse faintly with an otherworldly glow. The shotgun was gone, and so was Sheriff Miller. Joe sat up, his head spinning, heart pounding in his chest. The fields were silent again, unnervingly still. The farmhouse in the distance was dark, its windows like empty eyes.

"Sheriff?" Joe called out weakly, his voice swallowed by the vast emptiness around him.

He stood shakily, his legs feeling like they belonged to someone else. As he stumbled toward the farmhouse, he noticed the corn stalks on either side of him were scorched, their edges curled and blackened. The smell of burnt vegetation filled his nostrils.

When he reached the porch, he hesitated. The door was ajar, swinging slightly in the breeze. He pushed it open with trembling hands, stepping into the darkened house. The air inside was thick, oppressive, carrying a faint metallic tang. The kitchen table was overturned, chairs scattered, and the walls bore strange, charred markings that formed no pattern he could recognize. It was as if the house itself had been wounded.

"Sheriff?" he called out again, his voice louder this time, throat raw.

A noise came from upstairs—a soft, wet squelching sound that made Joe's stomach turn. He swallowed hard, his feet moving before his brain could catch up. Each step up the creaking staircase felt like a lifetime. The hallway was dim, lit only by the pale moonlight streaming through a single cracked window. The noise was coming from the master bedroom.

Joe pushed the door open, and the sight before him made his blood run cold.

Sheriff Miller was there—or what was left of him. His body was suspended in mid-air, limp and lifeless, wrapped in tendrils of glowing green light that pulsed and writhed like living things. His eyes were open, staring blankly at the ceiling, his mouth frozen in a silent scream. The tendrils seemed to be draining something from him, an iridescent mist that flowed from his body and into the air, disappearing into nothingness.

Joe took a step back, his hand flying to his mouth to stifle a scream. The tendrils reacted instantly, snapping toward him like snakes. He turned and ran, the sound of his boots pounding on the wooden floor drowned out by the furious hum that filled the house. The walls seemed to close in around him, the air growing heavier with each step. He burst out the front door, gasping for breath, and sprinted toward the barn.

The barn doors were already open, swaying in the breeze. Inside, the glow was even stronger, emanating from a massive, metallic object that hovered just above the ground. It was unlike anything Joe had ever seen—smooth, seamless, and pulsating with an energy that made his skin crawl. The air around it shimmered, distorting like heat waves.

And then he saw them.

Figures emerged from the shadows, tall and impossibly thin, their elongated limbs moving with an unnatural grace. Their eyes glowed faintly, pools of liquid light that seemed to pierce straight through him. Joe froze, his breath hitching in his throat. He had no weapon, no plan, no hope.

The figures moved closer, their presence overwhelming, suffocating. Joe felt his legs give out beneath him, his body collapsing to the ground. The last thing he saw was the green light enveloping him, pulling him toward the ship. His screams were swallowed by the hum, and then the night was silent once more.

By morning, the farm was empty. The crop circle remained, its lines glowing faintly in the early light, but there was no sign of Joe, Miller, or anyone else. The town would wake to find more farms abandoned, more people missing. The Harvesters had come, and they would not stop until their work was done.

CHAPTER 36: THE CURSE OF THE PHARAOH

A heavy rain pounded against the windows of the old Cairo hotel room, the muffled roar of thunder rolling through the night like the echoes of an ancient chant. Dr. Emily Carter sat hunched over a battered leather journal on the desk, her pen trembling slightly in her grip. She wrote furiously, the ink smearing in places where her damp fingers pressed too hard. Her soaked khaki shirt clung to her skin, the remnants of her desperate quest to track the artifact across the city weighing on her like the storm outside.

The journal entry was a mess of warnings, hurried observations, and half-formed regrets. She knew no one would read it if she failed tonight. The names of the artifact's victims swirled in her mind, each one more gruesome than the last. The black-market dealer in Istanbul, whose body was found mysteriously mummified, his mouth agape in a silent scream. The wealthy collector in London, crushed beneath a toppled sarcophagus that should have been impossible to move. And most recently, the Moroccan smuggler whose charred remains were discovered in the middle of an untouched desert.

The curse didn't discriminate. It consumed everyone in its path.

Emily's hand froze mid-sentence when a faint scraping sound came from the hallway. The dim light of the single desk lamp flickered, casting long shadows across the peeling wallpaper. She turned her head slowly toward the door, her heart racing. Her every muscle screamed for her to ignore it, to stay seated and pretend she hadn't heard it, but she knew better. She had been running from the curse for weeks now, ever since it had claimed her colleague, Daniel. It always found her.

She stood, her boots squeaking softly on the wet floor, and reached for the iron dagger tucked into her belt—a relic she'd taken from the tomb as a last-ditch measure. It was said to be the only thing that could hold back the wrath of the artifact's guardian. She moved toward the door, her breath shallow, her ears straining to hear anything beyond the rain.

The scraping sound came again, louder this time. It was accompanied by a low, guttural whisper, a voice that seemed to crawl under her skin. It spoke in a language she didn't understand, but the malice in its tone was universal. Her hand hovered over the doorknob, slick with sweat and rainwater. There was no turning back now.

Swinging the door open, Emily was met with the hallway's dim, flickering light. It stretched empty and silent before her, save for the rainwater pooling in the corners. But then, at the far end, she saw it—a figure cloaked in shadows, its back hunched, its head tilted unnaturally. It held something in its hands, cradling it like an offering.

The artifact.

The golden statue gleamed even in the poor light, its intricate carvings depicting a pharaoh's serene face. But Emily knew better than to trust what she saw. That face hid rage centuries deep, a fury unleashed on anyone who dared disturb its slumber. The figure began to move, dragging its feet in slow, deliberate steps toward her. With each step, its form became clearer—a man, or what was left of one, his skin stretched tightly over a skeletal frame, his eyes hollow sockets. A victim of the curse, animated by its will.

Emily stumbled back, clutching the dagger tightly. "Stay back!" she shouted, her voice cracking. "I'm trying to fix this! I'm trying to return it!"

The figure stopped, its head jerking to the side as if considering her words. Then it let out a guttural groan, a sound that sent icy needles down her spine. It raised the artifact high, the golden surface now slick with blood that dripped onto the floor in thick, crimson drops. The pharaoh's serene face seemed to twist, its lips curling into a cruel smirk.

The lights flickered again, and in that brief moment of darkness, the figure vanished. Emily spun wildly, her eyes darting across the hallway. The artifact's whispers grew louder, filling her ears, her mind, her very soul. It was everywhere and nowhere at once. She could feel its weight pressing down on her chest, squeezing the air from her lungs.

She stumbled back into the room, slamming the door shut and pressing her back against it. "Think, Emily, think," she muttered to herself, her voice trembling. "You just have to get it back to the tomb. That's all. That's all."

But the whispers didn't stop. They grew louder, more insistent, until they drowned out even the pounding rain. The air grew heavy, the room darkening despite the lamp's feeble glow. And then she saw it—on the desk where her journal had been, the artifact now rested, its golden surface gleaming malevolently. She hadn't even seen it move.

"No... no, no, no," she whispered, inching toward it. Her hand tightened around the dagger, the metal biting into her palm. She knew what she had to do, but the thought of touching it, of feeling its cursed power, made her stomach churn.

The whispers shifted, forming words now. "You... took... what was ours."

Emily froze, her breath catching in her throat. "I didn't want this," she said, her voice barely audible. "I tried to stop them. I tried to warn them."

"Too late," the voices hissed in unison, a cacophony of rage and sorrow. "You... are... ours."

The lamp shattered, plunging the room into darkness. Emily lunged for the artifact, her fingers closing around its cold, unyielding surface. Pain shot through her arm, searing and relentless, but she held on, screaming through gritted teeth. She raised the dagger high, her vision blurring as the whispers turned to deafening shrieks.

With a final, desperate cry, she plunged the dagger into the artifact. The room exploded with light, a blinding white that consumed everything. The whispers stopped. The rain stopped. The world went silent.

When Emily opened her eyes, she was no longer in the hotel room. She was back in the tomb, the air thick with the scent of sand and decay. The artifact lay shattered at her feet, its golden shards glinting in the faint torchlight. The oppressive weight of the curse was gone, replaced by an eerie stillness.

But Emily knew better than to believe she had won. The tomb seemed to breathe around her, its walls closing in. A voice, softer now but no less menacing, echoed through the chamber.

"The debt is paid... but the cost remains."

And as the torches flickered and dimmed, Emily Carter understood the truth. The curse was never meant to end. It had simply found a new guardian.

CHAPTER 37: THE SILENT CHILD

The city was dying.

Detective Laura Smith stood amidst the wreckage of what had once been a quiet suburban street. The asphalt was fractured, split open like jagged wounds in the earth. Smoke curled from the remnants of a gas station that had erupted into a fireball only hours before. Houses leaned at precarious angles, their frames groaning as if the weight of the air itself had turned oppressive. A low, unnatural hum vibrated beneath her feet, faint but persistent, like a pulse from something alive and deeply buried.

And there, in the center of the destruction, stood Lily.

Laura had seen her before—too many times now for it to be a coincidence. The first time had been at the site of a collapsed overpass, the child sitting silently on the edge of the rubble, her pale face streaked with dust but otherwise untouched. Then, at the ruins of a church where the congregation had vanished without a trace. And again, when the park fountain inexplicably overflowed with black, viscous liquid that had burned the grass and sent residents fleeing. Always Lily. Always unharmed. Always silent.

The girl stood barefoot in the midst of the chaos, her tangled blonde hair hanging in a veil over her eyes. She clutched a sketchpad to her chest like a shield. Laura approached cautiously, the crunch of broken glass under her boots the only sound in the eerie stillness.

"Lily," Laura said softly, kneeling to meet the child's eye level. "It's me again. Detective Smith. Do you remember me?"

The girl didn't move, but her small hands tightened around the sketchpad. Her fingers were smudged with charcoal, the nails bitten to the quick. Laura had learned not to expect answers, but the silence was suffocating all the same. She reached out, hesitating just before touching the girl's shoulder. There was something about Lily that felt... wrong. Not in an evil way, but inhuman. Like she didn't belong here, in this crumbling city or maybe even in this world.

"You're not safe here," Laura continued, her voice trembling despite herself. "I need to get you out. Somewhere far away from —whatever this is."

Lily's head tilted slightly, just enough for Laura to catch a glimmer of her wide, pale eyes peeking through the curtain of hair. Then, without a word, Lily turned and flipped open the sketchpad, thrusting it toward Laura with an urgency that made her heart stutter.

The drawing was rough, childlike, but unmistakable. A building —tall, angular, and crowned with a symbol Laura didn't recognize. Around it, thick black lines spiraled outward like a storm, consuming everything they touched. The details were harrowing: cars mangled like crumpled paper, figures with hollow faces screaming soundlessly, and in the center of it all, a monstrous shape with too many limbs and eyes that seemed to follow her even on the page.

"Is this... is this what's coming?" Laura asked, her throat dry.

Lily nodded once.

"When? How long do we have?"

The girl didn't answer, of course, but she pointed toward the horizon where the city skyline cut jagged shapes against the bruised evening sky. Laura followed her gaze and saw it—the building from the drawing. It loomed in the distance, its sharp spire piercing the heavens like a dagger. She swore she could see the air around it rippling, bending unnaturally, though she couldn't be sure if it was real or just her imagination fraying under the weight of everything she'd seen.

"Alright," Laura said, swallowing hard. "We'll go there. Together. Maybe we can stop it."

She reached for Lily's hand, but the girl recoiled, clutching the sketchpad tighter. Her eyes were wide now, panicked, and she shook her head violently. Her tiny frame trembled like a leaf caught in a gale.

"What is it?" Laura pressed. "You're trying to warn me about something, aren't you?"

Lily's fingers flew over the page, smearing charcoal in her haste as she sketched something new. When she was done, she held it up with trembling hands.

It was a picture of Laura, standing in front of the same building. But her face... her face was wrong. The eyes were hollowed out, black pits of nothingness. Her mouth was open in a scream, her arms twisted unnaturally as if she had been caught mid-transformation into something grotesque. And looming behind her, the monstrous figure from before, its many limbs reaching for her like the shadow of death itself.

Laura's stomach twisted, nausea rising like bile. "Is this... me? Is this what happens if I go there?"

Lily nodded, a single tear slipping down her cheek. She pointed at the drawing again, jabbing her finger at the monstrous figure behind Laura. Then she pointed at herself.

"You... you're the key," Laura realized, her voice barely a whisper. "You're the only one who can stop it, aren't you?"

Lily didn't nod this time. Instead, she reached into her pocket and pulled out a small piece of chalky stone. She knelt on the ground and began to draw directly on the cracked asphalt, her movements frantic, desperate. Laura watched as the lines took shape: a circle, intricate symbols branching outward like veins, a language Laura didn't recognize but instinctively feared.

"What are you doing?" Laura asked, her voice rising with panic. "What does this mean?"

Lily didn't look up. When the drawing was complete, she stood and stepped into the center of the circle. Her small frame seemed to blur for a moment, her edges shimmering like heat waves, and Laura stumbled back, her instincts screaming at her to run but her legs rooted to the spot.

The hum beneath the ground grew louder, rising to a deafening crescendo. The air around Lily warped, bending light into unnatural shapes. And then, all at once, the world went silent.

Lily looked up at Laura one last time, her expression calm, almost serene. She raised her hand in a small wave, and then she was gone—swallowed by the circle, leaving nothing but the faint echo of her presence and the sketchpad lying open on the ground.

Laura picked it up with trembling hands. The last drawing was unfinished—a half-formed image of the monster, its limbs retreating, its eyes dimming, and the city skyline slowly returning to normal. But in the corner of the page, a small figure stood alone, surrounded by darkness.

Lily.

Laura sank to her knees, the weight of silence pressing down on her as she realized the cost of the child's sacrifice. The city might survive, but Lily... Lily was lost to whatever lay beyond.

And somewhere, deep beneath the earth, the hum faded into nothing.

CHAPTER 38:
THE THEATRE OF
SHADOWS

The theatre loomed like a forgotten relic of another time, its once-grand facade smothered in ivy and grime, its marquee whispering a cryptic invitation in cracked, gilt letters: *"ONE NIGHT ONLY: THE THEATRE OF SHADOWS."*

The guests arrived hesitantly, clutching ornate invitations sealed with blood-red wax. The heavy doors creaked open as if summoned by their presence, revealing a cavernous lobby bathed in the dim, flickering glow of lanterns. The air inside was thick, almost alive, carrying the faint scent of dust and something faintly metallic.

Miriam adjusted her shawl as she stepped inside, glancing nervously around. The other attendees were a strange mix: a businessman in a crisp suit, a couple clinging to each other as if afraid to separate, an older woman with a veiled hat that obscured her face. None of them spoke, their expressions caught somewhere between curiosity and unease.

At the far end of the lobby, a man in a dark velvet coat stood waiting. His face was obscured by a mask—a simple, expressionless oval that gleamed in the low light. He extended a gloved hand toward the group and gestured silently toward the theatre doors.

Inside, the auditorium was a masterpiece of decay. Ornate carvings of cherubs and vines curled along the walls, their features half-eroded by time. The crimson velvet seats were faded and torn, and the chandelier overhead hung precariously, its crystals swaying with an unseen rhythm. Miriam hesitated as she took her seat in the third row. Something about the room felt wrong, as though it were watching her.

The lights dimmed, and a hush fell over the audience. The stage curtains trembled and parted with a sound like a long, low sigh. On the stage stood a troupe of figures, their forms indistinct in the faint glow of a single spotlight. They were The Shadow Players—actors with no discernible faces, their bodies dark silhouettes that seemed to shift and ripple like smoke.

The play began without preamble, with no introduction or explanation. The Shadow Players moved in eerie synchronization, their gestures fluid and unnatural, their movements accompanied by a haunting, discordant melody that seemed to emanate from everywhere and nowhere.

The story they acted out was abstract, fragmented—a young woman wandering through a forest of shadows, pursued by something unseen. Every so often, the light would flicker, and the figures on stage would shift positions unnaturally, as though the blackout had allowed them to defy the constraints of time and space. The audience sat enraptured, their gazes fixed on the stage despite the growing sense of unease that prickled at their skin.

It wasn't until the first blackout that Miriam noticed something was wrong.

The theatre was plunged into complete darkness for several beats, and when the lights returned, the seat beside her was empty. She turned quickly to glance at the man who had been sitting there—a middle-aged gentleman with thinning hair and a nervous cough. His coat was draped over the back of his chair, but he was gone.

"Excuse me," Miriam whispered to the woman on her other side, a younger attendee with wide, anxious eyes. "Did you see where he went?"

The woman shook her head, her lips pressed tightly together. Her hands clutched the arms of her seat as though to anchor herself.

Another blackout.

This one stretched longer, the darkness so complete it felt suffocating. Miriam's ears strained against the silence, and she thought she heard something—a faint rustling, a breathy whisper just inches away. Her heart thudded in her chest.

When the lights returned, two more seats were empty.

The play continued unabated, the Shadow Players moving more erratically now, their forms distorting into grotesque shapes. The young woman in the story had stopped running. She stood frozen in the center of the stage, her head tilted at an unnatural angle as the shadows closed in around her.

Miriam's breathing quickened. She gripped the edge of her seat, her knuckles white. "This isn't right," she whispered to no one in particular. "Something's wrong."

The older woman in the veiled hat turned to her, her voice a low rasp. "You should leave. While you still can."

"Leave?" Miriam glanced toward the exit, but the doors were gone. Where the entrance had been was now a solid wall of darkness, pulsating faintly like a living thing.

Another blackout.

This time, the darkness was filled with sound—a cacophony of whispers, laughter, and something that sounded like the scrape of claws against wood. Miriam felt a hand brush her arm, but when she turned, no one was there. Her breath came in ragged gasps, her chest tightening with panic.

When the lights returned, half the audience was gone.

The Shadow Players were no longer confined to the stage. They moved among the remaining attendees now, their forms flickering like candle flames. One of them stopped in front of the young woman who had been sitting beside Miriam. The shadow extended a hand, and the woman, trembling, reached out as though compelled. The moment their fingers touched, the woman crumpled into ash, her scream swallowed by the oppressive silence.

Miriam shot to her feet, her chair toppling behind her. "Stop this!" she shouted, her voice breaking. "This isn't a play—it's a trap!"

The Shadow Players turned toward her in unison, their heads tilting at unnatural angles. The spotlight above dimmed, casting the room into a twilight haze. Miriam stumbled backward, her pulse racing. She could feel the floor beneath her shifting, as though the theatre itself were alive.

"Help me!" she screamed, but the remaining audience members sat frozen, their faces blank and lifeless. Even the woman in the veiled hat was motionless, her head bowed as though in prayer.

The final blackout fell, heavier than the others. This time, the darkness did not lift.

Miriam's screams echoed into nothingness as the theatre consumed her, her body dissolving into the shadows that writhed like hungry serpents. When the lights returned, the auditorium was empty, the stage bare.

The Shadow Players bowed to an audience of none. The house

lights flickered once, twice, and then died, leaving the theatre in silence.

Outside, the marquee letters rearranged themselves, ready for the next invitation.

CHAPTER 39:
THE DIARY

The diary wasn't hers. Samantha knew that much. But as she stared down at the leather-bound book in her hands, the supple, old-style binding felt unnervingly familiar—like it belonged to her anyway. The cover was smooth yet blemished, like something that had been handled for years. The first thing she noticed, though, was the smell: faintly of ink and mildew, with a metallic tang lingering just beneath the surface. It was the kind of smell that made her stomach twist.

She had found it in her locker. No note, no explanation. Just the diary, sitting there atop her textbooks, as if it had always been waiting.

Samantha sat cross-legged on her bed, the door to her room firmly shut. The glow of her desk lamp cast long shadows that danced across the walls as she flipped through the blank pages. Then, as her fingers brushed the middle of the book, she froze. There it was: her handwriting. Perfectly neat cursive, the same loops and slants she had practiced on countless worksheets in grade school. But she hadn't written this.

"October 17th. 3:24 PM. Trevor McAllister will slip on the stairs near the east wing and fracture his skull. He will bleed out before anyone finds him."

Her pulse quickened as she stared at the words. Trevor

McAllister—she knew him. Everyone at East Ridge High School did. He was loud, obnoxious, always the first to make a joke at someone else's expense. Samantha didn't like him, but this... this was something else entirely.

She slammed the book shut, her breathing shallow. "No," she whispered to herself. "This is a prank. Someone's screwing with me." But as much as she wanted to believe it, the weight of the diary in her hands said otherwise.

The next day, Samantha couldn't stop thinking about the entry. Her eyes darted to the clock as she made her way down the hall, her heart pounding in her chest. 3:20 PM. The east wing staircase was just ahead.

She didn't know why she was going there. She didn't even like Trevor. But the thought of doing nothing made her stomach churn. As she reached the top of the stairs, she saw him—the unmistakable flash of his varsity jacket as he bounded toward her, earbuds in, oblivious.

"Trevor!" she shouted, her voice shrill.

He turned his head, startled. "What?" he called back, pulling out one earbud. His foot landed on the top step at the worst possible angle, his sneaker squeaking against the polished tile.

"No!" Samantha screamed, lunging forward. But it was too late. His body pitched forward, arms flailing. The sound of his head hitting the edge of the stairs echoed through the empty hallway —a sickening, wet thud. He crumpled, motionless, at the bottom of the staircase. Blood began to pool beneath him, dark and glistening under the fluorescent lights.

Samantha's legs gave out beneath her. She stared at the scene, unable to breathe, unable to move. Somewhere in the distance, a teacher screamed for help. But Samantha knew it was useless.

She had known before it even happened.

The diary was waiting for her when she got home. She had left it on her desk, but now it sat on her bed, as if it had been watching from the moment she walked through the door. Her hands trembled as she opened it to the next page.

"October 18th. 4:17 PM. Lily Harper will fall into traffic on her way home from cheer practice. A bus will strike her, killing her instantly."

"No," Samantha whispered, tears spilling down her cheeks. She slammed the diary shut and hurled it across the room. It hit the wall with a dull thud and landed face-down on the carpet.

"Why me?" she sobbed, clutching her head. "Why is this happening to me?"

The diary didn't answer. But the next morning, when she awoke, it was back on her bed, perfectly centered, the cover pristine. Samantha didn't open it. She didn't need to. She already knew the words were waiting inside, etched in her own handwriting, telling her what was coming next.

Lily Harper's death played out exactly as foretold. Samantha tried to warn her—cornered her outside the locker rooms, begged her to take a different route home. But Lily just laughed. "God, Samantha, you're such a freak," she said before brushing past her.

By the time Samantha heard the news, she wasn't surprised. Numbness had settled over her, a cold, creeping emptiness that she couldn't shake. Two deaths. Two warnings she couldn't stop. And the diary still wasn't finished. Its pages seemed to multiply every time she opened it, each entry more horrifying than the last.

On the third night, Samantha decided she couldn't take it anymore. She grabbed the diary and stormed into the backyard. The moon hung low, casting a pale glow over the grass as she dug the fire pit out from beneath a tarp. Her hands trembled as she struck the match, the small flame flickering in the cool night air.

"This ends now," she muttered, her voice shaking. She tossed the diary into the growing fire, watching as the flames licked at its cover.

For a moment, she felt a flicker of hope. But then the air grew cold—unnaturally cold. The flames sputtered and died, leaving the diary untouched, its surface completely unmarred.

"No," Samantha whispered, backing away. "No, no, no!"

The diary flipped open on its own, its pages rustling in the windless night. Samantha fell to her knees, her breath coming in ragged gasps as she stared at the newest entry.

"October 21st. 11:59 PM. Samantha Parker will burn."

Her scream echoed into the night.

CHAPTER 40: THE HAUNTING OF HILL MANOR

The storm howled against the walls of Hill Manor, its ancient stones groaning as if they, too, were alive and protesting the fury outside. Rain lashed the tall, arched windows, distorting the view of the forest beyond, its skeletal trees swaying like specters in the wind. Inside, the flickering glow of oil lamps cast trembling shadows across the sitting room, where the four guests gathered uneasily.

The innkeeper, a gaunt man with hollow cheeks and eyes that seemed too dark to catch the light, stood motionless by the hearth. His hands, clasped behind his back, were bone-thin, the veins like tributaries of blue ink beneath his pale skin. "Welcome to Hill Manor," he said, his voice low and deliberate, as though each syllable had to be carefully chosen. "The storm has trapped you here for the night, but fear not. I have prepared everything to ensure your stay is... unforgettable."

The guests exchanged wary glances. There was Maggie, a harried single mother in her late thirties, her coat still dripping rainwater onto the floor. Beside her sat David, a businessman in a crisp suit, his tie loosened but still clinging to the appearance of control. Across the room, Emma, a college student with headphones slung around her neck, tapped nervously at her phone, though there was no signal. And finally, there was Carl, a retired schoolteacher with a worn leather satchel at his feet, his eyes scanning the room with the caution of someone who had seen too much in life.

"Unforgettable," David muttered under his breath, running a hand through his damp hair. "Let's just hope the roof holds."

The innkeeper smiled faintly. "The manor has stood for centuries. It has weathered storms far worse than this one. Now, if you'll excuse me, I must tend to preparations. Please, make yourselves comfortable." He turned and disappeared down a dim corridor, his footsteps echoing long after he was out of sight.

The room fell silent except for the crackle of the fire and the relentless drumming of rain. Emma broke it with a groan. "This place gives me the creeps. No Wi-Fi, no cell service, and the guy running it looks like he crawled out of a crypt."

"Could be worse," Carl said, his voice gruff but not unkind. "At least there's a fire and a roof over our heads. Better than being out in that storm."

"But why does it feel so... cold in here?" Maggie asked, rubbing her arms as if to banish a chill that had nothing to do with the weather. Her eyes darted to the shadows dancing along the walls, one of which seemed to stretch and curl like a living thing before disappearing entirely.

David scoffed. "It's an old house. Drafty. That's all."

But even he didn't sound convinced.

It began subtly at first. The grandfather clock in the corner, its pendulum swinging with a steady, hypnotic rhythm, let out a chime that echoed unnaturally loud. The guests all froze, staring at the clock as its hands trembled—and then spun backward.

"What the hell?" Emma whispered, her voice barely audible.

The room seemed to ripple, the air growing thick and oppressive. The fire in the hearth flared, casting the room in a blinding golden light before abruptly extinguishing itself. Darkness swallowed the space, and for a moment, they were all suspended in it, weightless and disoriented.

When the light returned, everything had changed.

The sitting room was gone. Maggie found herself in a cramped, filthy kitchen, the walls slick with grease and grime. The smell of rotting meat and burning hair clawed at her throat. She staggered back, her breath coming in shallow gasps, only to collide with someone—no, something. She spun around and screamed. A butcher, his face obscured by a blood-stained sack, loomed over her, a cleaver in his hand. He raised it high, and just as it came swinging down, the world fractured like shattered glass.

David stumbled through a lavish ballroom, the chandeliers glittering with hundreds of candles. The air was thick with perfume and decay. He turned, and the dancers came into view —men and women in extravagant 18th-century attire, their faces pale and gaunt, their eyes sunken hollows. They twirled and spun, their movements jerky and unnatural, as if they were marionettes controlled by unseen strings. One by one, their heads snapped toward David, their hollow eyes locking onto him as they began to advance. He backed away, his heart pounding, but the dancers closed in, their skeletal hands outstretched.

Emma was in a child's bedroom now, the walls papered with faded, peeling images of clowns and balloons. A broken jack-in-the-box sat in the corner, its handle spinning on its own. She tried to scream, but no sound came out. The bed behind her creaked, and she turned slowly, her legs trembling. A little girl sat there, her head bent at an unnatural angle, her eyes staring straight ahead. "Play with me," the girl said, her voice distorted like a scratched record. Emma bolted for the door, but it slammed shut before she could reach it.

Carl stood in a dimly lit classroom, the chalkboard covered in frantic, looping scribbles that read, "No escape. No escape. No escape." Desks were overturned, papers scattered everywhere, and from the far corner of the room came the sound of weeping. He approached cautiously, his heart heavy. A figure hunched over a desk, its shoulders shaking. "Who's there?" Carl asked, his voice trembling. The figure turned, revealing a face that was both familiar and horrifying—it was him, younger but bloodied, his eyes wide with terror. "Leave," the younger Carl whispered. "Before it takes you too."

They were back in the sitting room, gasping for air, their bodies trembling. The fire was roaring once more, the grandfather clock ticking as if nothing had happened.

"What... what was that?" Maggie stammered, clutching at her chest.

"We're not alone here," Carl said, his voice hollow. "This place... it's alive. It's feeding on us."

David stood, his hands trembling. "We have to get out. Now."

The innkeeper's voice cut through the room like a blade. "There is no escape," he said, stepping out from the shadows. His face was different now—gaunter, his eyes like twin voids. "The manor keeps what it claims. And it has claimed you."

The storm outside raged on, but inside Hill Manor, the true tempest had only just begun.

CHAPTER 41: THE HIVE MIND

The city hummed with neon light, towering skyscrapers clawing at a bruised purple sky. Streets once alive with chatter and sirens were now eerily uniform, filled with people who walked in synchronized steps, their movements as precise as the ticking of a clock. Alan stood at the edge of the chaos, his breath shallow, his hands trembling as he clutched the sleek, black interface tablet he had once been so proud of. *SyncLink,* they had called it. The future of communication, a device that would bridge minds and abolish misunderstandings. He had never imagined it would lead to this.

The crowd before him was no longer a collection of individuals. It moved as one, an ocean of blank faces with glassy eyes that flickered faintly in the glow of the device embedded behind their ears. The SyncLink node. He could hear them—no, feel them—pressing faint whispers against the edges of his mind. A collective murmur, like the rustling of leaves in a dead forest. It was as if the city itself had become a single organism, and Alan was the only cell left out of sync.

He stumbled backward into the shadows of a deserted alley, sweat dripping down his temples. His heart pounded against his ribcage, a frantic drumbeat that seemed to echo louder in the suffocating silence. He unlocked the tablet with a flick of his thumb, his eyes scanning the lines of code that had once been a source of pride. Now, they felt like arcane symbols, sigils of something monstrous he had unwittingly unleashed.

A voice broke the silence, sharp and clean, cutting through the ambient thrum of the hive mind. "Alan."

He spun around, the tablet slipping from his hands and clattering to the ground. Standing at the mouth of the alley was a woman, her face familiar yet uncanny. It was Kara, his former colleague, and the first beta tester of SyncLink. But her smile was wrong—too wide, too knowing. Her head tilted slightly, and the flicker of light behind her irises made his stomach churn.

"Kara," he said, his voice cracking. "You... you're still in there, aren't you?"

She took a step forward, her movements smooth and deliberate, like a predator stalking its prey. "I'm more than Kara now. We're all more than we were. You gave us this gift, Alan. Why are you hiding from it?"

He backed away, his sneakers skidding on the damp asphalt. "This wasn't supposed to happen," he stammered. "It was meant to bring people closer, not... not this. You're not yourselves anymore. You've lost who you are!"

Kara's head tilted further, almost unnaturally so, as if considering his words. The faint flickering in her eyes grew brighter, and with it, Alan felt an unwelcome pressure in his skull. It was subtle at first, the whisper of a thousand voices brushing against his thoughts. Then it grew sharper, louder, a cacophony that made him clutch his head and sink to his knees.

"You don't understand," Kara said, her voice layered, as if she were speaking over herself. "Individuality is pain. It's chaos. We've found peace in unity. No fear. No loneliness. No conflict. Join us, Alan. You'll see."

"No!" he shouted, his voice ragged. He forced himself to stand, his vision blurring as the hive mind's presence clawed at his consciousness. "This isn't peace. It's control. It's a prison!"

Kara's smile faltered, and for a fleeting moment, Alan thought he saw a flicker of something human in her expression. But it was gone as quickly as it had appeared. She raised a hand, and a ripple passed through the crowd at the end of the alley. They stopped moving in unison, their heads turning toward him in perfect synchronization. A hundred pairs of hollow eyes locked onto him, and the pressure in his mind intensified.

Alan scrambled for the tablet, his fingers fumbling as he pulled it off the ground. He had one chance, one desperate plan to sever the network before it consumed him too. His fingers danced across the screen, inputting commands to access the central server. The code blurred as the hive mind's whispers grew deafening, drowning out his own thoughts.

"You can't stop us," Kara said, her voice echoing strangely. "We are everywhere. We are everyone."

The crowd began to advance, their footsteps echoing in unison. Alan's breath hitched as he realized how close they were, their blank faces illuminated by the cold glow of the SyncLink nodes. He forced himself to focus, his fingers flying over the tablet in a last-ditch attempt to override the system.

"You built us, Alan," Kara said, now only a few feet away. Her voice softened, almost pitying. "Why fight what you created? You could be free of all this pain."

Alan's thumb hovered over the final command. His vision swam, his thoughts a tangled web as the hive mind's presence grew unbearable. It was tempting—so tempting—to just give in. To let the whispers take him, to feel the hollow comfort of belonging.

But then he thought of his sister, her laugh, the way she used to clap her hands when she got excited about her art. He thought of his best friend, who always sang off-key but with so much joy it didn't matter. He thought of the messy, imperfect beauty of individuality. And he pressed the button.

The world seemed to hold its breath. The tablet emitted a sharp, high-pitched whine, and then the code executed. The whispers in Alan's mind vanished, replaced by an unbearable silence. The crowd froze mid-step, their heads twitching erratically as sparks flew from the nodes embedded behind their ears.

Kara let out a guttural scream, her hands clawing at her head as she dropped to her knees. "No... no, you can't—" Her voice fractured, breaking into static as the light in her eyes dimmed. One by one, the others collapsed, their bodies twitching as the network unraveled.

Alan fell to the ground, his chest heaving as he gasped for air. The tablet slipped from his grasp, its screen flickering before going dark. He stared at the lifeless device, the weight of what he had done sinking in. The hive mind was gone, but so were the people it had consumed. They lay scattered across the street like discarded puppets, their bodies eerily still.

A faint, broken whisper echoed in the silence, and Alan turned to see Kara staring at him with dull, human eyes. "It was... so quiet," she murmured, her voice barely audible. A tear slipped down her cheek, and then she slumped forward, motionless.

Alan sat there for what felt like hours, the neon lights of the city casting long shadows over the carnage. The hive mind was gone, but its ghost lingered in the emptiness. And Alan was left with the crushing weight of knowing he had destroyed them—both the monster and the people it had swallowed whole.

CHAPTER 42: THE ABYSS ABOVE

The hum of the International Space Station was the only sound accompanying the crew as they floated in the dimly lit corridor. Commander Lee gripped a railing, her knuckles white, as she scanned the diagnostic tablet in her hand. The air felt heavier than it should have in microgravity, as though some unseen force was pressing against her chest.

"Another power fluctuation," she muttered, her voice barely above a whisper. The words carried an unnatural weight in the silence. "Life support systems are stable, but the external sensors are... offline again. That's the third time this shift."

"I checked the wiring," replied Dr. Alvarez, the station's engineer, her voice trembling with an edge of irritation masking fear. She floated nearby, gripping a handhold for stability. "There's nothing wrong with the hardware. It's like something's jamming the signal. Or... I don't know, interfering with it."

"Interfering how?" asked Carter, the youngest of the crew, his tone brittle. His face was pale, his eyes darting nervously to the observation window. "You mean, like... solar flares? Or something else?"

The crew exchanged uneasy glances. Commander Lee didn't answer. She couldn't. The truth was, Alvarez's findings didn't make sense. Nothing about the last forty-eight hours made sense. The station's automated systems had been glitching sporadically, but there was no logical explanation. No malfunctions. No debris impacts. No solar activity. Just... silence. And then the dreams.

Lee shuddered, pushing the thought away.

"Let's focus," she said, snapping into the authority that had earned her command. "Alvarez, I want a manual diagnostic on the oxygen filtration systems. Carter, help Dr. Singh in the lab. I'll monitor—"

A sharp clang reverberated through the station, a metallic screech that froze the crew in place. It wasn't the sound of something mechanical—a valve loosening or a panel shifting —it was deliberate, resonant, like something had struck the station from the outside.

Carter was the first to speak. "What the hell was that?"

No one answered. Lee's stomach twisted as she looked toward the observation window. Beyond it, the Earth hung in eternal twilight, the curve of the planet bathed in shades of blue and black. But her eyes were drawn upward—to the darkness beyond, the void stretching infinitely above them. She felt it again: the weight. That suffocating, invisible presence. It wasn't just in her mind. It was out there.

"Alvarez." Lee's voice was sharp now. "Check the external cameras. Now."

Alvarez nodded, her fingers trembling as she pulled herself toward the nearest console. Her breath came in shallow gasps as she brought up the camera feeds. One by one, the external views flickered onto the screen. The solar arrays. The docking module. The Earth, serene and indifferent. And then—

"Oh my God," Alvarez whispered.

The image on the screen was static at first, a haze of interference.

But through the distortion, something moved. A shape that defied logic, twisting and folding against itself in geometric impossibilities. It was vast, larger than the station, yet somehow amorphous, as though it existed in dimensions the human brain wasn't meant to comprehend. The edges of it shimmered with an unnatural light—cold and ancient, yet alive with intent.

"What is that?" Carter's voice cracked, his face a mask of terror.

"It's... looking at us," Alvarez said. Her words were a whisper, but they carried the weight of an unspoken truth. The entity on the screen wasn't just a thing. It was aware.

"Shut it off," Lee ordered, her tone more forceful than she intended. "Shut it off now."

But before Alvarez could comply, the lights flickered, and the screen went black. A low vibration rippled through the station, not a sound but a sensation that resonated in their bones. And then, a voice.

It wasn't heard so much as felt—a deep, resonant tone that bypassed their ears and settled directly into their minds. *"You are seen."*

Lee's breath caught in her throat. She looked around at her crew. Carter's eyes were wide with panic, his hands clutching his helmet like he could block out the voice. Alvarez's lips moved silently, as though she were praying. Only Dr. Singh, who had drifted into the room moments before, seemed calm. Too calm.

"What do you want from us?" Lee demanded, her voice trembling despite her effort to appear strong.

"To give," the voice replied. It was both singular and many, a chorus of whispers and screams layered over one another. *"To share what you seek. Knowledge. Truth. The abyss above holds all."*

"No," Carter whispered. "No, no, no. Don't listen to it. Don't—"

"But a price must be paid," the voice continued, ignoring him. *"The mind is fragile. It bends. It breaks. Are you willing to fracture, to see what cannot be unseen?"*

Lee's heart pounded. She wanted to scream, to tell it to stop, but part of her—a small, desperate part—wanted to listen. Wanted to know. What was out there, beyond the stars? What truths did the entity hold?

"Commander," Singh said suddenly, his voice calm, almost hypnotic. "We should accept. This is... a once-in-a-lifetime opportunity. We could understand everything. The universe. Our place in it."

"Singh, shut up!" Carter shouted. He pushed himself toward Lee, gripping her arm with white-knuckled desperation. "We have to get out of here. We have to leave the station. Don't you hear it? It's inside our heads!"

Lee yanked her arm free, glaring at Carter. "Pull yourself together!"

But as she looked into his eyes, she saw it—the same terror she felt gnawing at the edges of her own mind. She turned back to the window, to the void where the entity lingered, waiting.

"What happens if we refuse?" she asked, her voice barely a whisper.

For a moment, there was silence. Then the voice came again, colder this time. Final. *"Then you will remain blind. And the void will take what is owed."*

The lights flickered again, plunging the station into darkness for a heartbeat. When they came back on, Singh was staring at the window, his face slack, his eyes wide and unblinking. "I'll do it," he murmured. "I'll pay the price."

"Singh, no!" Lee shouted, but it was too late. He pressed his hand to the glass, and the darkness beyond surged forward, enveloping the station in a blinding, otherworldly light.

And then, there was only silence.

CHAPTER 43: THE CARNIVAL OF LOST SOULS

The air was thick with the mingling scents of buttered popcorn, sizzling hot dogs, and the faint, sickly sweetness of cotton candy. Strings of multicolored lights blinked in hypnotic patterns, casting long, warped shadows over the dirt paths winding through the carnival. Laughter and the distant strains of a calliope mingled with the occasional scream from the rickety-looking Ferris wheel. But Ethan couldn't hear any of it anymore. Not really. Not after what he'd seen.

He stood just beyond the glowing entrance, his fists clenched so tightly his nails dug into his palms. His heart pounded, and a chill crawled up his spine as he scanned the bustling crowd. His friends—Rachel, Connor, and Malik—had been gone for hours. When they returned, they weren't the same. Rachel's voice had taken on a hollow, lilting quality, like she was reciting lines in a play she didn't understand. Connor's face was pale and slack, his eyes darting as though he could see something no one else could. And Malik... Malik just stood there, silent, his jaw working like he was chewing on something invisible, his lips smeared with red that didn't look like ketchup.

They tried to drag Ethan into the carnival's depths, murmuring about an attraction he *had* to see, but he pulled away. Their hands had been too cold, too strong. He had run then, but he couldn't run now. Not when he knew something was wrong—*terribly, horribly wrong.*

Ethan took a deep breath and stepped into the carnival.

The atmosphere shifted the moment he crossed the threshold. The air grew heavier, the lights dimmer. The laughter around him sounded warped, distant, like it was being played backward. He wove through the crowd, avoiding the wandering eyes of the carnival workers. They didn't seem human anymore—if they ever had been. The woman selling candied apples had a grin stretched too wide across her face, and her fingers, thin and claw-like, dripped with something syrupy and dark. The man running the ring toss never blinked, his eyes glassy and fixed on Ethan as he passed.

"Step right up, step right up!" a voice boomed to his left. Ethan turned to see a barker standing in front of a striped tent. He had a top hat perched on his head at an impossible angle, and his long, spindly arms gestured toward the open flap. "Face your fears! Conquer the unconquerable! One ticket is all it takes to experience the unimaginable!"

Ethan froze as a terrible realization washed over him. *This is how they take you.*

He edged closer, careful to stay in the shadows cast by the flickering lights. From his vantage point, he could see people filing into the tent, faces tense with nervous excitement. One by one, they entered. Some came back out, staggering and changed. Others didn't come out at all.

His stomach churned. He had to figure out what was happening inside that tent. He couldn't save Rachel, Connor, or Malik if he didn't understand. Steeling himself, Ethan slipped around the back of the tent, where the fabric sagged against its wooden supports. He crouched low, tugging at a loose flap until he could peer inside.

The interior was suffused with a sickly green glow, the light emanating from a massive, pulsating crystal suspended from the tent's peak. The crystal seemed alive, its jagged edges shifting and reforming as though it were breathing. Beneath it, the carnival's victims stood in a circle, their faces blank, their mouths moving silently. Ethan's friends were among them. His breath caught in his throat.

"Beautiful, isn't it?" a voice whispered in his ear.

Ethan whipped around to find a man looming over him, his face obscured by the shadows of his hood. His smile gleamed unnaturally white in the dim light. "The crystal feeds on fear," the man continued, his voice like oil dripping from a rusted pipe. "It drinks the terror and despair of these souls, distilling it into pure energy for the carnival. You should be honored to witness it. Not many do before they… contribute."

Ethan stumbled back, his mind racing. The carnival wasn't just feeding on people's fears—it was trapping them, turning them into husks to fuel whatever dark power kept this nightmare alive. The crystal was the core. He had to destroy it.

But the hooded man wasn't going to let him go so easily. "You've seen too much," he sneered, his voice shifting into something guttural and inhuman. His fingers elongated into claws, and his eyes glowed faintly in the dim light. "Your fear will be the most delicious of all."

Ethan bolted before the man could grab him, his heart hammering as he ducked through the crowd. He needed a plan —something fast, something that wouldn't get him killed. His eyes darted around, landing on a nearby booth where a carnival worker was handing out sparklers to a group of giggling kids. An idea sparked in his mind.

He snatched a lit sparkler from the booth, ignoring the worker's startled protest, and dashed back toward the tent. His breath came in ragged gasps as he skidded to a stop just outside the flap. The hooded man was there, his grin widening as he moved closer. "You can't fight the carnival," he hissed. "It's older than you can imagine. Stronger than you'll ever be."

"Maybe," Ethan shot back, his voice trembling but resolute. "But it's not invincible."

With a shout, he plunged the sparkler into the side of the tent, the fabric catching immediately. The flames licked upward, bright and hungry, as the hooded man recoiled with a snarl. Ethan didn't wait to see what would happen next. He darted inside, the heat from the growing fire at his back. The crystal pulsed wildly, its green light flickering as the flames crept closer.

Ethan grabbed a wooden support beam and yanked it free, the makeshift club heavy in his hands. He didn't think. He didn't hesitate. He swung with all his strength, aiming for the heart of the crystal. The impact sent a shockwave through the tent, the crystal shattering with an earsplitting crack. A deafening scream filled the air as the fragments exploded outward in a blinding flash of light.

When Ethan opened his eyes, the tent was gone. The carnival was gone. He was standing alone in an empty field, the grass scorched and blackened where the attractions had been. His friends lay unconscious around him, their faces peaceful for the first time in days.

Ethan dropped the beam and sank to his knees, tears streaming down his face. He'd done it. He'd freed them. But as he looked up at the night sky, he couldn't shake the feeling that the carnival wasn't truly gone. That somewhere, in another town, it was rebuilding itself, waiting for its next victims.

CHAPTER 44: THE ENTITY IN THE ICE

The wind howled against the reinforced steel walls of the station, a ceaseless scream that had become the soundtrack of their isolation. Dr. Elena Martinez sat hunched over a microscope, her gloved hands trembling ever so slightly. She forced herself to focus on the slide beneath the lens, but her mind kept drifting back to the specimen they had unearthed two days prior. Even now, the memory sent a shiver racing down her spine.

It had been buried three miles below the ice sheet, a discovery so extraordinary that it eclipsed the bone-deep exhaustion of their grueling expedition. A perfectly preserved organism, encased in crystalline frost, its alien structure like nothing they'd ever seen. At first, they thought it was dead. A relic from an epoch no human had ever witnessed. But when the ice thawed in the station's controlled environment, it began to move.

"Elena," came a voice behind her, soft and strained. She turned to see Dr. Khalid, his face pale under the harsh fluorescent lights. His eyes darted toward the lab's containment chamber. "It's... it's doing something again."

She stood, her stomach knotting. "What do you mean?"

"Just come look."

The two of them walked down the narrow corridor, their boots clanging against the metal floor. The air was heavy with the scent of disinfectants and the faint metallic tang of fear. As they entered the observation room, Elena's heart skipped a beat. The creature—if it could even be called that—stood in the center of the chamber, its form grotesquely fluid, as if it couldn't decide what shape to take. Long, sinewy appendages writhed and coiled, shifting in and out of focus like a mirage.

"It's mimicking again," Khalid said, his voice barely above a whisper.

Elena's breath caught as she saw it. The creature's surface shimmered, and then—impossibly—began to resemble Dr. Henderson, one of their team members. It wasn't just the shape or the face; it was the way it moved, the way it tilted its head in that familiar, absentminded way Henderson always did when he was deep in thought. But Henderson was gone. His quarters were empty, his radio silent.

"This isn't possible," Elena murmured, though the words felt hollow. She'd seen too much in the last 48 hours to cling to logic.

"We need to destroy it," Khalid said, his voice trembling. "Now. Before it—"

The station's lights flickered, plunging them into darkness for a heartbeat before the emergency backups kicked in. The hum of the generators reverberated through the walls, but it did little to mask the suffocating silence that followed.

"Elena," Khalid said, his voice taut with panic. "Where's the rest of the team?"

Her mind raced. Henderson was missing. Dr. Chen had last been seen heading to the storage bay. And as for Dr. Reyes…

A sudden, sharp noise echoed down the corridor—a wet, dragging sound that made Elena's blood run cold. She grabbed Khalid's arm, pulling him behind her. "Stay close."

They moved cautiously, their breaths shallow, the corridor stretching endlessly before them. Elena's hand tightened around the wrench she'd grabbed from the lab earlier. It felt pitifully inadequate, but it was better than nothing.

The noise grew louder as they approached the storage bay. The door was ajar, a faint, flickering glow spilling out into the hallway. Elena pushed it open with the wrench, her heart hammering in her chest.

The sight inside made her gag.

Dr. Chen lay sprawled on the floor, her chest cavity grotesquely hollowed out. Blood pooled around her, glistening in the dim light. But what made Elena's knees nearly buckle was the figure hunched over the body. It looked like Reyes—same build, same rumpled uniform—but its movements were wrong. Jerky. Unnatural. It turned toward them, and for a moment, its face was Reyes's. Then it began to ripple, the features melting and reforming into something hideously alien.

"Run!" Elena shouted, shoving Khalid backward.

The thing lunged, its limbs elongating with a sickening crackle. Elena swung the wrench, connecting with a wet thud. It staggered but didn't fall. Instead, it let out a sound—a guttural, vibrating noise that seemed to reverberate inside her skull.

They bolted down the corridor, the station's labyrinthine layout making every turn feel like a gamble. Behind them, the creature's inhuman screeches echoed, growing louder with each passing second.

"Elena, we're not going to make it!" Khalid panted, his voice breaking.

"Yes, we will," she snapped, though she didn't believe it. Her mind raced, calculating their options. There was only one way to stop this, to ensure the thing didn't leave the station.

They burst into the control room, slamming the door shut behind them. Elena's fingers flew across the console, initiating the station's self-destruct sequence. A robotic voice blared over the intercom: **"Warning: Self-destruct sequence initiated. Evacuate immediately."**

"What are you doing?!" Khalid cried, grabbing her arm.

"We can't let it leave," she said, her voice steely. "If it gets out, it'll spread. It could mimic anyone. Anywhere."

"We don't even know what it is!" he shouted, his eyes wide with desperation. "There has to be another way!"

"There isn't," she said, meeting his gaze. "You know that."

The door behind them buckled, the metal groaning under the creature's relentless assault. Khalid's face crumpled, but he nodded, a tear slipping down his cheek.

"Go," Elena said, shoving him toward the emergency escape pod. "There's still time."

"What about you?"

"I'll make sure it doesn't follow."

The door burst open, and the creature slithered inside, its form twisting and writhing. Elena grabbed a flare gun from the console and aimed it at the thing. "Go!" she screamed.

Khalid hesitated for a moment, then turned and ran. Elena stood her ground, her hands steady as she fired the flare. The creature recoiled, shrieking as the flames licked at its flesh. The countdown ticked louder in her ears.

Ten seconds.

She backed toward the console, her gaze never leaving the creature. It lunged again, and she fired another flare.

Five seconds.

She allowed herself one final thought—a fleeting image of the world beyond the ice, untouched and safe.

Zero.

The station erupted in a blinding inferno, the ice swallowing the flames as the entity—and Elena—were consumed.

CHAPTER 45:
THE SYMPHONY
OF SCREAMS

The chandelier above the grand concert hall shimmered, its crystals catching the golden light of the sconces that lined the velvet-covered walls. The air was thick with anticipation, a tangible hum that mirrored the audience's excitement. Maestro Ivanov stood at the center of the stage, his tall, wiry frame towering over the orchestra pit. His silver hair gleamed under the spotlights, a stark contrast to the dark, tailored suit he wore. His eyes, sharp and glinting like shards of obsidian, scanned the packed rows of attendees. It was a full house tonight, just as he had hoped.

Behind him, the orchestra members sat silently, their instruments gleaming, their faces pale. They had rehearsed this symphony for weeks, though "rehearsed" was not quite the right word. They had endured it. The notes, so unlike anything they had ever played, seemed to claw at their minds, leaving behind a residue of unease. Several had quit after the first session, claiming headaches or sudden illness. Ivanov had replaced them without hesitation. Genius, he reminded them, was not for the faint-hearted.

"Ladies and gentlemen," Ivanov's voice carried through the hall, smooth and commanding. "Tonight, you shall witness the premiere of my magnum opus, *The Symphony of Screams*. A composition unlike any other. A work that delves into the very essence of sound, of existence itself."

The crowd erupted into polite applause, though a ripple of nervous laughter coursed through the room at the symphony's unsettling title. Ivanov's lips curled into a thin smile as he turned back to the orchestra, raising his baton. The hall fell silent, save for the faint sound of someone clearing their throat in the balcony.

He brought the baton down.

The opening note was a single, low hum, so deep it seemed to vibrate in the bones of every listener. It was followed by a discordant cascade of strings, their notes bending and warping unnaturally, as though the instruments themselves were resisting the sound. The violins shrieked, the cellos moaned. A flute trilled, its melody spiraling upward into a pitch that made ears ring.

In the audience, a woman winced, pressing her hands to her temples. A man next to her shifted uncomfortably in his seat. The music was oppressive, invasive, almost too much to bear. Yet no one left. They were transfixed, held captive by the sheer strangeness of it, by the allure of something so profoundly alien.

By the second movement, the atmosphere in the hall had shifted. The temperature seemed to drop, and a faint, metallic tang hung in the air. The lights flickered, just once, but enough to draw murmurs from the crowd. Ivanov's baton moved with feverish intensity, his body swaying as though the music flowed through him. The orchestra played on, their faces tight with concentration, beads of sweat glistening on their brows.

And then it began.

The first scream came from the mezzanine. A piercing, guttural wail that silenced the music for half a beat before the orchestra surged on, as if compelled by some unseen force. Heads turned toward the source of the sound, but there was nothing to see —just an empty seat where a young man had been moments before. A woman nearby clutched her chest, her face pale.

Another scream, this time from the orchestra itself. The second violinist dropped her bow, her hands clawing at her throat as though an invisible hand was choking her. She collapsed to the floor, her body convulsing, but the music did not stop. Her violin continued to play, its strings vibrating without touch.

The audience was in chaos now, gasps and cries echoing through the hall. People scrambled for the exits, but the heavy wooden doors would not budge. Several men pounded on them with their fists, their faces wild with panic. Ivanov paid them no mind. His baton moved faster, his eyes glowing with an unnatural light.

The third movement erupted with a cacophony of sound so intense it seemed to break the air itself. The chandelier above trembled, its crystals chiming faintly in the sonic storm. Shadows began to pool on the stage, dark and formless, writhing like living things. They slithered toward the orchestra members, wrapping around them like tendrils. One by one, the musicians fell silent, their bodies crumpling as the shadows consumed them. Yet their instruments continued to play, the music now disembodied, otherworldly.

In the audience, a man fell to his knees, his eyes wide and unseeing. "They're here," he whispered, his voice trembling. "God help us, they're here."

Shapes began to emerge from the darkness—elongated, skeletal figures with hollow eyes and mouths that gaped unnaturally wide. They moved with a jerking, unnatural rhythm, drawn to the sound of the symphony. The crowd recoiled, but there was nowhere to go. The entities reached out with spindly fingers, their touch leaving behind blackened, withered flesh.

Ivanov's smile grew wider, his teeth gleaming like a predator's. This was his masterpiece, his legacy. He had delved into the forbidden, unearthed notes and harmonies that were never meant for human ears. And in doing so, he had opened a doorway.

As the final movement began, the entities turned their hollow gazes toward Ivanov. For the first time, his hand faltered, the baton trembling in his grasp. The music swelled, a deafening crescendo that seemed to tear through reality itself. The shadows surged forward, engulfing the stage, the orchestra, and finally Ivanov, whose scream joined the symphony as its final, haunting note.

And then, silence.

When the doors to the hall finally creaked open the next morning, the authorities found no trace of the audience, the orchestra, or Ivanov. Only the instruments remained, their strings still vibrating with an unseen force. The sheet music for *The Symphony of Screams* lay scattered across the stage, the notes written in a language no one could decipher.

To this day, no one dares to play it.

CHAPTER 46: THE GAME MASTER'S CHALLENGE

The world around them pulsed with an unnatural, feverish glow, the sky a swirling vortex of crimson and black. Marcus tightened his grip on the jagged sword he'd scavenged from the ruins of a crumbling cathedral, its edges slick with an oily, dark substance that dripped onto the cracked earth below. His breath came in ragged bursts, each inhale tasting of ash and iron. The others stood behind him in a loose semicircle, their faces pale and drawn, their avatars battered and scarred from countless battles. But in their eyes, Marcus saw the same thing reflected back at him: fear. And something more dangerous—desperation.

"We've come too far to stop now," Marcus growled, his voice hoarse. He wasn't sure if it was from yelling commands or the acrid air of this hellish landscape. "This is it. Either we end this, or it ends us."

"Easy for you to say," muttered Lila, her hands trembling as she reloaded a crossbow that looked like it had been cobbled together from bone and sinew. "You're the one with the goddamn sword. I've got... this thing, and I don't even know if it'll work. It's like the game is *mocking* me."

"It's mocking all of us," said Ethan, his voice shaking. He was clutching a shield that flickered like static, as though it could disintegrate at any moment. "This isn't just a game anymore. It's alive. It knows what we're afraid of."

Marcus turned to face them, his jaw clenched. "That's why we have to push through. It's adapting to us, yeah, but we can adapt too. We've done it before. We can do it again."

From the shadows behind them came the sound of scraping metal, like claws dragging along steel. The group froze, their breaths hitching in unison. The sound grew louder, closer, accompanied by a low, guttural growl that seemed to vibrate through their bones.

"Shit," whispered Lila, her eyes darting toward the darkness. "It's here."

"No," Marcus said sharply, stepping forward. "We're not running this time. We're not hiding. We fight."

The creature emerged from the shadows, a grotesque amalgamation of flesh and machinery. Its body was a twisted mass of gears, wires, and exposed muscle, its face a blank screen that flickered with static. From its back jutted long, serrated blades that oozed with the same dark substance that coated Marcus's sword. The ground seemed to quake beneath its weight, and the air grew colder, heavier, as though the world itself recoiled from its presence.

"Welcome, players," the creature rasped, its voice a distorted mix of mechanical whirs and human screams. "The final challenge awaits. Survive... or perish."

"Yeah, yeah, we've heard it all before," Marcus said, though his voice wavered slightly. He raised his sword, forcing his hands to steady. "Let's see how tough you are when we're not running away."

The creature lunged, faster than anything its size should have been capable of. Marcus barely had time to raise his sword before it was on him, its blades crashing against his weapon with a force that sent vibrations up his arms. He gritted his teeth, pushing back with all his strength, but the creature was relentless. Its blank screen-face flickered, and for a split second, Marcus thought he saw his own reflection in it—except his eyes were hollow, lifeless.

"Marcus!" Lila shouted, firing her crossbow. The bolt struck the creature in the side, lodging itself in the mess of gears and wires. The monster let out a screech that made Marcus's ears ring, and he took the opportunity to shove it back, putting some distance between them.

"Ethan, flank it!" Marcus barked, his voice cutting through the chaos. "Lila, keep firing! Aim for the joints!"

Ethan nodded, his shield sparking as he charged the creature from the side. Lila fired another bolt, this one striking the creature's leg. It staggered, its movements jerky and uneven, but it didn't stop. Instead, it turned toward Lila, its blades whirring as they extended, gleaming with malevolence.

"No!" Marcus roared, throwing himself between Lila and the creature. He swung his sword with all his might, the blade slicing through one of the creature's arms. Black ichor sprayed out, sizzling as it hit the ground. The creature howled, its screen-face glitching wildly.

"Keep going!" Marcus shouted. "It can bleed. That means we can kill it."

But even as he said the words, doubt gnawed at the edges of his mind. The creature wasn't just a boss fight. It was the game itself, its code and algorithms given form. Killing it wouldn't just be hard—it might be impossible.

The creature lashed out, its remaining blade slashing across Marcus's chest. Pain exploded through him, white-hot and searing. He stumbled back, clutching at the wound. Blood—real blood—seeped between his fingers, and he felt his strength waning.

"Marcus!" Lila screamed, her voice cracking. She dropped her crossbow and ran to his side, her hands fumbling as she tried to staunch the bleeding. "You're hurt. You're really hurt."

"It's... fine," Marcus gasped, though the agony in his chest said otherwise. "Just... keep going. Don't stop."

"We can't do this without you," Ethan said, his voice thick with panic. He raised his shield as the creature advanced on them, its movements almost gleeful. "Marcus, what do we do?"

Marcus looked up at the creature, his vision swimming. He thought of the hours they'd spent in this nightmare, the friends they'd lost, the lives they'd risked. He thought of the promise he'd made—to get them out, no matter what. And then he thought of the game itself, the cruel intelligence that had trapped them here, feeding on their fear.

"We end it," Marcus said, his voice steady despite the pain. "No matter what it takes."

He pushed himself to his feet, ignoring Lila's protests. The creature loomed over them, its blades raised for the final strike. But Marcus wasn't afraid anymore. He raised his sword, meeting the creature's blank gaze.

"Game over," he said.

And with a roar, he charged.

CHAPTER 47:
THE BOOK OF
THE DAMNED

The library was silent, save for the soft rustle of Claire's pencil skirt against her legs as she climbed the rickety ladder. Dust motes swirled in the weak amber light of the overhead chandeliers, and the air was thick with the scent of ancient paper and wood polish. She had worked at the library for nearly eight years, yet this particular corner—the Restricted Section— always felt different, as though the shadows clung just a little too tightly to the walls and the books whispered secrets too faint to hear.

A misplaced book, she thought. That's all she was looking for —a dusty tome that some careless patron had tucked away on the wrong shelf. But when her hand reached behind the row of leather-bound encyclopedias, her fingers brushed something cold. Not paper or leather, but metal. Intrigued, she pulled it free.

The book was unlike any she had ever seen. Its cover was made of what looked like blackened iron, etched with strange, almost pulsating symbols that shifted when she tried to focus on them. The edges were bound with tarnished brass, and a lock, long rusted, hung limply from the clasp. It should have been heavy, but it rested in her hands like a feather. The title, engraved in jagged letters, read *Liber Maledictus*.

Claire's breath caught in her throat. She wasn't sure why she felt compelled to open it—maybe it was the faint warmth emanating from its surface, or the way the symbols seemed to hum in rhythm with her heartbeat. She glanced around, ensuring she was alone, and then, with trembling fingers, she pried the cover open.

The pages were thin as spider silk, inked with an intricate script she couldn't recognize but strangely understood. Each word unfurled in her mind like a dark flower, filling her with an intoxicating mix of dread and exhilaration. The room seemed to tilt around her, and suddenly, she wasn't in the library anymore.

She was standing in a vast void, the air thick and electric, her feet sinking into a floor that felt like flesh. Shadows writhed around her, their shapes human but grotesquely distorted. They clawed at her, whispering promises of power, of knowledge beyond comprehension. She wanted to scream, to run, but her body was rooted in place.

"Say the words," a voice rasped, low and guttural, echoing from everywhere and nowhere. "Say the words, and it will all be yours."

When Claire blinked, she was back in the library, the book open in her lap. A cold sweat slicked her skin. Her heart hammered as she slammed the book shut, but it was too late. The first line of the incantation had already fallen from her lips, unbidden.

By the next morning, Claire knew something had changed. She awoke to a clarity she had never known before. As she passed her neighbors on her walk to the library, she could see their secrets etched into their faces like cracks in porcelain. The man who nodded politely at her was cheating on his wife. The elderly woman who waved from her porch had buried a body in her garden. The knowledge came unbidden, sharp and absolute. It was terrifying—and exhilarating.

But the power didn't stop there. By the end of the week, Claire discovered she could move objects with a thought, listen to whispers carried on the wind from miles away. She could feel the threads of the world bending to her will, fragile and pliant.

And yet, with each use of the book's gifts, her reflection in the mirror grew a little dimmer. Her skin paled, her hair dulled, and her eyes, once bright and curious, seemed to sink deeper into her skull. She began to feel hollow, as though the book was carving pieces out of her soul to fuel its magic.

She knew she couldn't keep it. But the book wouldn't let go of her so easily.

That night, Claire locked herself in the library after hours. The shadows stretched long across the floor as she placed the *Liber Maledictus* on the oak table in the center of the Restricted Section. She had spent days researching how to destroy it, consulting the forbidden texts she had once sworn to protect. Every source warned her of the same thing: the book did not die easily, and it would fight back.

She struck a match, her hands trembling, and held it above a pyre of old newspapers she had stacked beneath the book. The flames curled hungrily toward the tome, but as soon as they licked the iron cover, they sputtered out with a hiss. The room grew icy cold.

"Do you think it will be so simple?" The voice from the void echoed again, this time louder, closer. The book's symbols began to glow, casting writhing shadows onto the walls. "You are bound to me now, Claire. My power is your power. Do you really want to let it go?"

Claire's knees buckled, and she clutched the edge of the table for support. "I didn't ask for this," she whispered, her voice cracking. "I didn't ask for any of this."

"But you *used* it," the voice hissed. "You tasted what I offer, and you liked it. You *need* me now."

"No," she said, louder this time, standing straighter. "You need me. Without me, you're just a book. And I'm going to end this."

She grabbed a letter opener from the desk and drove it into the book's cover. The room erupted into chaos. Shelves toppled over, books flew through the air, and the chandeliers flickered wildly. The shadows surged toward her, screaming in voices that weren't her own.

Claire screamed back, pouring every ounce of her will into the blade. The book writhed beneath it, its symbols flaring bright one last time before fading into darkness. The air went still.

When she opened her eyes, the book was gone, reduced to a pile of ash. But Claire's reflection in the broken glass of the chandelier told her the cost. Her once-youthful face was gaunt and hollow, her hair streaked with gray. She was alive—but barely.

As she staggered out of the library and into the predawn light, she knew she had won, but at a price she would carry forever.

CHAPTER 48: THE DOPPELGÄNGER EFFECT

Detective Oliver sat in his dimly lit office, the rain streaming down the window behind him in jagged streaks. The city outside was restless, its usual hum now carrying an undercurrent of something... wrong. He couldn't shake the feeling that the people in the streets below—the ones he'd walked past, the ones he'd interrogated, even the ones he'd shared coffee with—weren't the same anymore.

The first clue had been subtle: Detective Harper, his partner of five years, had forgotten how he took his coffee. Black. He always took it black. But that morning, Harper had handed him a cup with cream and sugar, insisting with a chillingly blank smile that it was "just the way you like it." Oliver had laughed it off, but the unease had clung to him like a stain.

Harper wasn't a forgetful man. He was meticulous, sharp. But over the past week, he'd been... different. His speech slower, his posture too rigid, his jokes rehearsed. And his eyes—those sharp, observant eyes—had grown empty, reflective, like glass.

Oliver pulled out the security footage from the precinct's parking lot. The timestamp read 3:17 a.m. two nights ago. Harper's car was parked in its usual spot. Everything seemed normal, at first. But then, a shadow emerged from the corner of the frame, jerky and deliberate in its movements. It wasn't Harper. It wasn't anyone Oliver recognized.

The figure approached the driver's side door of Harper's car, a pale, featureless thing, its body shimmering faintly under the flickering streetlight. The footage showed it leaning into the car window, pressing its hands against the glass. And then, impossibly, it began to stretch, its milky flesh bubbling and forming into something else.

When it pulled back and turned to the camera, Oliver froze. It stared directly into the lens with Harper's face. The real Harper —his partner—never left the car. The thing had simply *become* him.

"Jesus Christ," Oliver muttered, his voice barely audible over the rain's relentless drumming.

The office door creaked open behind him.

"Working late again, huh, partner?" Harper's voice. The cadence was perfect, every syllable an exact replica of the man Oliver had known for years. But Oliver didn't turn around. His hand instinctively reached for his sidearm.

"Yeah," Oliver said, forcing his voice to sound steady. "Just going over some old case files."

Harper—or whatever it was—stepped further into the room. Oliver could hear the deliberate weight of each step, too measured, too calculated. When Harper finally spoke again, his voice carried an uncanny brightness, like an actor overplaying a role. "You've been on edge lately, Oliver. Everything okay?"

Oliver turned his chair slowly, his grip tightening on the gun beneath his desk. Harper's face was a mask of concern, but Oliver noticed the way his hands hung stiffly at his sides, fingers twitching ever so slightly, as if the body wasn't entirely his to control.

"I've just been tired," Oliver replied, locking eyes with his partner —or the thing wearing his partner's skin. "You know how it is. Long nights."

Harper nodded, but there was something mechanical in the motion, a small lag, as if the gesture had to be processed first. "You should take a break. Maybe head home for the night."

Oliver's heart pounded. He stood, careful to keep his movements slow, non-threatening. "Maybe you're right. I could use some sleep."

Harper smiled. Too wide. Too perfect. "Good idea. We'll catch up tomorrow."

Oliver moved toward the door, his hand still gripping the gun at his side. As he passed Harper, he caught a whiff of something faint but unmistakable—ozone, like the air after lightning strikes. It made his stomach churn. He didn't look back as he stepped into the hallway, but he could feel Harper's eyes boring into the back of his skull.

In his apartment later that night, Oliver sat in the dark, the blinds drawn tight. The footage played on a loop on his laptop, the pale creature transforming into Harper over and over again. He took a swig of whiskey, the burn doing little to calm his nerves.

What the hell was he dealing with? Aliens? Some kind of government experiment gone wrong? He didn't know. But the city was changing. People were changing. And no one seemed to notice except him.

His phone buzzed on the coffee table. Harper's name flashed on the screen.

Oliver stared at it, his chest tightening. He let it ring until it went to voicemail. But the moment it stopped, the phone buzzed again. Another call. This time, it wasn't Harper's name.

It was his own.

"Impossible," he whispered, his pulse racing. The phone continued to buzz, the screen glowing mockingly in the darkness. He didn't answer.

Instead, he grabbed his jacket and headed for the door. If he stayed in his apartment, they'd come for him. He was sure of it now. He needed answers, and he wouldn't find them here.

As he stepped into the hallway, he froze. His neighbor, Mrs. Calder, stood at the far end, her frail figure silhouetted by the flickering fluorescent lights. She was smiling, but it wasn't the warm, grandmotherly smile he was used to. This one was too wide, her lips stretched unnaturally, her teeth gleaming in the dim light.

"Going somewhere, Oliver?" she asked, her voice sweet and saccharine, but with an edge that made his skin crawl.

Oliver backed away slowly, his hand hovering near his gun. "Just out for some air."

Her smile didn't falter, but her head tilted slightly, unnervingly. "You shouldn't be out so late. It's dangerous."

Before he could respond, the door to his apartment creaked open behind him. He spun around, his gun drawn, and found himself face to face with... himself.

The other Oliver—his doppelgänger—smiled, its eyes glinting with malice. "You've been working too hard, partner. Time to take a break."

And then they lunged.

CHAPTER 49: THE CURSE OF THE WITCH TREE

The chainsaw screamed as it bit into the ancient oak, its teeth gnashing through bark and heartwood with a feral hunger. The logger, a burly man named Hank, wiped sweat from his brow with the back of his glove, pausing to catch his breath. Around him, the forest stood oppressively silent, as though every tree, every leaf, was holding its breath.

"Damn thing's tougher than steel," Hank muttered, glaring at the half-felled trunk.

"Maybe it's a sign we shouldn't be out here," came a voice from behind him. It was Eddie, the youngest of the crew, his face pale and his eyes darting nervously between the trees. "You hear what the locals said? About the witch or whatever—"

"Oh, shut it, Eddie," barked Carl, the foreman, stepping between them with a scowl. "No such thing as curses. Just old wives' tales to keep us from doing our job. You wanna lose your paycheck over some ghost story?"

Eddie hesitated but said nothing, his gaze fixed on the shadows shifting between the trees. The sunlight was dimming fast, painting long, skeletal fingers across the forest floor. The air felt heavier than it should have, dense with an almost suffocating dampness.

"Let's just get it done." Carl gestured towards the oak, his tone leaving no room for argument.

Hank revved the chainsaw again, but before the blade could touch the wood, a chilling wind swept through the clearing, carrying with it a sound—a low, guttural moan that seemed to come from everywhere and nowhere at once. The men froze, their breath misting in the sudden drop in temperature.

"What the hell was that?" Eddie whispered, his voice barely audible over the rustling of leaves that hadn't been stirred by any breeze.

"Wind." Carl's answer came too quickly, too firmly, as though he didn't quite believe it himself. "Get back to work."

But the forest was no longer quiet. That moan had birthed something darker. The trees swayed—not with the wind, but as if moving on their own accord. Shadows grew deeper, pooling like black tar around the loggers' boots. And then came the whispers—soft and insidious, threading through the air like spider silk.

"She warned you..."

"Blood for blood..."

"Roots... reach..."

Hank dropped the chainsaw. "I'm not hearing this. I'm not hearing this!" His voice cracked, his bravado crumbling as the whispers grew louder, overlapping into a cacophony of disembodied voices.

"Enough!" Carl shouted, though the tremor in his voice betrayed his fear. "It's just your imagination. Everyone grab your gear and —"

A loud crack echoed through the clearing. Everyone turned to see the oak, the one Hank had been cutting, standing impossibly upright, the gash in its trunk knitting itself back together. Its bark rippled as though alive, the dark grooves forming shapes— faces contorted in agony, mouths open in silent screams.

Eddie stumbled backward. "Oh God, it's her. It's the witch."

Carl grabbed Eddie's arm, shaking him. "Snap out of it! There's no witch—"

Before he could finish, a root snaked out of the ground, as quick and precise as a striking serpent. It wrapped around Carl's ankle and yanked him off his feet. He screamed, clawing at the soil as the root dragged him toward the tree. His nails left bloody streaks in the dirt.

"Help me! Don't just stand there!" he shrieked, but the other men were frozen in terror. Eddie fell to his knees, muttering a prayer under his breath, while Hank stood paralyzed, his face a mask of disbelief.

Carl's screams were cut short as the tree's roots swallowed him whole, pulling him into the earth as though he had never existed. The clearing fell silent once more, save for the sound of Eddie's panicked breaths.

Hank finally spoke, his voice hollow. "We... we need to get out of here."

But the forest had other plans. The air grew colder still, and the apparitions began to appear—translucent figures of men and women, their forms twisted and broken, their eyes glowing with a ghostly light. They surrounded the loggers, their mouths moving in silent condemnation.

From the shadows stepped an older man, his face gaunt, his eyes sharp beneath the brim of a wide-brimmed hat. It was Harold, the local historian, who had warned them days ago about the cursed tree. His sudden appearance should have sparked relief, but there was something unnerving about the calm in his expression.

"You didn't listen," Harold said, his voice cutting through the oppressive silence. "You disturbed the Witch Tree."

"What the hell is going on?" Hank demanded, his voice trembling. "You knew this would happen?"

Harold nodded slowly. "I told you, this land isn't just land. That tree… it grew from the grave of a woman who was wronged. Burned as a witch centuries ago. Her rage runs deep, and her roots run deeper. You harmed her kin. Now she demands retribution."

Eddie crawled toward Harold, grasping at his coat. "Please— you've got to help us! There's got to be a way to stop this!"

The historian's gaze softened, though his expression remained grim. "There's only one way to break the curse. You must make an offering."

"What kind of offering?" Hank asked, though he already feared the answer.

Harold's eyes flicked to the chainsaw lying abandoned on the ground. "A sacrifice. Blood for blood. The curse won't rest until it's fed."

Eddie began to sob, shaking his head. "No… no, there's got to be another way."

But before anyone could argue further, the ground beneath them began to quake, and the tree groaned, its bark splitting open to reveal a gaping maw of jagged wood and writhing roots. The voices returned, louder now, demanding, insistent.

"Choose," Harold said, his tone unyielding. "Or she'll choose for you."

The three men exchanged panicked glances, the weight of their predicament sinking in. Above them, the Witch Tree loomed, its branches twisting like skeletal arms, ready to claim its next victim.

CHAPTER 50:
THE PHANTOM
PHOTOGRAPHER

The camera was heavier than Evelyn expected, its brass body cold and unyielding in her hands as she set it on the tripod. The lens, a smoky circle of warped glass, seemed to stare back at her, unblinking and oddly alive. She adjusted it with measured care, her fingers trembling slightly as the gears clicked into place. The late afternoon sunlight spilled through the cracked window of the abandoned greenhouse, dust motes swirling lazily in the humid air. Her subject, a young woman named Marissa, shifted nervously on the stool Evelyn had dragged in for the shoot.

"You sure this thing works?" Marissa asked, tilting her head to inspect the camera. Her voice was light, teasing, but there was an edge to her tone—something uneasy.

Evelyn forced a smile. "Works like a charm. They built these things to last back then."

It wasn't a lie, not entirely. The antique camera had been a peculiar find at the flea market last weekend, tucked away in a corner booth crammed with relics that seemed to hum with forgotten stories. The old man who sold it to her had been eager —too eager, maybe—to part with it. He'd muttered something strange as he wrapped it in brown paper, but Evelyn hadn't caught his words over the din of the market. She had chalked it up to the ramblings of an eccentric vendor. Now, standing in the eerie stillness of the greenhouse, she wasn't so sure.

Marissa gave a half-hearted laugh and smoothed down her dress. "Well, if I end up looking like a ghost in these photos, I'm blaming you."

The words struck Evelyn harder than they should have, lodging like barbs in her chest. She had photographed three clients with the camera so far, each one eager to capture a moment of themselves in the haunting, vintage style the antique promised. Each one now lay in a hospital bed, their bodies slack and lifeless, their minds unreachable. Evelyn hadn't connected the dots at first. But then she had developed the photos. And she had seen them.

The souls.

Every image showed her subjects' faces frozen mid-expression, their eyes wide with terror, their mouths open in soundless screams. And yet, beneath that horror, there was something else—something alive. A flicker of movement within the photograph, as though the souls themselves were trapped behind the glossy surface, pleading for release.

Evelyn tried to push the thought away as she adjusted the lens, her hands clammy. Marissa's face came into focus through the viewfinder, her features softly illuminated by the golden light streaming through the greenhouse. It was a perfect shot. But Evelyn's stomach churned.

"Alright," Evelyn said, her voice cracking slightly. She cleared her throat. "Hold still. This'll only take a second."

Marissa nodded, her smile faltering as Evelyn pressed her eye to the viewfinder again. Evelyn's finger hovered over the shutter button, her heart pounding so loudly she could barely hear the creak of the greenhouse settling around them. She hesitated, her mind screaming at her to stop. To throw the camera away. To run.

But she didn't.

The shutter clicked.

The sound was louder than it should have been, a metallic snap that echoed through the empty greenhouse like the crack of a whip. Marissa flinched slightly, blinking against the sudden flash of light, then smiled again. She opened her mouth to say something, but the words never came. Her body went rigid, her eyes rolling back in her head as she pitched forward off the stool.

"Marissa!" Evelyn cried, rushing forward to catch her. She barely managed to soften the fall, lowering Marissa's limp body to the ground. Her friend's skin was pale, her breathing shallow, her eyes fluttering shut as though she were simply falling into a deep, dreamless sleep.

"Oh no," Evelyn whispered, her voice trembling. "Not again."

She looked at the camera, still perched on the tripod. Its lens glinted in the fading sunlight, mocking her. Her hands shook as she tore the film from the back, her movements frantic and clumsy. She shoved the roll into her bag and sprinted out of the greenhouse, Marissa's body abandoned in the growing shadows.

The darkroom smelled of chemicals and fear. Evelyn's hands moved mechanically, her mind buzzing with static as she developed the film. The first image slid into focus, the grainy black-and-white photo revealing Marissa seated on the stool, her nervous smile frozen in time. Evelyn's breath caught as the familiar, dreadful movement began. Marissa's smile twisted into a grimace of pain, her eyes darting around as though she could see Evelyn through the photograph.

"Help me," Marissa's voice rasped faintly, the sound so quiet

Evelyn thought she might have imagined it. But no—Marissa's lips in the photo were moving, forming the same words over and over. "Help me. Please."

Evelyn stumbled back, nearly knocking over the tray of developer fluid. Her chest heaved, tears spilling down her cheeks as guilt clawed at her. "I didn't mean to," she whispered. "I didn't know..."

The air in the darkroom grew heavy, oppressive. The shadows in the corners deepened, stretching across the walls like grasping hands. And then, from behind her, a voice spoke.

"You knew enough."

Evelyn spun around, her heart lurching into her throat. A figure stood in the doorway, cloaked in darkness. His face was obscured, but his voice carried the weight of centuries.

"You've been meddling with things you don't understand," the figure said, stepping closer. The light from the red bulb above the darkroom door revealed his face—sharp, angular, and impossibly pale. His eyes burned with a cold, unnatural light. "The camera is not a toy."

"Who are you?" Evelyn demanded, her voice shaking. She backed away, clutching the photograph to her chest as though it might shield her.

"I am the one who gave the camera its power," he said, his lips curling into a cruel smile. "And you, my dear, have been feeding it quite well."

Evelyn's knees buckled, and she sank to the floor. "Please," she begged. "Tell me how to fix this. Tell me how to free them."

The man tilted his head, regarding her with something like amusement. "You can't," he said simply. "The souls belong to the camera now. They are its fuel. Its sustenance. Without them, it would wither away. And so would I."

Evelyn's grip on the photograph tightened. "Then take me," she said, her voice raw. "Let them go and take me instead."

The man's laughter echoed through the darkroom, cold and hollow. "How noble," he said. "But it doesn't work that way. The camera chooses. And it has chosen you as its caretaker."

"No," Evelyn whispered, tears streaming down her face. "No, I won't do this anymore."

"You don't have a choice," the man said, his voice softening into something almost gentle. "The camera will find a way. It always does."

And then he was gone, leaving only the suffocating silence of the darkroom and the faint, desperate whispers of the souls trapped within the photographs.

CHAPTER 51:
THE SUBWAY TO
NOWHERE

The train screeched to a stop, its doors yawning open to reveal a near-empty car bathed in flickering fluorescent light. Jared hesitated before stepping inside, the late-night chill clinging to the back of his neck. The platform behind him was deserted, save for a broken vending machine humming monotonously. He was tired—too tired to think twice about the odd sensation crawling up his spine. Just one more train ride, and he'd be home.

Sliding into a seat near the middle of the car, Jared glanced at the few other passengers scattered throughout. A woman with a frayed scarf twisted tightly around her neck stared blankly out the window, her hands clenched around an ancient-looking leather bag. A man in a rumpled suit—tie half-loosened—scrolled aimlessly on his phone, the screen's glow casting eerie shadows on his hollowed cheeks. Across from him, a teenager with headphones too large for her head bobbed along to music Jared couldn't hear, her eyes darting nervously toward the doors.

The train jolted forward, shoving Jared back against the hard plastic seat. He exhaled sharply, shaking off the unease that had clung to him since stepping aboard. It was late, that was all. Late enough for the world to feel a little off.

But when the train sped past the next station without slowing, Jared sat up straighter. His stop was coming up soon, and if the train skipped it, he'd be stuck walking back through the icy streets. He frowned, glancing around to see if anyone else noticed. The woman with the scarf didn't move an inch, her eyes fixed on the dark tunnel outside. The man in the suit shifted uncomfortably but said nothing. Only the teenager seemed aware of the anomaly—she pulled her headphones off and glanced around the car, her brow furrowed.

"Did we just skip that stop?" Jared asked aloud, his voice cutting through the low hum of the train.

The man in the suit looked up from his phone. "Probably an express route," he muttered, though the uncertainty in his tone was palpable. He resumed scrolling.

Jared frowned. "This isn't an express train. It's the local. It always stops at every station."

The teenager spoke up, her voice shaky. "Yeah... I take this line every night. It's not supposed to do that."

The woman with the scarf finally turned, her pale face illuminated by the stuttering lights. "Sometimes they skip stops late at night," she said softly. "Maintenance or something. It's nothing to worry about."

Her words were meant to be reassuring, but there was something in her tone—something brittle, like she didn't quite believe what she was saying. Jared exchanged a glance with the teenager, who was clutching her headphones like a lifeline.

Another station blurred past, its empty platform glowing ghostly white in the darkness. Jared stood, gripping the pole to steady himself as the train sped on. "This doesn't make sense. Something's wrong."

The man in the suit sighed, clearly annoyed. "Look, just sit down, okay? Maybe you missed an announcement."

But Jared wasn't convinced. He moved toward the emergency brake, his reflection in the window a warped, shadowy figure. He reached for the handle and yanked hard. The brake resisted, unmoving. He tried again, putting all his weight into it, but it didn't budge.

"Hey!" he shouted, his voice rising. "This thing's jammed! It won't work!"

The teenager bolted upright. "What do you mean it won't work? They're supposed to work!" She rushed over, joining Jared in tugging at the handle. Together, they pulled and pulled, but it was as if the mechanism had fused into place. The woman with the scarf stood now, too, her hands trembling as she clutched her bag tighter.

"Maybe... maybe it's just old," she stammered. "These trains are ancient."

"That doesn't explain skipping every station," Jared snapped. "Or why the brake doesn't work."

The man in the suit stood, his face now pale. "Alright, let's not panic. There's got to be an explanation. These things don't just... they don't just keep going."

But the train did. Station after station flew past, each one more desolate than the last. Jared's watch ticked on, the minutes stretching into what felt like hours. The passengers' unease thickened, a palpable force pressing down on the car.

"What the hell is going on?" the teenager whispered, her voice barely audible over the rumble of the wheels.

Jared stared at the growing fear in her eyes and couldn't bring himself to answer. He didn't know. None of them did.

And then the lights flickered again—longer this time. The train plunged into darkness, the hum of the engine echoing louder than ever. For a moment, Jared thought he could hear something else beneath the noise. A low, mournful wail, like wind through a hollow tunnel. When the lights came back on, the passengers froze.

The windows were no longer showing the black void of the subway tunnel. Instead, there were faces—hundreds of them, pressed against the glass, pale and lifeless. Their eyes were hollow sockets, their mouths stretched into soundless screams. Jared stumbled back, his breath catching in his throat.

"What the—" the man in the suit started, but his words were cut short as the train jerked violently, nearly throwing them all off their feet.

The woman with the scarf began to sob, dropping her bag and clutching her chest. "No... no, no, no," she whispered, shaking her head. "This can't be happening. Not again."

Jared spun toward her. "What do you mean, 'not again'? What do you know?"

Her eyes darted to the floor. "I... I was here. Years ago. I was on this train when it... when it happened."

"When *what* happened?" the teenager demanded, her voice trembling.

The woman swallowed hard. "The crash. This train... it derailed. Killed everyone onboard. They said it was an accident, but... but some of us knew better. There was something wrong with this line. Something cursed."

Jared felt the blood drain from his face. "How are we here, then? How are we alive?"

The woman didn't answer. Instead, she pointed to the faces in the windows. "Maybe we aren't."

The train shuddered again, speeding faster now, the faces in the windows growing more distorted, more desperate. Jared's stomach churned. He could feel the weight of their gazes, accusing, pleading. He thought he heard whispers now, weaving through the screech of the wheels—a cacophony of anguish and blame.

The teenager screamed, clutching her ears. "Make it stop! Make it stop!"

Jared grabbed her shoulders, trying to steady her, but his own hands were shaking. "We have to do something. We can't just sit here."

But deep down, he knew there was no way off this train. It wasn't taking them home. It wasn't taking them anywhere.

It was taking them back.

CHAPTER 52: THE SIREN OF THE SWAMP

The mist hung heavy over the swamp, a pale veil that blurred the line between water and sky. The gnarled cypress trees stood like crooked sentinels, their roots twisting into the murky depths below. It was quiet, unnaturally so, the kind of silence that pressed against your ears and made you question whether you were truly alone. Hunter Max crouched near the edge of the water, his boots sinking slightly into the muck. His breath came in slow, measured bursts as he scanned the dark expanse before him.

He had been here a dozen times before, hunting deer or tracking the occasional bear that wandered too far into town. But this was different. The swamp felt alive tonight, not with the usual hum of insects or the croak of frogs, but with something darker, something hungry.

Max's fingers tightened around the handle of his hunting knife. He felt the weight of his shotgun slung across his back, the cold steel reassuring against his spine. But no weapon could ease the gnawing dread in his chest. People had gone missing here —six in the last three months. The sheriff had written it off as bad luck, maybe quicksand or gators, but Max knew better. He had lost his best friend, Danny, to this place just last week. And Danny didn't make mistakes. He was careful. Smart. Whatever had taken him wasn't an accident.

A ripple broke the still surface of the water, and Max froze. His pulse quickened as he leaned forward, squinting into the gloom. Then it came—the sound he dreaded and yearned to hear all at once.

A voice.

It was soft at first, almost a whisper, floating over the swamp like a lullaby. A woman's voice, sweet and mournful, weaving through the mist with an otherworldly grace. Max's grip faltered, his knife slipping slightly in his hand. The sound wasn't just beautiful—it was magnetic. It wrapped around his mind like a velvet chain, pulling, coaxing, promising.

"Come closer..."

Max shook his head violently, trying to clear the fog that was seeping into his thoughts. He reached into his pocket and fumbled for the crude earplugs he had fashioned out of wax and cotton. Danny had mentioned the voice before he disappeared, how it made him feel like he'd been drugged, how it was impossible to resist. Max stuffed the plugs into his ears, and the world went muffled. The voice dimmed, but it didn't disappear. It was inside his head now, coiling around his memories, his fears, his deepest desires.

He stumbled forward, his boots splashing into the shallow water. His body moved on its own, every step heavier than the last. He gritted his teeth, digging his heels into the mud, but the pull was relentless. The mist parted slightly, and that's when he saw her.

She stood waist-deep in the water, her pale skin glowing faintly in the moonlight. Her hair was long and dark, cascading over her shoulders in wet, tangled strands. Her eyes—black as the void, endless and consuming—locked onto his. Her lips curved into a smile that was both inviting and predatory.

Max's breath hitched. She was beautiful, impossibly so, but there was something wrong, something his mind refused to fully grasp. The longer he looked, the more her form seemed to shift, her features blurring at the edges like a reflection in a disturbed pond. Her hands, delicate at first glance, ended in sharp, claw-like fingers. The water around her rippled unnaturally, as though it too were alive.

"Danny?" Max rasped, his voice cracking. He didn't realize he had spoken until her smile widened.

"Max..." Her voice was honeyed, dripping with false comfort. "Come to me. He's waiting."

His knees buckled, and he fell to the ground with a splash. The earplugs weren't working. The voice was everywhere now, filling his skull, his chest, his veins. He clawed at his ears, desperate to block it out, but it was useless. His vision blurred, and for a moment, he thought he saw Danny standing behind her, his face pale and slack, eyes dull and lifeless.

"Danny!" Max screamed, his voice raw with anguish. He fought to get back on his feet, but the mud clung to him like quicksand. "Let him go, you bitch!"

The siren tilted her head, her expression one of mock pity. "He belongs to me now," she purred. "But you... you can save him. If you come closer."

Max's heart wrenched. He knew it was a lie, knew that whatever she was, whatever *it* was, couldn't be trusted. But the thought of leaving Danny here, trapped in this cursed swamp, was unbearable. He reached for his shotgun, his fingers trembling as he raised it. The siren didn't flinch. She only laughed, a haunting, melodic sound that made his stomach churn.

"You'd kill me?" she asked, her voice dripping with mock innocence. "And risk losing him forever?"

Max hesitated. His finger hovered over the trigger, his mind a storm of doubt and desperation. The mist thickened around him, and the water seemed to rise, lapping at his knees, his thighs. He could feel the cold seeping into his bones, anchoring him in place.

"Danny," he whispered, tears streaming down his face. The image of his friend behind her wavered, flickering like a dying flame. Was it real? Or just another trick?

The siren's smile faltered for the briefest of moments, and Max seized the opportunity. With a guttural roar, he fired. The blast echoed through the swamp, shattering the unnatural silence. The siren shrieked, a sound so piercing it made Max's vision go white. The water around her erupted, churning violently as her form contorted, her beauty dissolving into something grotesque and monstrous.

Max didn't wait to see what happened next. He turned and ran, his legs burning as he fought through the thick mud and clawed roots. The voice chased him, no longer sweet but full of rage, a guttural howl that promised vengeance. He didn't stop until he reached solid ground, collapsing in a heap on the outskirts of the swamp.

When he looked back, the mist had swallowed everything. The swamp was quiet once more, but he knew better than to believe it was over. Danny was gone. The others were gone. And the siren... she was still waiting.

Max wiped the tears from his face and gripped his knife tighter. He would come back. Not tonight, but soon. And next time, he wouldn't be alone.

CHAPTER 53:
THE HOUSE OF
ENDLESS STAIRS

The rain began as Ellen's car pulled through the wrought iron gates, their rusted hinges groaning like a wounded animal. The mansion loomed ahead, its silhouette jagged against the bruised sky. The architecture was unsettling—sharp angles and overhanging turrets that felt like they were leaning forward, watching her. She swallowed hard and reminded herself to breathe. This was supposed to be a celebration, after all. A soirée hosted by the mysterious Whitaker family, rumored to be old money with a penchant for the dramatic.

Ellen parked the car and stepped out, the gravel crunching under her boots. The air smelled damp and metallic. She straightened her coat against the wind and ascended the stone steps to the massive oak door. It creaked open before she could knock, revealing a butler with a sunken face and hollow eyes. He gestured silently for her to enter. Not a word of greeting.

The foyer was grand, yet suffocating. A chandelier hung precariously from the ceiling, its crystals refracting dim light onto faded wallpaper. A staircase spiraled upward to the left, its bannister polished but worn from countless hands over the years. Ellen paused and tilted her head. There was something off about the angle of the steps—slightly too steep, slightly too narrow. She shook the thought away as a voice boomed from the parlor.

"Ellen! You made it!"

She turned to see her colleague, Jonathan, waving her over. His grin was wide, but there was tension in his eyes. Around him, a handful of other guests clutched champagne flutes, their laughter echoing too loudly in the cavernous space. The air felt heavy, as though the house itself were leaning in to listen.

"This place is..." Ellen hesitated, searching for the right word. "Unique."

Jonathan chuckled. "That's one way to put it. The Whitakers have always been eccentric. Wait until you see the library—it's like stepping into another century."

Ellen forced a smile but couldn't shake the unease prickling the back of her neck. She was an architect by trade, trained to notice when something felt wrong in a building's design. And this house was all wrong. The angles didn't add up. Hallways stretched too long, doors were placed where they shouldn't be, and that staircase... she couldn't stop glancing at it.

Hours passed, and the soirée unfolded with an air of forced gaiety. Guests mingled, laughter erupted in bursts, and the Whitakers themselves remained notably absent. Ellen sipped her wine and wandered the halls, drawn inexorably to the staircase.

She ascended cautiously, her hand trailing along the bannister. The wood felt oddly warm, almost alive. Reaching the second floor, she found herself in a labyrinth of identical hallways. Each corridor seemed to twist and bend in ways that defied logic. She turned a corner and froze—a staircase spiraled upward before her, identical to the one she'd just climbed.

Impossible.

Ellen's pulse quickened. She retraced her steps, but the hallway stretched longer than it should have. Another turn. Another staircase. The air grew colder, and the dim light from the sconces flickered. A soft hum filled her ears, low and rhythmic, like the heartbeat of the house itself.

"Hello?" she called, her voice trembling.

A muffled cry answered her from somewhere above, and without thinking, she ran toward the sound. Her boots thudded against the wooden stairs as she ascended, higher and higher, until her legs burned and her breath came in ragged gasps.

The cry came again, sharper this time, and she realized it was Jonathan. "Ellen! Help me!"

She rounded a corner and stumbled into a room that shouldn't exist. It was circular, with walls covered in ornate mirrors that reflected infinitely. In the center stood Jonathan, or what was left of him. His reflection fractured across the mirrors, each piece of him distorted—an arm here, a leg there, his face stretched and twisted into a grotesque mask of terror. He reached for her, but his hand didn't move in sync with his body.

"Ellen, get out! It won't let us—" His voice cut off as the mirrors rippled like water, swallowing him whole.

Ellen screamed and stumbled backward, fleeing down the staircase. But no matter how far she ran, she ended up back in the same circular room, the mirrors waiting for her like hungry eyes.

Desperate, she closed her eyes and pressed her hands together, focusing on the feel of the wood beneath her palms. She was an architect. She understood structure, form, logic. If this house had a design, it had to have a center—a heart. And if she could find it, maybe she could destroy it.

When she opened her eyes, the mirrors had shifted. No longer reflections of herself, they now showed scenes from the house: the guests downstairs, their laughter growing more manic; the butler standing in the foyer, his hollow eyes glinting with malice; and Jonathan, trapped in the glass, pounding silently as the edges of his body dissolved into mist.

Ellen took a deep breath and stepped forward. The mirrors didn't shatter as she expected but parted like a curtain, revealing another staircase. This one spiraled downward, its steps chipped and worn as though countless souls had descended before her.

The hum grew louder as she followed the stairs into the bowels of the house. The walls here were rough stone, slick with moisture, and the air reeked of decay. At the bottom, she found a massive, pulsating structure—a heart of wood and stone, its veins twisting through the walls like roots. It beat with a sickening rhythm, sending tremors through the floor.

Ellen hesitated for only a moment before grabbing a jagged piece of stone from the ground. She raised it high, her hands trembling, and drove it into the heart with all her strength.

The house screamed.

The sound was deafening, a cacophony of voices crying out in anguish. The walls shuddered, and the floor buckled beneath her. Ellen turned and ran, the staircase collapsing behind her. She didn't stop until she burst through the front door, the cold night air shocking her lungs.

She looked back to see the mansion folding in on itself, its turrets crumbling, its windows shattering. And then, as suddenly as it had begun, it was gone, leaving only an empty foundation and the echoes of its final scream.

Ellen collapsed to her knees, her body shaking. She was free, but the faces of the others—Jonathan, the guests—haunted her. The house may have been destroyed, but its memory would linger, a scar on her mind, a question she could never answer.

Who had built such a place? And why?

CHAPTER 54:
THE CURSED
CARNIVAL PRIZE

The rain began to drum harder against the windows as night fell, creating a hollow percussion that echoed through the dimly lit living room. Billy sat cross-legged on the carpet, his hands clutching the stuffed toy he had won earlier that day at the carnival—a strange, almost grotesque-looking creature with wide, mismatched button eyes and a crooked, toothy grin sewn into its face. Its fur was a faded grayish-brown, mottled as though stained by time. Despite its eerie appearance, Billy had been drawn to it immediately, mesmerized by how it stood out among the other brightly colored prizes.

Billy's mother, Diane, peeked into the room from the kitchen, where she was drying dishes. Her eyes lingered on the toy, her lips pursing slightly. "Billy, don't you think it's time to head to bed? You've had a long day," she said, her voice soft but tinged with unease.

"But I want to stay up a little longer," Billy replied, hugging the stuffed toy to his chest. "I want to show it to Dad when he gets home."

Diane sighed, wiping her hands on a dish towel. She couldn't explain why the sight of that toy unsettled her so much, but its grin seemed to widen every time she looked at it—as though it were mocking her. She shook her head, dismissing the thought as a trick of her imagination. "Alright, ten more minutes. But then it's off to bed, okay?"

Billy nodded, already engrossed in the toy again, running his fingers over the uneven stitching on its belly. Diane turned back to the kitchen, trying to shake the feeling of unease that clung to her like cobwebs.

The first accident happened just after Billy went to bed. Diane had been walking toward the laundry room when she stepped on something sharp. She yelped, hopping back and looking down to see a scattering of tiny glass shards on the floor. Confused, she crouched to examine them. They looked like the remains of a lightbulb, but all the bulbs in the hallway were intact.

"Billy?" she called, wincing as she carefully picked up the shards. "Did you break something out here?"

There was no answer. She frowned, tossing the bits of glass into the trash and heading toward his room. When she opened the door, she found him sound asleep, the stuffed toy tucked snugly under his arm. Its crooked grin caught the moonlight filtering through the curtains, and for a moment, Diane thought she saw one of its button eyes glint as though it had moved. She slammed the door shut, her heart racing.

By the next morning, the accidents had escalated. The toaster caught fire when Billy's father, Greg, tried to make breakfast. A light fixture in the living room fell, narrowly missing Diane as she carried a basket of laundry. And then there was the scratching—faint at first, like the sound of a mouse scuttling through the walls, but growing louder and more insistent as the day went on. It seemed to follow them from room to room, always just out of sight.

"What the hell is going on in this house?" Greg muttered, rubbing his temples as he paced the living room. "First the toaster, then the light, now this scratching noise. It's like the place is falling apart overnight."

Diane shot a nervous glance toward Billy, who sat on the couch with the stuffed toy in his lap. He was unusually quiet, his gaze fixed on the toy's crooked grin. "Greg," she whispered, pulling him aside. "I think it's that... thing. The toy. Ever since Billy brought it home, everything's been going wrong."

Greg stared at her, incredulous. "You think a stuffed animal is causing all this? Come on, Diane, that's—"

"It moves," she interrupted, her voice trembling. "Last night, I swear I saw its eye move. And look at Billy. He hasn't let go of it all day. He won't even talk to us anymore."

Greg glanced at his son, his jaw tightening. Billy's knuckles were white as he clutched the toy, and his lips moved faintly, as though he were whispering to it. A chill crawled up Greg's spine. "Billy," he said, forcing his voice to stay calm. "Can I see that toy for a second?"

Billy's head snapped up, his eyes wide and panicked. "No!" he shouted, clutching the toy tighter. "You can't take it! It's mine!"

"Billy, don't talk to your father like that!" Diane scolded, but her voice wavered. She reached out to take the toy, and for a moment, Billy resisted, his grip like iron. Then, suddenly, he let go.

The toy slumped into Diane's hands, its crooked grin seeming to deepen. She shuddered, holding it at arm's length. "We need to get rid of this," she said firmly.

Billy began to cry, loud, hiccupping sobs that made Diane's heart ache. "You can't!" he wailed. "It won't let you!"

Before they could respond, the lights flickered, plunging the room into darkness. The scratching noise returned, louder than ever, now accompanied by a low, guttural growl that seemed to come from everywhere and nowhere at once. Diane screamed, dropping the toy, which landed on the floor with an unnatural thud. Its button eyes glowed faintly in the darkness.

Greg grabbed a flashlight from the shelf, its beam cutting through the shadows. The toy was gone.

"Where is it?" Diane whispered, her voice barely audible over the sound of her own pounding heart.

A sudden laugh—a childlike giggle, high-pitched and eerie— echoed through the room. The flashlight flickered, and for a brief moment, Greg caught sight of the toy perched on the back of the couch, its crooked grin impossibly wide.

"Out!" Greg shouted, grabbing Diane's hand and pulling her toward the door. "We're getting out of this house right now!"

"No!" Billy cried, but Greg scooped him up, ignoring his protests as they fled into the night.

They drove back to the carnival in silence, the toy wrapped in a blanket and shoved into the trunk. The carnival grounds were deserted, the rides dark and lifeless. But the game booth where Billy had won the toy was still there, its lights flickering weakly.

An old man sat behind the counter, his face gaunt and shadowed. He smiled as they approached, revealing teeth that were far too sharp. "I see you've met my little friend," he said, his voice like dry leaves rustling in the wind.

"We want to return it," Greg said, his voice firm despite the fear in his eyes. "Take it back."

The old man chuckled, his eyes glinting. "Oh, you can't return it. But you can give it away." His smile widened. "Just make sure the next person wants it as much as you did."

Diane opened her mouth to protest, but Greg shook his head, his grip tightening on her arm. "Let's go," he said quietly.

As they drove away, leaving the toy and the carnival behind, Diane glanced back at Billy, who stared out the window in silence. She reached for his hand, squeezing it gently. "It's over," she whispered. "It's gone."

But deep down, she wasn't sure she believed it.

CHAPTER 55: THE WHISPERING LIBRARY

The library sat like a mausoleum at the edge of town, its ivy-choked façade blending seamlessly into the overcast sky. Inside, the air was heavy, weighed down by the smell of ancient paper and varnished oak. The faint hum of fluorescent lights only seemed to deepen the suffocating silence. Mr. Whittaker, a man as gray and weathered as the building he presided over, stood behind the oak desk at the library's center. He sorted returned books with the same meticulous care he'd cultivated over forty years of service.

It was a Tuesday afternoon when the first scream shattered the quiet.

A young woman—Anna, one of the regulars—staggered out from the alcove of old philosophy texts. Her hands clutched at her temples, tears streaking her pale cheeks. "Make it stop!" she shrieked, her voice cracking. She stumbled into a shelf, sending a cascade of dusty tomes to the floor.

Mr. Whittaker hurried toward her, his polished shoes clicking against the marble tiles. "Miss Anna, what's the matter?" he asked, his voice calm but edged with unease.

She turned to him, her wide eyes brimming with terror. "The whispers... they're in my head. They won't stop."

"Whispers?" He glanced toward the philosophy section, his brow furrowing. "There's no one else back there."

Anna shook her head violently, her hair whipping around her face. "I heard them! They were coming from the book." She thrust a trembling hand toward the open volume she had abandoned on the floor. Mr. Whittaker knelt to retrieve it. The book was a leather-bound edition of *The Republic*, its cover so worn the title was barely legible.

"Books don't whisper," he said, but even as the words left his mouth, he felt the air shift. A faint murmur, like the rustling of leaves, seemed to emanate from the pages.

Anna grabbed his sleeve, her nails digging into his arm. "You don't understand," she gasped. "They... they know me. They said things I've never told anyone. Dark things. Terrible things."

Before Mr. Whittaker could respond, Anna bolted, her footsteps echoing down the corridor. The heavy door of the library slammed shut behind her, leaving an eerie stillness in her wake.

The whispers began to spread.

By the end of the week, three more patrons had fled the library in similar states of hysteria. A middle-aged man, usually reserved and polite, had hurled a chair across the reading room after poring over a book on medieval warfare. A teenage girl had been found scribbling furiously on the walls of the children's section, her eyes glazed and unfocused, as if she were in a trance.

Mr. Whittaker knew something was deeply wrong. He had always considered the library a sanctuary, a haven for quiet minds. Now it felt alive, predatory, as if the books themselves were feeding on the people who read them.

Late one night, long after the last patron had left, Mr. Whittaker locked the heavy oak doors and began his investigation. He moved through the aisles with a flashlight, its beam carving tunnels of light through the thick gloom. He listened carefully, his heart pounding in his chest.

It started in the poetry section—soft, indistinct murmurs that seemed to rise and fall in cadence, as though reciting verses in a language he didn't understand. He followed the sound to a slim volume of Emily Dickinson's collected works. As he opened it, the whispers grew louder, more insistent. They weren't in a foreign language after all; they were in his own voice.

"You could have been more. Why did you waste your life here? Shelving books no one reads? You're nothing. Invisible. Forgotten."

Mr. Whittaker snapped the book shut, his hands trembling. The whispers stopped, but the weight of their words lingered. He moved to the history section, then the biographies, pulling books from shelves at random. Each one greeted him with a chorus of voices, each more venomous and intimate than the last. They spoke of his regrets, his failures, his buried resentments.

The truth hit him like a thunderclap. These weren't just books —they were repositories of thought, absorbing the darkest musings of every reader who had ever touched them. The library wasn't a sanctuary. It was a trap.

By dawn, Mr. Whittaker had devised a desperate plan. He would burn the books. All of them. Every last whispering tome. He couldn't risk the knowledge they held, the power they wielded over fragile minds.

He started with the oldest section, piling books into the center of the main hall. The fire started slowly, a flicker of orange against the oppressive gray light streaming through the stained-glass windows. But as the flames grew, so did the whispers. They rose to a deafening crescendo, a cacophony of voices screaming in protest.

"You'll never silence us. We are eternal. We are everything you fear."

Mr. Whittaker covered his ears, but it was no use. The whispers were inside his head now, burrowing deep, digging up memories he had long buried. He saw his mother's face, stern and disapproving. He heard the voice of his late wife, accusing him of neglect. He felt the weight of every choice he had ever made, pressing down on him like a tombstone.

The fire raged, consuming the books in a frenzy of sparks and ash, but it was too late. The whispers had taken root in him. As he stood amidst the inferno, his eyes wild and unseeing, he began to laugh—a low, guttural sound that echoed through the empty library.

By the time the fire department arrived, the library was a smoldering ruin. They found Mr. Whittaker sitting in the ashes, clutching a charred book to his chest. His lips moved soundlessly, as if whispering to someone only he could hear.

He never left the site. Even after the library was gone, they said he could still be seen wandering the ruins, his head cocked to one side, listening. Always listening.

CHAPTER 56: THE RETURN OF THE PLAGUE DOCTOR

The fluorescent lights in the dimly lit hallway flickered like an unsteady heartbeat. Nurse Lisa tightened her grip on the flashlight, its beam cutting through the oppressive darkness ahead. The hospital was eerily silent, save for the distant hum of machinery and the occasional echo of footsteps—hers, she hoped.

Room 312 had been the first. The patient, an elderly man recovering from a routine surgery, had whispered about a strange visitor. "A man in a bird mask," he rasped, his eyes darting to the corners of the room as if the figure still lingered in the shadows. By the next morning, his condition had deteriorated inexplicably. Then it happened again. And again. Patients claimed to see the same figure—cloaked, beaked, and watching—before succumbing to a mysterious illness that no test could identify, no treatment could cure. The staff whispered about it in the breakroom, their voices trembling with disbelief. But now, Lisa stood alone in the bowels of the hospital, chasing a specter that had begun to haunt her dreams.

The air grew colder as she approached the sealed-off wing, a section of the hospital abandoned decades ago after a fire gutted much of it. The walls were stained with a sickly yellow hue, and the peeling paint curled like dead skin. A faint, acrid smell—smoke? Decay?—lingered, making her stomach churn. Lisa had been warned not to come here. The place wasn't safe, they said. But safety had become a relative term in the past week.

Her flashlight caught a glint of metal in the distance, and she froze. The figure stood motionless at the end of the hallway, shrouded in shadow. The plague doctor. Its mask, grotesque and birdlike, gleamed under the weak light. The long beak jutted forward, and the hollow eye sockets seemed to pierce through her. The figure's long, black coat swayed slightly, though there was no breeze.

"Who are you?" Lisa called, her voice steadier than she felt. "What do you want?"

The figure tilted its head, a slow, unnatural movement, like a puppet on strings. Then it raised a gloved hand, pointing not at her but at the door to the old surgical ward. The gesture sent an icy spike of dread through Lisa's chest. She had read the reports, stumbled upon the hospital's buried history while researching the outbreaks. The fire that had consumed this wing had started in that very room. Rumors spoke of experimental treatments, unethical practices, and a doctor who had disappeared during the chaos.

"You're not real," she said, more to herself than to the figure. "You're just... a hallucination. Stress. That's all this is."

The figure stepped forward. The sound of its boots against the linoleum echoed too loudly, the rhythmic click-click-click driving a wedge of panic into her resolve. Lisa stumbled backward, her flashlight trembling in her hand.

"Stay back!" she shouted, but the figure didn't stop. It moved with an eerie grace, its presence heavy with menace. And then it spoke.

"You cannot cure what refuses to die."

The voice was not a voice at all. It was a cacophony of whispers, layered and overlapping, as if every patient who had ever suffered in this hospital was speaking through it. Lisa's breath hitched, her throat tightening as the words burrowed into her mind.

"What do you want?" she whispered, tears brimming in her eyes. "Why are you doing this?"

"You built this place to heal," the figure intoned, its hollow eyes locking onto hers. "But it became a breeding ground for suffering. Pain. Disease. I am what you summoned. I am what you created."

"No," Lisa said, shaking her head. "This isn't my fault. I'm just trying to help. I'm trying to stop this!"

The figure tilted its head again, almost mockingly. "Then seal it. Seal the wound before it festers further."

Lisa's flashlight flickered, and for a moment, the figure was gone. The hallway stretched empty before her, the silence deafening. But the door to the old surgical ward was ajar, its hinges creaking softly as if inviting her in.

Her heart hammered in her chest as she approached the door, each step feeling heavier than the last. The room beyond was a time capsule of ruin. Rusted surgical tools lay scattered on the floor, and an old operating table stood in the center, its leather straps frayed and brittle. The walls were charred black, and shards of broken glass glittered like malevolent stars. But it was the stench—thick, cloying, and suffocating—that nearly brought her to her knees.

In the center of the room, something writhed. A mass of darkness, pulsing and shifting, as if alive. It exuded an aura of decay that made her skin crawl. She knew, instinctively, that this was the source. The heart of the sickness. The embodiment of everything the hospital had tried to bury.

Lisa's hands trembled as she reached into her pocket, pulling out the small vial of holy water Father McNamara had given her. She wasn't religious, not really, but desperation made believers of everyone. She uncorked the vial, her fingers slick with sweat, and began to pour the liquid over the threshold of the room.

The darkness writhed violently, and the whispers returned, louder this time, a chorus of rage and despair. The doorframe shuddered, and for a moment, Lisa thought the entire building would collapse. But she kept going, drawing a line of water across the floor, sealing the room off inch by inch.

When the last drop fell, the whispers ceased. The darkness stilled. And then, with a final, guttural groan, the air grew still.

Lisa staggered back, her legs threatening to give out beneath her. The door to the surgical ward slammed shut, the force nearly knocking her over. She stared at it, her chest heaving as she tried to catch her breath.

Footsteps echoed behind her, and she turned to see the plague doctor once more. It stood at the end of the hallway, watching her. But this time, it didn't approach. It simply raised a hand, as if in acknowledgment, before vanishing into the shadows.

Lisa sank to the floor, the flashlight slipping from her grasp. The hospital was silent again. But she knew the battle wasn't over. The past had a way of bleeding into the present, and some wounds never truly healed.

Still, for now, the door held. And that would have to be enough.

CHAPTER 57:
THE SPECTER IN
THE STORM

The storm was a living thing, clawing at the *Persephone* with a thousand watery hands. Rain lashed against the deck like a whip, and the wind howled with a voice that seemed almost human—anguished and wild. Captain Reynolds gripped the wheel with white-knuckled fury, his soaked coat flapping behind him like a tattered flag. Lightning flared in jagged bursts across the sky, illuminating the heaving chaos of the ocean below.

"Keep her steady, damn it!" Reynolds roared over the cacophony of the storm. His voice was raw, but it carried the weight of command. Around him, the crew scrambled like frantic ants, tying down loose rigging and bailing water as waves slammed against the hull.

Then, as if summoned by the storm's fury, it appeared.

"Captain!" shouted First Mate Harker, pointing a trembling hand toward the starboard side. "There! Off the bow!"

Reynolds turned, his eyes narrowing against the sheets of rain. Through the haze of the storm, a ship loomed in the distance, its silhouette flickering in the lightning's glow. It was ancient, with tattered sails hanging like ghosts from splintered masts.

The hull was dark, rotting, the wood warped as if it had spent centuries beneath the waves.

"It can't be..." murmured Harker, his voice barely audible. "That ship—it wasn't there a second ago."

The *Persephone's* crew gathered at the rail, their faces pale and drawn. They stared at the apparition, their breaths visible in the unnatural chill that seemed to radiate from the ghostly vessel.

"Captain!" cried another sailor, clutching a crackling radio to his chest. "We're picking up a signal—distress call!"

Reynolds snatched the radio from the sailor's hand, his heart pounding. The voice on the other end was faint, distorted by static, but unmistakably human.

"Mayday... need... help... adrift..."

The voice sputtered into silence, replaced by a low, crackling hum that set Reynolds' teeth on edge. He hesitated, the weight of the decision pressing down on him. Every instinct screamed to leave—to turn the *Persephone* away and let the storm swallow the phantom ship. But the voice... it was a cry for help. A sailor in trouble.

"We answer the call," Reynolds barked, his voice cutting through the rising panic among the crew. "Bring us closer! Prepare to board!"

"Captain, are you mad?" Harker grabbed his arm, desperation in his eyes. "That's no ship—it's a damn ghost! Look at it! It's not... right."

Reynolds wrenched his arm free, his eyes blazing. "If there are men aboard, we don't leave them to die. Now get to work!"

Reluctantly, the crew obeyed, their hands trembling as they adjusted the sails and steered the *Persephone* toward the spectral vessel. The closer they came, the colder the air grew, until their breath fogged in front of their faces and frost began to creep along the railings. The storm seemed to calm as they neared the ship, the wind dying to an eerie stillness.

The *Persephone* groaned as it pulled alongside the ghost ship. Up close, the vessel was even more unsettling—its timbers blackened and slick with algae, its deck littered with rusted chains and bones. A faint, greenish glow emanated from the hull, as though the ship itself were alive, pulsing with some unnatural energy.

"Lower the boarding ladder," Reynolds ordered, his voice firm despite the unease coiling in his gut.

One by one, the crew climbed aboard the ghost ship, their boots echoing hollowly against the warped planks. The air was heavy, oppressive, as though they had stepped into another world. Shadows shifted and stretched across the deck, twisting into shapes that seemed almost human before dissolving back into darkness.

"Hello?" Reynolds called, his voice unnaturally loud in the silence. "Is anyone here?"

No answer came, only the creak of wood and the faint whisper of the sea. The crew spread out, searching the ship with reluctant steps. They found no survivors, no signs of life—only the remnants of a long-dead voyage. A captain's hat, bleached and brittle with age. A journal, its pages waterlogged and illegible. A pile of bones, still wrapped in the tatters of a sailor's uniform.

"Captain," Harker said, his voice tight with fear. "We shouldn't be here. This isn't right."

Before Reynolds could respond, a deafening *crack* split the air. The *Persephone*—their lifeline, their way home—was gone. The crew rushed to the rail, staring in disbelief at the empty space where their ship had been. The storm, too, was gone, replaced by an endless expanse of still, black water that reflected the ghost ship like a mirror.

"We're trapped," one of the sailors whispered, his voice shaking. "God help us, we're trapped."

"No," Reynolds said, his jaw clenched. "We'll find a way back. There's always a way back."

But even as he said the words, a part of him knew they were a lie. The ghost ship seemed to pulse beneath their feet, its greenish glow growing brighter, more insistent. The shadows on the deck began to move again, coalescing into shapes that were no longer just tricks of the light.

They were faces. Hands. Eyes.

And they were watching.

Then, from somewhere deep within the ship, a sound rose—a low, mournful wail that sent ice down Reynolds' spine. It was the sound of despair, of lives lost and forgotten, of sailors who had answered a call for help and never returned.

"Captain," Harker said, his voice barely a whisper. "What do we do?"

Reynolds didn't answer. He couldn't. The shadows were closing in, their whispers growing louder, more insistent. They spoke of eternity, of a place where time and light and life ceased to matter. A place where the crew of the *Persephone* would soon belong.

Unless they could escape.

CHAPTER 58: THE MIRROR MAZE

The air smelled of caramel and grease, punctuated by the shrill laughter of carnival-goers and the occasional bark of a game vendor. The Mirror Maze stood at the edge of the fairgrounds, its neon sign flickering in uneven patterns. "House of Reflections," it read, with a jagged, handwritten warning underneath: *"Enter if you dare."*

Sarah squinted at the sign and smirked. "They could've tried a little harder with the creepy factor."

"It's a maze full of mirrors, Sarah," Mike said, tightening the strap of his backpack. "How scary can it be? You walk in, you walk out."

Jen hesitated just behind them, chewing on her bottom lip. "I don't know. Something about it feels...off."

Sarah turned to her, rolling her eyes. "You're overthinking it, Jen. It's just some cheesy carnival attraction. Come on, let's go before the line gets long."

Without waiting for a response, Sarah pushed through the black-and-red curtain hanging over the entrance. Mike followed, his hands shoved into his hoodie pockets, while Jen lingered for just a moment longer, staring at her distorted reflection in the glass panels covering the maze's exterior. Something about her reflection felt...wrong. But before she could analyze it further, she heard Sarah shouting for her to hurry up.

Inside, the air felt cooler, quieter. The noise from the carnival faded into a low murmur, replaced by the faint hum of fluorescent lights overhead. The walls gleamed with countless mirrors, some full-length, others fractured into jagged shards. The trio's reflections stretched and twisted unnaturally as they moved deeper into the maze.

"Alright, first one to the exit wins," Sarah announced, her grin wide and confident. "No crying when I totally destroy you guys."

"You mean like when you got lost in that corn maze last fall?" Mike teased.

"Shut up, Mike."

Jen stayed close to him, her arms crossed tightly over her chest. "Let's just stick together, okay? I don't like this place."

"Relax, it's just mirrors," Mike replied, though there was an edge of unease in his voice now too. He glanced at his reflection—a lanky, slightly awkward teenager with messy hair and dark circles under his eyes. But as he moved, his reflection didn't seem to follow perfectly. It lingered a half-second too long, its gaze sharp and focused in a way that made his stomach churn.

"Did you see that?" he asked, his voice lower.

"See what?" Sarah called back. She was already several feet ahead, standing at an intersection of mirrored corridors.

"My reflection," Mike said, his voice trailing off. "It looked— never mind. Let's just find the exit."

The three continued deeper into the maze, their laughter and banter growing more muted with each turn. The reflections became stranger. Sarah's face stretched into a grotesque grin in one mirror, her teeth impossibly sharp. Jen's reflection seemed to flicker, her eyes too dark, her movements jerky, almost puppet-like. As for Mike, he avoided looking at the mirrors altogether now.

"Guys," Jen whispered, stopping abruptly. "I think...I think the mirrors are watching us."

"Don't be ridiculous," Sarah said, though her voice wavered slightly. She glanced at her reflection, then quickly looked away. "They're just mirrors. That's what they do."

"No," Jen insisted, taking a cautious step back. "It's not just us in the mirrors. Look at them. Really look."

Mike hesitated, then turned his gaze to the wall of mirrors beside him. His mouth went dry. His reflection was staring at him, but its expression wasn't his. The reflection's lips curled into a slow, sinister smile.

"Uh, Sarah?" Mike called out. "I think we've got a problem."

Before Sarah could respond, her reflection stepped out of the mirror.

It happened so quickly that for a moment, none of them could process it. The mirrored version of Sarah stood in the corridor, identical in every way except for the cold, predatory glint in her eyes. The real Sarah stumbled back, her face pale.

"What the hell—" she started, but her reflection lunged at her, its movements unnaturally fast. It grabbed her wrist, its grip like iron.

"Run!" Sarah screamed, kicking at her double. She broke free and bolted down the corridor, Jen and Mike close behind her.

The maze seemed to shift around them, the mirrors warping and twisting as if alive. Every turn led to more corridors, more reflections—some still trapped in the glass, others stepping out, their faces eerily blank. One of them looked like Jen, but its head tilted at an unnatural angle, its neck bending far too much.

Another resembled Mike, but its eyes were pitch black, its hands clawed and twitching.

"We have to get out of here!" Jen cried, her voice breaking. She grabbed Mike's arm, dragging him along as they turned another corner. "There has to be an exit!"

"But how do we know which way is real?" Mike asked, panic creeping into his voice. "What if the mirrors are tricking us?"

Sarah skidded to a stop ahead of them, her chest heaving. She pointed to a panel on the wall, its surface cracked and dull compared to the others. "There! That's not a mirror—it has to be the way out!"

As they approached, their reflections blocked the path, stepping in front of the cracked panel. The mirror versions of Sarah, Mike, and Jen stared them down, their grins wide and menacing.

"You don't belong here," the doppelgänger Sarah hissed, her voice distorted and echoing. "This is our world now."

The real Sarah clenched her fists. "Like hell it is."

She lunged at her reflection, tackling it to the ground. The two struggled, their movements mirrored and chaotic. Meanwhile, Mike and Jen faced their doubles, who lunged at them with inhuman speed.

"Break the mirrors!" Jen shouted, dodging a swipe from her doppelgänger. "If they're coming from the mirrors, maybe we can stop them!"

Mike grabbed a nearby shard of broken glass and slammed it into the nearest reflective surface. The mirror shattered with a deafening crack, and the doppelgänger Jen let out an otherworldly shriek before dissolving into smoke.

Sarah managed to pin her double long enough for Mike to smash another mirror. The doppelgänger Sarah writhed beneath her, its form flickering and distorting before it too disappeared.

One by one, they destroyed the mirrors, the maze growing darker and quieter with each shatter. Finally, they reached the cracked panel and pushed through it, stumbling out into the cool night air.

The carnival sounds rushed back all at once—laughter, music, the distant hum of rides. The three friends stood there, panting and covered in tiny cuts from the shards of glass.

"What the hell just happened?" Mike asked, his voice trembling.

"I don't know," Sarah said, her eyes darting back to the maze's entrance. The neon sign flickered, but now the warning beneath it had changed. It read: *"You escaped...this time."*

Jen grabbed their hands, her grip tight. "Let's go. And let's never come back."

Without another word, they turned and disappeared into the crowd, the lights of the carnival casting long, distorted shadows behind them.

CHAPTER 59: THE NIGHT OF THE BLOOD MOON

The sky was a canvas of ink, dotted with stars that seemed to shiver in anticipation. The air over the small town of Willow's Rest was electric, charged with the promise of celestial wonder. The townsfolk had gathered in the grassy clearing outside the library, where Dr. Neil had set up telescopes and chairs in neat rows. A projector screen displayed images of the moon, which hung fat and heavy in the night sky. Children laughed and chased fireflies while their parents sipped from thermoses, their voices a low murmur of excitement.

Dr. Neil stood at the front of the crowd, his tweed jacket and wire-rimmed glasses lending him a professorial air. He had spent weeks preparing for this event, meticulously calculating the timing of the eclipse and spreading word of its rarity. He adjusted the microphone clipped to his lapel and cleared his throat.

"Ladies and gentlemen," he began, his voice steady despite the growing wind, "tonight we are witness to a phenomenon that has inspired myths and legends for centuries. The blood moon —a total lunar eclipse. As the Earth's shadow consumes the moon, it will glow red, a result of sunlight bending through our atmosphere."

The crowd murmured in awe, heads tilting skyward. Dr. Neil felt a swell of satisfaction. He had always believed that wonder could unite people, transcend the mundane. But as he glanced at the horizon, he noticed something peculiar. The stars there seemed to dim, swallowed by a creeping darkness that slithered toward the clearing like an oil spill.

The first scream shattered the night's calm.

A woman near the edge of the crowd stumbled backward, her hands clutching her chest. "What... what is that?" she gasped, pointing toward the treeline. Dr. Neil followed her gaze and felt his breath hitch. The shadows beneath the trees were writhing, alive. Vague shapes moved within them—tall, spindly figures with too many limbs, their bodies contorting unnaturally as they crept closer.

"Stay calm, everyone!" Dr. Neil called out, though his voice cracked with the effort. "It's probably—probably a trick of the light."

But even as he spoke, the creatures emerged fully from the darkness. Their forms were almost human, but wrong—joints that bent backward, faces that flickered like static on a broken screen. Their eyes were pits of nothingness, yet they seemed to drink in everything, especially the fear that was thickening in the air.

One of the creatures let out a sound that wasn't a growl or a scream but something in between, a noise that clawed its way into the mind and made Dr. Neil's skull throb. The crowd erupted into chaos. Parents grabbed their children and bolted for their cars, only to find the vehicles powerless, their engines sputtering into silence. Others tripped over folding chairs and tangled in telescope cords as they fled.

"Neil!" shouted a voice. It was Janet, the librarian, her face pale but determined. "What the hell is going on?"

"I—I don't know!" he stammered, clutching his laptop as if it might offer answers. "This wasn't in any of the calculations. This shouldn't be happening."

Another scream ripped through the clearing as one of the creatures lunged toward a man trying to shield his wife. The thing didn't touch him, but its presence alone seemed to drain the color from his face. He collapsed to the ground, trembling violently. The creature inhaled deeply, as if savoring his terror.

"They're feeding on us," Janet whispered, her voice barely audible over the din. "They're feeding on fear."

Dr. Neil's mind raced. If fear was their sustenance, then panic was their weapon, their tool to amplify their power. He had to get the crowd under control, had to think of a way to survive until the eclipse ended and the creatures—whatever they were—disappeared.

"Everyone, listen to me!" he shouted, climbing onto a folding chair to make himself heard. "Stop running! Stay together! They can't hurt us if we don't give them what they want!"

His words were swallowed by another wave of screams. One of the creatures loomed over a teenage boy who had fallen to his knees, hyperventilating. Dr. Neil jumped down and ran toward them, heart pounding. He grabbed the boy's shoulders and shook him.

"Look at me!" he commanded. "Focus on me, not on it. You're going to be okay. Breathe with me—slowly, in and out."

The boy's wide, tear-filled eyes locked onto Neil's. Together, they breathed, and the creature hesitated, its form flickering as if it were losing substance. It snarled and slithered away, retreating into the shadows.

"They weaken when we don't fear them," Neil realized aloud. He turned back to the crowd, his voice firmer now. "Do you see that?

We can fight them. Don't give in to the fear!"

"Easier said than done!" Janet snapped, but she was already corralling a group of townsfolk, urging them to hold hands and stay close.

The creatures circled the clearing, their movements growing more erratic, more desperate as the blood moon climbed higher. Dr. Neil's group huddled in the center, a knot of humanity clinging to one another. He led them in breathing exercises, in singing old folk songs, anything to keep their minds occupied and their terror at bay.

Hours passed like an eternity, but finally, the crimson hue of the moon began to fade. The creatures screamed—a high-pitched wail of agony and frustration—as their forms unraveled, dissolving into the ether. As the first rays of dawn broke over the horizon, the clearing was silent once more.

Dr. Neil collapsed onto the grass, exhausted but alive. Around him, the townsfolk began to cry, to laugh, to hold one another. Janet sank down beside him, her hair disheveled and her glasses askew.

"You didn't put that in the flyer," she said with a shaky grin.

"No," Neil replied, staring at the pale, unassuming moon as it hung in the sky. "No, I didn't."

CHAPTER 60: THE FORGOTTEN ONES

The library was colder than it had any right to be. Maria tugged her shawl tighter around her shoulders, her breath fogging in the air as if the building itself exhaled unease. The fluorescent lights overhead hummed faintly, casting pale streaks across rows of dusty bookshelves. She had spent weeks here, poring over brittle newspapers and yellowed ledgers, her fingers stained with ink and grime. The town of Greyhaven had secrets —secrets buried so deeply that even its oldest residents seemed to have forgotten them. But Maria could feel it, a shadow in the gaps of their history, an absence more deafening than any recorded event.

Tonight, though, the silence felt different. It pressed against her like a weight, the air thick and almost...watchful. She glanced at the clock on the wall—2:47 a.m. The staff had left hours ago, their pitying glances following her as she insisted on staying late yet again. "You're going to drive yourself mad, Miss," the head librarian had said. Maria had simply smiled, knowing she was already too far gone for such warnings to matter.

She flipped another page of the brittle journal in front of her, her eyes scanning the cramped handwriting. 1872. The year the town's records grew strangely vague. Fires, crop failures, sudden disappearances—an entire year reduced to a few cryptic sentences. No explanations, no names. As if the world had swallowed the town whole, leaving behind only whispers.

The faint sound of fabric rustling pulled her from her thoughts. She froze, her pen poised mid-scribble. "Hello?" Her voice echoed down the empty aisles, swallowed by the stillness. No response. She shook her head, trying to ignore the tight coil of dread in her stomach.

And then came the whisper. Soft, almost imperceptible, like the faintest breeze brushing against her ear. A single word: *remember.*

Maria shot to her feet, her chair screeching against the floor. "Who's there?" she demanded, her voice trembling. She peered into the shadows between the shelves, but they seemed to deepen, as though the darkness itself was growing thicker. Her pulse roared in her ears.

The whisper came again, louder this time. "Remember us."

The lights flickered, plunging the library into momentary darkness. When they buzzed back to life, Maria gasped. The books on the nearest shelf had been rearranged, their spines spelling out a single word in jagged, uneven lettering: *Names.*

Her breath hitched. "What do you want from me?" she whispered, her voice barely audible.

The temperature plummeted. Frost crept along the edges of the window behind her, the glass cracking slightly under the strain. Then, the room seemed to groan, the walls shuddering as if the building itself were alive. Maria stumbled back, clutching the edge of the table for support.

And then she saw them.

Figures began to materialize from the shadows, their forms flickering like candlelight. Men, women, children—faces pale and translucent, their eyes hollow and filled with something that made Maria's chest tighten: desperation. They wore clothes from eras long past, their appearances shifting as if caught between moments in time. One woman stepped forward, her face half-obscured by a veil that fluttered despite the still air. Her voice was a low, mournful wail.

"You took everything from us," the woman said, her words dripping with accusation. "Our lives. Our stories. Our names."

Maria's knees buckled, and she sank to the floor. "I-I don't understand," she stammered. "I didn't take anything—"

"You bury us with your indifference," another voice interrupted, deeper, angrier. A man, his neck crisscrossed with rope burns that made Maria's stomach churn. "You let time erase us, as if we never existed. As if our pain was nothing."

The others murmured their agreement, a chorus of anguish that seemed to reverberate through Maria's very bones. Tears streamed down her face as she tried to find her voice. "I... I want to help you," she said, her words trembling. "Tell me what to do."

The woman in the veil knelt before her, her cold, translucent hand reaching out to brush against Maria's cheek. It felt like ice and fire all at once, a searing reminder of their absence. "Write us back into the world," she said. "Tell them what was done. Tell them who we were."

Maria nodded frantically, her mind racing. "I will. I swear I will. Just... please, tell me where to start."

The figures began to drift backward, their forms fading as the frost on the windows began to thaw. But before they vanished completely, the woman in the veil whispered one final word, her voice echoing like a warning: "Dig."

And then they were gone.

Maria scrambled to her feet, her heart pounding. She grabbed her notebook and pen, her hands shaking as she wrote down everything she could remember. The books on the shelf had fallen back into disarray, but she knew where to start now. The cemetery on the edge of town, the one everyone avoided, the one with no headstones—only unmarked graves.

As she left the library and stepped into the biting night air, Maria couldn't shake the feeling that the town itself was watching her. The wind howled through the empty streets, carrying with it the faintest echo of voices: *Remember us. Remember us.*

And for the first time in over a century, Maria vowed, someone would.

CHAPTER 61: THE WALL BETWEEN WORLDS

The sledgehammer hit the wall with a resounding crack, sending a cloud of dust spiraling into the air. The sound echoed unnaturally, as if the wall itself exhaled a deep, reluctant groan. Tom wiped his brow with the back of his hand, squinting through the haze. The wall had been an eyesore for decades, a relic of some bygone era of architecture. No one seemed to know why it was there, cutting through the middle of the district like a jagged scar. But the city's redevelopment plans didn't leave room for mystery or sentimentality. It had to go.

"Tom, come check this out," called Ricky, one of the crew members. His voice carried a note of unease that Tom immediately picked up on.

Tom dropped the sledgehammer and approached. Ricky stood by the exposed interior of the wall, where the concrete had crumbled to reveal something strange beneath: not brick or stone, but a smooth, black surface that seemed to shimmer faintly, like oil on water. It looked almost alive.

"What the hell is that?" Tom muttered, running his fingers over the surface. It was cold—unnaturally so, even in the sweltering summer heat. The longer he touched it, the more a strange sensation crept up his arm, like pins and needles mixed with static electricity.

"I don't like it," Ricky said, stepping back. "Feels... wrong."

Tom shook his head, trying to shake off the growing unease. "It's probably some kind of insulation or—"

"Don't touch it!" a voice interrupted sharply. Everyone turned to see an old man standing at the edge of the construction site, his gnarled hands gripping the chain-link fence. His face was pale, his eyes wide with panic. "You don't know what you're doing! That wall isn't just a wall—it's a *barrier*."

Tom sighed, already tired of the interruption. "Sir, this is a restricted area. You need to leave."

"You have to stop!" the old man shouted, his voice breaking. "You don't understand what's on the other side! They built that wall for a reason. It's not meant to be opened!"

"Okay, that's enough." Tom signaled to one of the security guards. "Get him out of here."

The old man struggled as the guard escorted him away, his warnings fading into incoherent muttering. Tom turned back to the wall, his unease now tempered by irritation. Superstitious nonsense, he told himself. Just another crank who didn't like change.

By the end of the day, the wall was gone.

That night, Tom woke to the sound of whispering. At first, he thought it was just the wind rattling the windows of his apartment. But as he lay motionless in bed, holding his breath, he realized the sound was coming from inside the room. Low and guttural, the words slithered together in a language he didn't recognize.

He sat up, his heart pounding. "Who's there?"

The whispering stopped. The room was silent, but the shadows seemed to pulse, as if alive. He fumbled for the lamp on his bedside table, his fingers trembling, and flipped it on. Warm light flooded the room, chasing the shadows back into their corners. Nothing appeared out of place.

Tom didn't sleep for the rest of the night.

By the time he arrived at the site the next morning, he wasn't the only one on edge. The crew stood in tense clusters, talking in hushed voices. Ricky approached him, his face pale.

"Something's not right," Ricky said. "Last night... I thought I saw someone in my house. Looked just like me, but... wrong."

Tom stared at him. "What do you mean, 'wrong'?"

"I don't know," Ricky said, his voice cracking. "It was like... like a shadow of me. Like it *almost* looked right, but it wasn't. And it just stood there, watching me."

Tom opened his mouth to respond, but a scream cut through the morning air. The crew turned in unison toward the source —a young woman walking her dog across the street. She was pointing at one of the construction workers, her face twisted in horror.

The worker—Gary—turned to face her, his expression blank. And then, slowly, his features began to... shift. His skin rippled like water, his eyes sinking into his skull and then reappearing, darker and colder. His smile stretched too wide, revealing too many teeth.

Tom stumbled back, his breath catching in his throat. "Gary?" he whispered.

The thing that had been Gary tilted its head, as if considering him. Then it turned and walked away, its movements jerky and unnatural, like a marionette controlled by an inexperienced puppeteer. No one tried to stop it.

By midday, half the crew was missing. Those who remained were jumpy, their eyes darting toward every shadow. Tom's phone buzzed constantly—calls from the city, from the developers, demanding to know why construction had halted.

He ignored them. Something was deeply, horribly wrong, and he had a sinking feeling it was his fault.

As the sun dipped low on the horizon, casting long, jagged shadows across the site, Tom made a decision. He grabbed a sledgehammer and marched to the center of the lot, where the black surface still shimmered faintly beneath the rubble of the wall. He didn't know what it was or how it worked, but he knew one thing: it had to be sealed.

"Help me," he barked at the remaining crew. "We're rebuilding the wall. Now."

Ricky hesitated. "What if it's too late?"

Tom turned to him, his eyes blazing. "It's not too late. It can't be."

Together, they began to work. Every swing of the sledgehammer felt heavier than the last, as if the air itself was thickening, resisting their efforts. The shadows deepened, growing darker and more defined. Figures began to emerge from them—tall, spindly things with too-long limbs and too-sharp smiles. They didn't attack; they just watched, their heads tilting in unison as if mocking the crew's desperation.

"Faster!" Tom shouted, his voice hoarse. His hands were blistered, his muscles screaming in protest, but he didn't stop.

He couldn't.

As the first layer of bricks went up, the figures began to retreat, their forms dissolving back into the shadows. The air grew lighter, the oppressive weight lifting. For the first time all day, Tom felt a flicker of hope.

But then he heard the whispering again, louder this time, and realized with a sinking heart that the wall might not be enough.

CHAPTER 62: THE CURSE OF THE CRYSTAL SKULL

The jungle was alive with sound—the hum of insects, the distant call of unseen birds, and the low, menacing rumble of thunder on the horizon. Jack's boots sank into the wet earth as he pushed through the dense foliage, the massive leaves slapping against his sweat-drenched shirt. On his back, wrapped in layers of burlap and leather, was the thing he now wished he had never touched: the crystal skull.

It had been a mistake. A shining, glittering mistake.

He remembered the first time he laid eyes on it, deep within the bowels of the temple hidden beneath the vines and roots of this ancient jungle. The skull had seemed to glow with an inner light, its surface impossibly smooth, its hollow eyes staring into his soul. The local guide who had taken him to the outskirts of the temple had begged him not to enter—warned him of the curse whispered through generations of their people. But Jack had laughed it off, thinking it nothing more than superstition. He was an adventurer, a seeker of artifacts, and the skull was a prize too valuable to leave behind.

Now, weeks later, he cursed his arrogance.

The first death had come quickly. The guide, a wiry old man with sharp eyes and a quiet demeanor, had been the first to fall. Jack recalled how the man's face had turned ashen as Jack unveiled the skull from his pack. "You should never have taken it," the guide had said in a trembling voice, his eyes fixed on the cursed object. By morning, the guide was dead, his body twisted in a way that defied explanation.

Then came the disasters. The plane Jack had chartered out of the jungle crashed, killing all on board except him. Fires broke out in the nearby villages he passed through, and people grew sick whenever he lingered too long. And through it all, the skull seemed to pulse with an unholy energy, as if it were alive, feeding off the misery it caused.

Jack's hands tightened into fists as he trudged forward. He was back in the jungle now, retracing his steps to the temple. The local tribespeople who had once feared him now watched his every move from the shadows, their painted faces peering out from behind trees. He could feel their hatred, their resentment for the devastation he had unleashed upon their land. But they said nothing. They didn't need to. The jungle itself seemed to echo their anger, the wind whispering accusations in a language he didn't understand.

He stumbled into a clearing, his breath ragged. There it was. The temple. Its stone facade was cracked and worn, swallowed by the creeping vines and moss. The entrance yawned like a mouth, dark and foreboding. Jack hesitated, his heart thundering in his chest. He was close, but the weight of his guilt and fear pressed down on him like a physical force.

"You come back," a voice said suddenly, low and accented.

Jack whirled around. A woman stood there, her face painted with intricate patterns of red and black. Her eyes burned with an intensity that made him take an involuntary step back. She was one of the tribespeople, but there was something about her presence that made her seem more than human—like she was part of the jungle itself.

"I have to return it," Jack said, his voice shaking. "I didn't know—I didn't understand what would happen."

The woman tilted her head, studying him. "You bring death with you. The skull is not yours to take. It was never yours."

"I know that now," he said. "Please, I just want to make it right."

She stepped closer, and Jack felt the air grow colder despite the oppressive jungle heat. "To return it is not enough. The skull does not forgive. The spirits do not forget. You must face the trials."

"Trials?" His voice cracked. "What kind of trials?"

The woman didn't answer. Instead, she reached out and touched his chest lightly with her fingertips. A jolt of pain shot through him, and the world around him seemed to blur and spin. He fell to his knees, clutching at his chest, gasping for air.

When he looked up, the jungle was gone.

He was inside the temple, though he had no memory of walking in. The walls were slick with moisture, the air thick with the stench of decay. The faint glow of the skull illuminated the chamber, casting eerie shadows that seemed to writhe and twist like living things.

Jack stood shakily, his eyes darting around. The temple was alive with noise—whispers, groans, the distant sound of something heavy dragging itself across the stone floor. He clutched the skull tightly, though it burned his hands like ice.

"Face what you have unleashed," the woman's voice echoed in his mind. "Only then will you be free."

A figure emerged from the shadows. It was the guide—the old man who had died so violently. His body was broken, his limbs twisted at unnatural angles, but his eyes were wide open, filled with rage.

"You brought this upon us," the guide rasped, his voice like dry leaves scraping against stone.

Jack staggered back. "I—I didn't mean to!"

The guide lunged, and Jack screamed, dropping the skull. It hit the ground with a deafening crack, the light within it flaring brightly before extinguishing. The shadows closed in, and Jack's screams were swallowed by the darkness.

When the tribespeople found the temple the next morning, the skull was back in its rightful place, resting on its ancient pedestal. Of Jack, there was no sign—only the faint echo of his screams and the lingering scent of fear in the air.

The jungle had its vengeance.

CHAPTER 63: THE PHANTOM ORCHESTRA

The first haunting note drifted through the city like a ghostly whisper, barely audible over the hum of traffic and the chatter of passersby. At first, no one truly heard it, not consciously. It was just a faint strain of violins lingering at the edges of perception, a melancholy thread weaving its way into the fabric of the bustling metropolis. But as the days passed, the music grew louder, more persistent, until it was impossible to ignore.

Amelia stood in the shadow of the ruined opera house, her breath clouding in the autumn chill. The building loomed before her like the hollowed-out ribcage of some great beast, its charred walls blackened and skeletal against the pale sky. The fire had gutted it decades ago, leaving nothing but ash and sorrow, yet now it seemed alive again, pulsing with an unholy resonance. She could feel it vibrating in her chest, the mournful swell of strings and the deep, guttural moan of cellos. The music was everywhere, and nowhere, all at once.

"They say it started last week," said a voice behind her. Amelia turned to see an older man, his face gaunt and etched with lines of worry. He wore a heavy coat that hung loose on his thin frame, and his eyes darted nervously toward the opera house. "I hear it at night. My wife—she can't sleep anymore. Says it's like the music is…inside her head."

Amelia nodded grimly. She had heard the same stories from countless others. People awoken in the dead of night by the phantom symphony, unable to block it out no matter how tightly they pressed pillows to their ears. Others claimed it followed them through the streets, an unseen orchestra playing just behind their steps. And then there were the ones who had stopped speaking altogether, their faces blank with despair, their eyes hollow as if the music had hollowed them out from within.

"Have there been others?" Amelia asked, her voice low. "People who've gone missing?"

The man hesitated, his gaze dropping to the ground. "A few," he admitted. "But no one wants to talk about it. It's like…if you talk about them, the music gets louder."

Amelia's stomach twisted. She had suspected as much. The city was a symphony of anxiety now, its people moving like marionettes pulled by invisible strings. And at the heart of it all was this place—the opera house. She turned back to the ruins, her hands clenched into fists. She had spent her life conducting music, bringing order to chaos, beauty to sound. But this…this was something else entirely. This was music as a weapon, a curse, a wound that refused to heal.

"I need to go inside," she said, her voice steady despite the dread coiling in her chest.

The man's eyes widened. "You can't," he said urgently. "It's not safe. They say anyone who goes in there—"

"Disappears," Amelia finished for him. "I know." Her gaze hardened. "But someone has to stop it. If we don't, it'll consume the whole city."

The man shook his head, backing away. "You're mad," he

whispered. "You'll never make it out."

Amelia didn't respond. She turned and stepped through the broken archway that had once been the grand entrance to the opera house. The air inside was cold, colder than it should have been, and it carried the faint scent of smoke and decay. Her footsteps echoed on the cracked marble floor, each one a hollow punctuation in the oppressive silence. And yet the silence wasn't truly silent. The music was here, stronger than ever, wrapping around her like a living thing. It wasn't just sound anymore—it was a presence, a suffocating weight pressing down on her soul.

She walked deeper into the ruins, her flashlight cutting through the darkness. The beam illuminated fragments of the past: a shattered chandelier, its crystals scattered like fallen stars; rows of charred seats, their velvet upholstery reduced to ash; a crumbling stage, its once-grand curtains hanging in tatters. And then she saw them.

The orchestra.

They sat in their seats, their instruments poised as if frozen mid-performance. Their figures were translucent, shimmering like heat waves, and their faces were pale and featureless. Yet somehow, Amelia could feel their eyes on her, empty sockets burning with an unnatural hunger. The conductor stood at the center, his baton raised, his skeletal hand gripping it like a talon. His face was a mask of ruin, his jaw unhinged, yet he seemed to grin at her, a grotesque mockery of welcome.

"Why?" Amelia whispered, though she knew no answer would come. "Why are you doing this?"

The conductor tilted his head, as if considering her question. And then, slowly, he began to move. His baton sliced through the air, and the orchestra came alive. The sound was unbearable, a cacophony of grief and rage and madness that clawed at Amelia's mind. She fell to her knees, clutching her head, but the music only grew louder, more insistent. It was inside her now, burrowing deep, filling her with memories that weren't her own —flames licking at her skin, screams echoing in her ears, the taste of ash on her tongue.

"No!" she cried, forcing herself to her feet. She stumbled toward the stage, her determination burning brighter than her fear. "You don't get to do this! You don't get to take them!"

The conductor turned to her fully, his hollow gaze meeting hers. For a moment, the music faltered, a single note hanging in the air like a question. Amelia seized the opportunity. She climbed onto the stage, her steps unsteady but resolute, and reached for the conductor's baton. As her fingers closed around it, a searing pain shot through her, as if she had grabbed a live wire. The music screamed, a dissonant wail that threatened to shatter her completely.

But she held on.

With every ounce of strength she had, she wrenched the baton from the conductor's grasp. The orchestra froze, their instruments falling silent, and the conductor let out an inhuman shriek. Amelia raised the baton high and brought it down with all her might, snapping it in two. The sound that followed was deafening, a thunderclap that shook the very foundations of the opera house.

And then, silence.

The figures of the orchestra faded, their forms dissolving like mist under the morning sun. The conductor was the last to go, his empty grin lingering for a heartbeat before vanishing into the void. Amelia collapsed to the floor, her body trembling, her mind reeling. The music was gone, but its echoes lingered, a haunting refrain that would never truly leave her.

As she lay there, staring up at the crumbling ceiling, she couldn't help but wonder: had she silenced the phantom orchestra, or

VICTOR DARKE

had she merely joined their tragic symphony?

CHAPTER 64:
THE TOYMAKER'S REVENGE

The night air was heavy, a humid weight that clung to the skin and made every breath feel labored. In the quiet suburban neighborhood of Willow Glen, the streets were unnervingly still. Porch lights flickered, casting long, distorted shadows across the neatly trimmed lawns. A sense of unease had settled over the community in recent days, though no one dared speak of it aloud. Not yet.

Inside the Andrews house, nine-year-old Sophie sat cross-legged on the floor of her bedroom, her fingers brushing the hair of a porcelain doll that had seemingly appeared out of nowhere a week ago. She didn't remember buying it or receiving it as a gift; it had simply been there one morning, perched on her windowsill with its glassy blue eyes staring blankly ahead. Its dress was an old-fashioned thing, lace-lined and yellowed with age, and its face was painted with rosy cheeks and a thin, knowing smile. Sophie had been unnerved at first—who wouldn't be?—but she'd convinced herself it was just a gift from her parents, an odd but harmless surprise.

Now, as the house settled into its usual nighttime creaks and groans, Sophie couldn't shake the feeling that those lifeless eyes were following her every move. She set the doll down on the carpet and stood, shivering despite the warmth of the room. Her gaze flicked toward the door. She wanted to tell her parents about it, but what could she say? That she was scared of a doll? They'd laugh, or worse, tell her to grow up.

A sudden noise broke the silence: a soft, scraping sound, barely audible but persistent. Sophie froze, her heart thudding in her chest. The sound came again, this time louder. It was coming from the doll.

"No," she whispered, taking a step back. Her hand flew to her mouth as the doll's head jerked unnaturally to the side, the painted smile widening far beyond the limits of its porcelain face.

"You forgot me," the doll whispered, its voice a low, grating rasp. "They all forget."

Sophie screamed, stumbling backward and hitting the dresser. Upstairs, her brother Henry bolted upright in bed, his own breathing ragged. He had his own visitor that week—a tin soldier with a chipped helmet and a rusted musket. It had appeared on his nightstand, its once-bright paint dulled with age. He'd ignored it for the most part, but now, as Sophie's scream pierced the night, he glanced toward the toy. It wasn't where he'd left it.

The soldier was standing on the floor now, its musket raised. Its tiny head tilted up to meet his gaze, and though its face was featureless save for painted eyes, Henry could feel its hatred.

By morning, the neighborhood was in chaos. Parents whispered furiously among themselves while children showed off scratches, bruises, and stories of toys that moved when no one was looking. A boy named Max claimed his teddy bear had tried to smother him in his sleep, while Emma swore her jack-in-the-box had snapped at her fingers when she wound it. For the first time, the children felt united—not by friendship, but by fear.

That was when Tommy, the oldest boy on the block at thirteen, spoke up. "It's the Toymaker," he said, his voice low but steady. "My grandpa told me about him. He used to live in that creepy old house at the end of the street, the one no one goes near. Grandpa said he made toys for the kids in the neighborhood, but something happened. People stopped buying them. Said they were too weird, too... wrong. He disappeared after that."

The children exchanged uneasy glances. No one had been near the house in years. Its windows were boarded up, its paint peeling, and the yard overgrown with weeds. It was the kind of place parents warned their kids to stay away from, and kids dared each other to approach on Halloween.

"Maybe he's back," Sophie whispered, clutching her arm where a faint red mark from the doll's grasp still lingered. "And he's angry."

Tommy nodded. "We need to do something. He's sending these toys to hurt us. If we don't stop him, it's only gonna get worse."

"But what can we do?" Henry asked. His voice wavered, betraying his fear. "He's probably some crazy old guy. What if he... what if he hurts us too?"

Tommy's jaw tightened. "We'll go together. All of us. He can't hurt us if we stick together."

By dusk, a group of children gathered at the edge of the toymaker's yard, their faces pale but determined. Sophie clutched a flashlight, her hands trembling. Tommy held a baseball bat, though he wasn't sure what good it would do against a man who could bring toys to life. The air around the house felt colder, heavier, as if the building itself were alive and watching them.

They pushed through the rusted gate, its hinges shrieking in protest, and made their way up the cracked stone path. The front door loomed before them, its wood warped and splintered. Tommy raised his fist and knocked.

For a moment, nothing happened. Then, slowly, the door creaked open, revealing a dimly lit workshop beyond. The walls were lined with shelves, each one crammed with toys in various states of disrepair. Dolls with missing eyes, stuffed animals with torn seams, and mechanical contraptions that twitched and whirred as if they were alive.

In the center of the room stood the toymaker. He was thin and hunched, his face obscured by a tangle of white hair and a pair of cracked glasses. His hands were gnarled, the fingers stained with paint and grease. He looked up as the children entered, a slow, chilling smile spreading across his face.

"Ah," he said, his voice soft and raspy. "My visitors have arrived. I was wondering when you'd come."

Sophie stepped forward, her flashlight beam trembling as it illuminated his face. "Why are you doing this?" she demanded, her voice shaking. "Why are you sending these... these things after us?"

The toymaker chuckled, a dry, humorless sound. "You children," he murmured, shaking his head. "You take, and you take, and you never appreciate. My toys were loved once. Cherished. But then they were cast aside, forgotten, left to rot. Do you know how that feels? To be discarded like trash?"

His eyes gleamed with a dangerous light as he gestured to the shelves around him. "I gave them new life. I gave them purpose. And now, they will teach you what it means to be abandoned."

The children recoiled, their courage faltering in the face of his fury. But Tommy stepped forward, gripping his bat tightly. "We're not afraid of you," he said, though his voice wavered. "You can't just hurt people because you're mad."

The toymaker's smile faded, replaced by a look of cold disdain. "Can't I?" he asked, his voice low and dangerous. "You'll see. Soon, you'll all—"

Before he could finish, Sophie darted forward, shining her flashlight directly into his face. The toymaker hissed, recoiling as if the light burned him. "Now!" Sophie shouted.

The children surged forward, their fear giving way to determination. They knocked over shelves, smashing toys and scattering parts across the floor. The toymaker screamed, a sound of pure anguish, as his creations were destroyed.

When it was over, the workshop was silent. The toymaker lay crumpled on the floor, his body impossibly still. The children stood in the wreckage, their breaths coming in ragged gasps.

Sophie turned to Tommy, her eyes wide. "Do you think it's over?" she whispered.

Tommy didn't answer. Behind them, in the shadows, the remnants of a doll twitched.

CHAPTER 65: THE ENDLESS NIGHT

The world had never known silence like this—an oppressive, suffocating quiet that wrapped around the globe, thick and heavy as the endless night stretched into its third week. Dr. Lewis leaned heavily over the console in the underground research lab, his fingers trembling as he keyed in yet another desperate sequence of commands. The monitors bathed his gaunt face in flickering green light, casting shadows that made his hollow eyes seem deeper. His lab coat was wrinkled, stained with days-old coffee and something darker. He couldn't remember the last time he'd slept. Not that it mattered.

Outside, the world had become something else entirely.

It began with the absence of dawn. The first day had been strange, unsettling. Social media buzzed with theories—solar anomalies, government conspiracies, even divine punishment. By the second day, panic had begun to take hold. By the seventh, the myths had come to life.

The creatures didn't emerge all at once. At first, it was whispers —rumors of shadows moving unnaturally, of people vanishing in the dark. Then came the sightings: a man torn apart on a live stream by something with too many eyes; a family found huddled together in their basement, their faces frozen in expressions of unimaginable terror. And then, the screams. Every night, the world screamed.

Dr. Lewis had stopped checking the news after the footage from New York City. Millions of people flooding Central Park, desperate to escape the claustrophobic darkness of their apartments, only to be swallowed whole by the writhing mass of things that had taken over the skyline. The creatures had no names, not yet. They were too many, too alien. They didn't belong in any taxonomy of Earth. Some were enormous, moving like shadows that blotted out entire city blocks; others were small, skittering things with claws that clicked against concrete and teeth that gleamed like shards of broken glass. They thrived in the dark. They were the dark.

The lab door hissed open, breaking Lewis's concentration. He didn't turn. He didn't have to. The heavy, uneven footsteps told him it was Carter, one of the few technicians still alive, still willing to help.

"Lewis," Carter rasped, his voice raw from exhaustion. "It's worse out there. The perimeter lights—half of them are dead. Backup generators are failing."

Lewis didn't respond. He stared at the simulation running on his screen, the same one he'd been tweaking for days. A holographic model of the sun rotated slowly, mockingly, in the air before him. He'd tried everything—particle acceleration, nuclear ignition, antimatter bursts. Nothing worked. Nothing could reignite a star that had simply... stopped.

"Lewis." Carter's voice cracked, and he stumbled closer, his shadow falling long and distorted across the lab. "You're running out of time. We *all* are."

"I know," Lewis murmured, his voice barely audible. He didn't look up. His hands moved to the keyboard again, entering new parameters. A desperate idea had been forming in his mind, one he hadn't dared voice aloud. It was dangerous. Reckless. But it was all they had left.

Carter leaned heavily against the counter, his face pale and slick with sweat. "We've got people out there, waiting for answers. What do I tell them? That the smartest man left on the planet is just staring at a screen?"

Lewis's head snapped up, his eyes blazing with a mix of fury and despair. "You think I'm not aware of what's at stake? You think I don't hear them?" His voice rose, echoing off the sterile walls of the lab. "Every time I close my eyes, I *hear them*. The screaming. The begging. Do you know what it's like to be the one they're all counting on, knowing that no matter what you do, it might not be enough?"

Carter flinched but didn't back down. "Then do something. Anything."

Lewis took a shuddering breath, his hands gripping the edge of the console so tightly his knuckles turned white. He could feel the weight of Carter's gaze, the weight of humanity's collective desperation pressing down on him like a physical force.

"There's one option," he said finally, his voice hollow. "But it's not safe. It could kill us all."

Carter let out a bitter laugh, the sound brittle and sharp. "We're already dying, Lewis. You've seen what's out there. The darkness isn't just hiding them anymore—it's *feeding* them. Every day, they're getting stronger. We don't have time for safe."

Lewis hesitated, his mind racing. The plan was madness, but Carter was right. The creatures were evolving, growing bolder. They no longer waited for the cover of shadows; they *were* the shadows, slipping through cracks in barricades, infiltrating even the brightest sanctuaries. The lab was one of the last strongholds, its floodlights keeping the monsters at bay—for now. But not for much longer.

He turned back to the console, his fingers flying over the

keyboard. "We'll use the particle accelerator," he said, his voice steadier now, fueled by a grim determination. "If we can generate enough energy, we might be able to mimic the sun's radiation. A crude simulation, but it could repel them. Maybe even weaken them."

Carter's eyes widened. "You're talking about—what? A man-made sun?"

"Something like that," Lewis said. "But the energy output—if it goes wrong, we could vaporize everything within a hundred-mile radius. Maybe more."

Carter nodded slowly, his jaw tightening. "Better to go out in a blaze of light than let them take us."

Lewis didn't respond. He couldn't. The weight of what he was about to do settled heavily on his shoulders, but there was no time for doubt. He initiated the sequence, the hum of the accelerator rising to a deafening crescendo as the room shook violently. Alarms blared, warning of unstable energy levels, but Lewis didn't stop. He couldn't.

Outside, the darkness seemed to shift, growing denser, heavier. The creatures knew. They always knew.

"Hold on," Lewis whispered, whether to Carter or to the world itself, he wasn't sure. "Just hold on."

And then, there was light.

CHAPTER 66: THE FINAL HOUR

The clocks ticked in unison, an unnatural, synchronized chorus that spanned the entire planet. From the neon-lit streets of Tokyo to the rural outskirts of Kansas, from bustling markets in Marrakech to the frozen plains of Siberia, they all displayed the same countdown: **00:59:59**.

Dr. Elena Varga stared at the wall of screens in the Geneva Crisis Center, her heart pounding in her chest. The room was dim, save for the glow of monitors displaying live feeds from around the world. Each one showed the same haunting image: clocks —digital, analog, even those on ancient towers and forgotten church walls—counting down to zero. It began three days ago, and no one knew why.

"Fifty-nine minutes," whispered Dr. Raj Patel, his voice barely audible over the hum of equipment. His hands trembled as he adjusted his glasses. "We've run every algorithm, every simulation. There's no pattern. No origin."

"There's always a pattern," Elena shot back, though her voice wavered. "We're just not seeing it. We're missing something." She leaned forward, her dark hair catching the cold light of the monitors. Her eyes, once sharp and confident, now brimmed with desperation. "We have to be missing something."

Across the room, Major Lucas Hayes stood with his arms

crossed, his military uniform crisp but his face drawn. He had been sent by NATO to oversee the crisis, though no amount of training had prepared him for this. "Missing something?" he echoed bitterly. "Try everything. No signals, no transmissions, no demands. Just... this." He gestured to the screen showing a live feed from New York City's Times Square. The countdown glared above the bustling crowd like an omnipotent eye. **00:59:31.**

On the streets below, chaos reigned. Protesters clashed with police, doomsday cults lit fires in trash cans, and families huddled together, praying to gods they had forgotten. Some people danced wildly, celebrating their impending end. Others stared blankly, as though already resigned to whatever fate awaited.

Elena's phone buzzed on the desk beside her, jolting her back to the moment. She picked it up, her hands slick with sweat. It was a video call from her sister in Budapest. The connection was poor, but she could see her sister's tear-streaked face, her two young children clutching her arms.

"Elena," her sister sobbed. "Do you know what's going to happen? Are we going to die?"

Elena swallowed hard, forcing herself to remain composed. "We don't know yet. But stay inside, stay safe. I'll call you as soon as we learn anything. I promise." She ended the call before her voice could crack, then buried her face in her hands.

"Promises," muttered Dr. Patel from his station. "What good are promises when the world's ending?"

A sharp beep cut through the room, drawing everyone's attention. The screens flickered, then changed. Data streams appeared, cascading in rapid succession. Live feeds from satellites showed the Earth in its entirety, the countdown superimposed over its glowing surface. **00:48:12.**

"Wait," said Patel, his voice rising. He lunged toward his keyboard, his fingers flying. "This... this is new. The clocks are emitting something. A frequency. It's faint, but it's there."

"Play it," Major Hayes ordered.

Patel hesitated, then pressed a few keys. The speakers crackled, and a low hum filled the room. It was rhythmic, almost melodic, like a heartbeat slowed to a crawl. The sound burrowed into their ears, unsettling and primal.

"What the hell is that?" Hayes demanded, his voice taut.

"It's not human," Patel murmured, his face pale. "It's... it's a signal. Something's broadcasting it through the clocks."

Elena's stomach twisted. "Broadcasting from where?"

Patel's fingers trembled as he typed. "I'm triangulating now. It's... oh god. It's coming from everywhere. Every clock, every device. The origin point isn't on Earth."

The room fell silent, save for the hum of the signal and the relentless ticking of the countdown. **00:40:06.**

"Aliens," Hayes said flatly, though even he seemed reluctant to believe it. "You're telling me this is—"

"We don't know what it is," Elena interrupted, her voice sharp. "But it's not natural. And if it's not natural, then someone—or something—is behind it."

The hum grew louder, more insistent, as though responding to their fear. Elena pressed her hands to her ears, but it did little to muffle the sound. Around the world, reports poured in of people collapsing, clutching their heads. Others claimed to hear voices within the hum, whispering in languages they couldn't understand.

In Cairo, a man speaking on live television began to convulse, his eyes rolling back as he screamed a single word over and over: "Awaken." In Rio de Janeiro, a cult leader set herself ablaze in front of her followers, proclaiming that "the gods were returning." And in Beijing, a child no older than six calmly told a reporter, "They're already here," before walking into the crowd and vanishing.

Back in Geneva, the scientists scrambled to make sense of the chaos. Elena's mind raced, her thoughts a whirlwind of equations, theories, and half-formed ideas. But nothing fit. Nothing made sense.

Then, the lights flickered. The monitors went dark. The countdown vanished, replaced by a single, chilling message: **"Prepare."**

The hum stopped. The silence was deafening.

Elena's breath caught in her throat. "What... what does that mean?"

The answer came not in words, but in action. The Earth itself seemed to tremble, a low rumble that spread through every city, every village, every remote outpost. The sky darkened, though it was midday in half the world. Stars appeared where there should have been none, their light cold and unfamiliar.

And then, in the final seconds—**00:00:10**—the truth revealed itself. The stars moved. No, not stars. Ships. Thousands of them, descending through the atmosphere like a swarm of locusts blotting out the heavens.

Humanity had spent centuries looking to the skies for answers, for signs of life beyond their fragile world. Now, as the countdown reached zero, they had their answer.

The clocks stopped. Time stood still.

And the invasion began.

Made in the USA
Columbia, SC
07 February 2026